Josh Lacey

BEARKEEPER

First published in the UK by Marion Lloyd Books,
An imprint of Scholastic Ltd
Euston House, 24 Eversholt Street
London, NW1 1DB, UK
Registered office: Westfield Road, Southam, Warwickshire, CV47 0RA

10 digit ISBN 1 407 10543 4
13 digit ISBN 978 1407 10543 7

A CIP catalogue record for this book
is available from the British Library

Typeset by M Rules
Printed by CPI Bookmarque Ltd, Croydon, CR0 4TD
Papers used by Scholastic Children's Books are made from
wood grown in sustainable forests.

1 3 5 7 9 10 8 6 4 2

www.scholastic.co.uk/zone

ABOUT THE AUTHOR

Josh Lacey was born in London and still lives there. He has worked as a journalist, a screenwriter and a teacher.

Josh has always wanted to go back in time and meet the people who lived in London four hundred years ago. When writing *Bearkeeper*, he didn't actually do that. But he did go to India and visit a sanctuary for rescued dancing bears. He's also read and seen all of Shakespeare's plays, and even acted in a couple.

ALSO BY JOSH LACEY

Writing as Joshua Doder

The Grk Series

A Dog Called Grk
Grk and the Pelotti Gang
Grk and the Hot Dog Trail
Grk: Operation Tortoise
Grk Smells a Rat

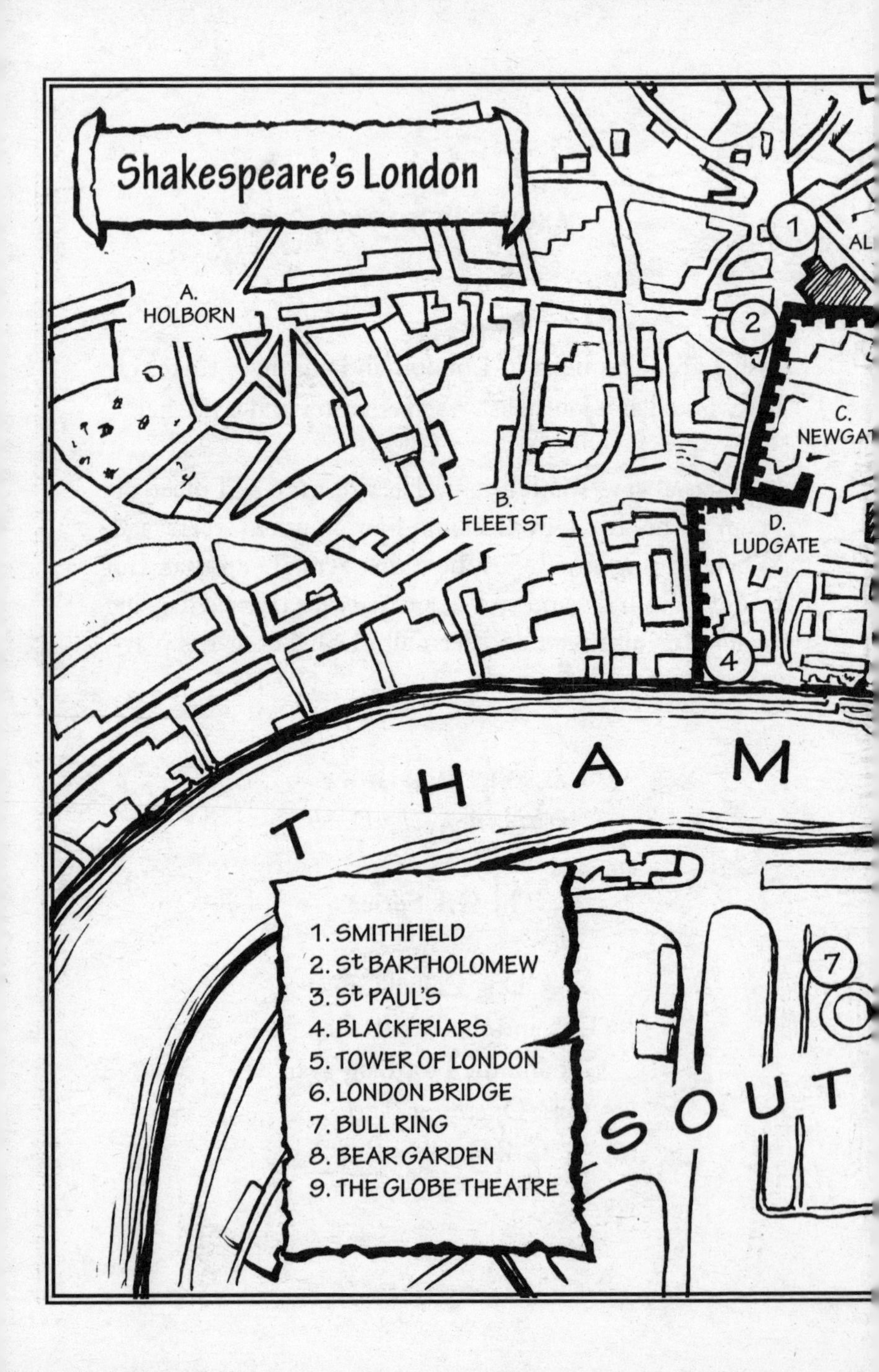
Shakespeare's London
A. HOLBORN
B. FLEET ST
C. NEWGAT
D. LUDGATE
1
2
4
7
T H A M
S O U T
1. SMITHFIELD
2. St BARTHOLOMEW
3. St PAUL'S
4. BLACKFRIARS
5. TOWER OF LONDON
6. LONDON BRIDGE
7. BULL RING
8. BEAR GARDEN
9. THE GLOBE THEATRE

G.
CRIPPLEGATE
H.
MOOREGATE
I.
BISHOPSGATE
E.
CHEAPSIDE
K.
ALDGATE
J.
EASTCHEAP
3
5
6
8
9
S
WARK

1

One Sunday afternoon, not much more than four hundred years ago, a boy named Pip walked into the woods. He moved quickly, never pausing to look around.

When Pip first started wandering through these woods alone, at the age of five or six, they'd terrified him. Day and night, bizarre sounds echoed among the trees. Not just snapping branches and rustling leaves but weird whistles, odd coughs and all kinds of other unidentifiable noises. He used to hear footsteps behind him and see strange shapes lurking in the shadows up ahead.

Now he never felt scared. Over the years, he'd seen ferrets, toads, voles, moles, snakes, rats, wild boars and other, even stranger creatures that he could not name, but his fear had faded. Day by day, year by year, he came to love the woods. He often got lost, but could usually find his way home quickly enough, wading through the undergrowth until he found a familiar landmark. Even the darkness lost its power to scare him. Most months, he would take advantage of the full moon and saunter through the woods at night, stopping to watch a family of deer or a foraging badger.

Just twice in the years that he had lived here, he had seen a shadowy pale shape which might have been a ghost. On both occasions it had stood between the trees for a few seconds, then melted into the air in front of him. The first time, when he told his mother about the ghost, she laughed. Since then, he'd never mentioned it to anyone.

That afternoon, as he walked through the woods, Pip saw nothing but birds chirruping wildly, and a single fox drinking from the stream.

He reached the clearing. Sunlight glistened on the wet leaves. A heavy rain had fallen overnight and the grass was still slippery. Pip would have to be careful. He didn't want to fall over and sprain his ankle or break his wrist.

He pulled his knife from its leather scabbard. Under his palm, he could feel the familiar pattern on the handle, the five-pointed star carved into the wood. He ran the fingers of his left hand along the blade, testing its sharpness. Yesterday morning he had sharpened it himself with a file, and it was still perfect.

He raised the knife, took up his position and waited for them to come. They would be here soon.

The first of them walks through the trees and emerges into the clearing. He is a heavyset man with a beard. Gripping his long sword with both hands, he stands opposite Pip.

They look into one another's eyes.

This is what Pip knows:

The more you have learnt about your opponent, the better you can fight him. You must watch him constantly. Study him. Search for his weaknesses. If he's brawny, use your speed. If he's scrawny, use your strength. If he has a limp in his left leg or a kink in his right arm, aim all your blows on that side.

Pip watches and waits.

Without any warning, hoping to take Pip by surprise, the bearded man hauls his sword into the air.

The bearded man is quick, but Pip is quicker. Twisting his body, he thrusts his knife forward and parries the blow.

A knife can often outwit a sword if you know how to use it, turning your opponent's strength against himself. The bearded man stumbles awkwardly, thrown off balance by the weight of his own weapon, and loses his footing.

Pip takes his chance. He plunges the knife into his enemy's throat. With a shriek, the bearded man staggers backwards, clutching his neck.

Pip turns a half-circle. Another man is already running out of the trees, armed with a short sword and a small round shield. At the last possible moment Pip ducks, letting the blade whistle over his head, then thrusts, slashing his opponent's fingers. Shocked by the pain, the man drops his sword. Pip stabs him twice between the ribs. *Squelch! Squelch!* The man falls to the ground and writhes on the grass, yelling, but Pip hardly hears him. He's whirled round already, turning to face the next of his enemies.

They keep coming. More and more of them. Short or tall, thin or fat, heavily armoured or bare-chested, they are all well armed. Between them, they carry every possible variety of weapon. Spears lunge at him. Swords slash him. Axes hack him. Voices taunt him, trying to distract him, but Pip's concentration is pure and clear. He ducks, darts, stabs and slices, then turns on the spot, knife raised, ready for the next one.

If you'd happened to be walking through the woods that afternoon, you would have seen a strange sight.

A boy was moving around a clearing. He was short and skinny. He had brown hair and brown eyes. His face was red and he was panting, but he never stopped to catch his breath.

In his right hand he was holding a short, sharp knife. He darted forward, plunged the knife into the empty air and twisted the blade. He jumped back, ducked, bent his body and thrust the knife in another direction. Once again he twisted the blade, withdrew and turned. And then he was off again, his hand carving the air, his feet dancing on the grass, his knife stabbing yet another imaginary opponent.

2

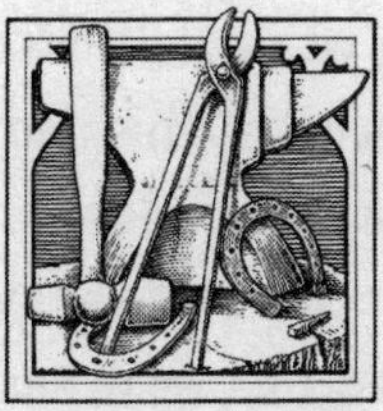

Six days a week Pip worked in the smithy with his mother's husband. Sunday was their day off. No one worked on the Sabbath.

Every Sunday morning the whole family walked to Mildmay, the nearest village, half an hour away, and went to church. On Sunday afternoons Pip was free. He could have picked blackberries, paddled in the stream, practised writing his alphabet or just fallen asleep in the long grass. Instead he walked into the woods, found a quiet spot and practised fighting with his father's knife. He spent the whole afternoon there, conjuring up opponents, giving them swords and spears, knives and axes, shields and helmets.

He was practising for the fighting competition at Bartholomew Fair. One day he was going to win it. Just like his dad did. That's what drove him onward through that long hot Sunday afternoon, ignoring the heat and his thirst and all the bits of his body begging him to stop. That's why he kept imagining new opponents for himself, clothing them and arming them, then watching them stroll out of the forest and take up their positions opposite him.

One August, a few years from now, he was going to walk to London, find Bartholomew Fair, pay his penny and enter the fighting competition. To win, he would have to defeat experienced swordsmen and battle-hardened soldiers. Against them, he would have only three weapons: his speed, his cunning and his father's knife.

Apart from the knife, Pip had nothing of his father's. He wasn't even sure that he could remember what his dad looked like. He had a few vague memories of George Stone's face and voice, although he couldn't help worrying that he'd invented them, stealing bits of other children's fathers for himself, borrowing the sound of a voice, the smell of wet cloth, the feeling of a hand on the top of his head.

Seven years ago Pip's father had walked out of the house and never returned. At first Pip's mother, Isobel, had simply said that George Stone had gone away on business. He would be back next week, she promised. Next week had turned into next month and then next year, but George never came back. He stayed away on business. What was his business? Where had he gone? No one seemed to know.

A couple of years after George had left the house for the last time, Isobel knelt beside Pip. "I have to tell you some bad news," she said. "Something horrible has happened. Your father is dead."

Pip stared at his mother. He didn't know what to say. He had a lot of questions but didn't ask any of them, just kept quiet and listened as she explained that George Stone had been killed in a brawl, stabbed almost accidentally while defending a friend. Through his own strong sense of loyalty, George had been drawn into a pointless fight and murdered.

"I want you to have this," said Isobel. She was holding a small knife in a leather scabbard. "It was his." She pressed the knife into Pip's hands.

Against the soft skin of his palm, he felt the five-pointed star carved into the knife's wooden handle.

A few weeks later a man moved into the cottage. Pip knew him already. His name was Samuel and he was the village smith. He shod horses, sharpened knives and made scythes for the farmers. He was rumoured to be rich, a miser who made lots of money but never spent anything.

"This is your new father," said Isobel.

Samuel smiled. "I think we're going to be good friends, Philip."

Pip stared up at the smith, wrinkling his nose and saying nothing. He didn't want a new father. He wanted his own father back again.

Since then George Stone's name had hardly ever been mentioned in the house.

You don't speak of the dead. You let them sleep in peace.

That's what his mother said anyway. Pip felt differently. He quizzed villagers about his father, gathering facts and anecdotes, never quite sure which were true. George Stone was a soldier, said someone, fighting for Queen Elizabeth against the Spanish. George Stone owned a pet parrot, said someone else. George Stone sailed across the ocean to strange islands in the New World and met black-skinned savages who had never seen a white man before. George Stone captured Spanish galleons laden with tobacco and chocolate, silver and gold. When George Stone returned to Europe he travelled to the Low Countries with the English army and fought alongside Sir Philip Sidney. During one of their battles, Sir Philip was shot in the thigh and died from loss of blood. That was why George Stone insisted on calling his own son Philip.

Of all the stories, there was only one which Pip felt sure must be true. When George Stone left the army and got married, he didn't have enough money to buy somewhere to live, so he entered the fighting competition at Bartholomew Fair.

Every August, thousands of people poured into London to celebrate the feast of St Bartholomew. They took over Smithfield, an empty pasture on the north-western edge of the city, just outside the walls. For most of the year Smithfield was used as a cattle market, but for a week each summer, starting on St Bartholomew's Day, the twenty-fourth of August, the enormous field was transformed into Bartholomew Fair, a riot of buying and selling, eating and drinking, performances and competitions. The most popular was the fighting competition. For an admission fee of one penny, anyone could enter, and the winner took home ten pounds.

Ten pounds might not sound like much to you, but it was a lot of money in 1601. Most working men – butchers, bakers, farm labourers – would be lucky to earn that much in a whole year. That's why several hundred men travelled from as far as fifty miles away carrying their weapons, and queued up at dawn to pay their penny. A crowd gathered to watch. As the day progressed, and only the better fighters were left in the competition, the crowd got bigger.

Most years, someone died. Many more lost a finger or an eye. And one was crowned champion.

About fifteen years before, Pip had been told, George Stone came to Bartholomew Fair and entered the fighting competition, armed with nothing but a knife. The other fighters laughed at him. A knife, they said. A knife! What are you going to do with that? Cut up your lunch?

George Stone just smiled and said nothing.

The other men showed him their weapons. One had a broadsword, almost as tall as himself. Another had a long-handled axe, big enough to chop down a tree with a single blow. A third had an Italian rapier forged by Antonio Petruccio, one of the finest swordmakers in Europe.

George Stone never said a word, just smiled and kept hold of his knife, fingering the five-pointed star carved into its wooden handle.

The competitors were called forward, two by two. The

crowd cheered and whistled. The fighters stood opposite one another, staring into their opponent's eyes, checking for signs of strength and weakness. When the referee shouted "Go!", they leapt forward and started fighting.

By the end of the day, George Stone was covered in cuts and bruises. His nose was broken. His clothes were soaked with blood, his own and other men's. But he had won ten pounds. Enough to buy a home for himself, his wife and the baby growing inside her womb.

3

When the sun had sunk low in the sky and the shadows had lengthened, Pip noticed he was tired. He slid his father's knife into its scabbard, left the clearing and strolled slowly through the woods towards home.

On the way, he glimpsed three deer, a hart and two hinds, but they bounded through the trees before he could get a good look.

He stopped to watch a scattered group of rabbits nibbling at the long grass. The nearest lifted its ears and tensed but didn't run away. Pip stood very still. After a moment, the rabbit relaxed and went back to its meal.

As Pip came closer to the house, he saw wisps of smoke rising above the trees and smelt cooking meat. Suddenly he felt hungry. On Sundays supper was always good. He quickened his pace and jogged to the door.

All his life Pip had lived in the same small cottage surrounded by trees, not much more than thirty miles north of London. Till he was five, he lived there with both his parents. Then he lived there for a couple of years with his mother, just the two of them. Now Pip shared the cottage with his mother and her second husband, Samuel Smith, and their two young daughters, Bridget, aged one, and Susannah, who was almost four.

Pip ducked through the low doorway and went into the main room, which served as the workshop, the bedroom, the kitchen, the living room and the dining room. A pot bubbled on the fire, tended by his mother. She looked up and smiled. "Hello, lambkin. Where have you been?"

"In the forest," said Pip.

"Doing what?"

"Nothing."

"Pip." His mother grinned. "You've been gone for hours. What have you really been doing?"

"Just walking." Pip shrugged his shoulders. "I saw a good place for rabbits. Might go back and catch a couple tomorrow."

"That would be nice. We haven't had rabbit for ages." Isobel stirred the pot with a long wooden spoon. "Are you hungry?"

"Quite."

"We'll have supper soon."

Once a week Pip's mother bought a chicken or a hunk of mutton from one of the farmers in Mildmay. They ate the meat on Sunday. On Monday morning Isobel boiled up the bones, adding onions, carrots, leeks, turnips or a few cloves of garlic, making a soup which kept them fed for several days, its taste thinner and weaker with each meal.

There were no shops in Mildmay – Pip had never been to a shop in his life – but you could buy just about whatever you needed from one of the villagers. For a penny or two someone was always happy to sell you a chicken, some apples, a big bunch of onions or whatever they happened to be harvesting. Anything else you could buy from one of the pedlars who arrived every few days. There was a weekly market in the nearest town, which you could reach in two or three hours at a brisk walk, but the residents of Mildmay rarely bothered. Many of the villagers went their entire lives without venturing more than a mile from their homes.

After supper, Isobel put Bridget and Susannah to bed. Samuel sat by the fire's dying embers, warming his feet. Pip said goodnight and went into the store, his bedroom, a tiny windowless space tucked into the back of the workshop. He had no candle, so he felt his way from the door to his bed. He pulled off his boots and sat down on the rectangle of cloth that served as his mattress.

Pip was used to the darkness. Before the invention of electricity most people went to bed at sunset. The rich used lanterns and candles, but the poor just adjusted the routines of their lives to follow the sun, sleeping more in winter, less in summer.

He knelt beside his bed, clasped his hands together and muttered a few words, thanking God for the gift of another day. When his prayer was finished, he undressed and lay down, sliding his father's knife under his pillow.

4

A couple of months ago I went to Mildmay. I caught the train from London. The journey takes about twenty-five minutes, stopping at all the small suburban stations in between. Just enough time to drink a cup of coffee and read the paper.

I don't suppose you've ever been to Mildmay?

No?

I'm not surprised. There's not much reason to. Unless you live there, of course. Or have family who do.

Oh, there's nothing wrong with Mildmay. It's a nice little town. People are polite and friendly. Neighbours always have time for a chat. Kids play football and cricket in the streets. The gardens are packed with flowers. There are lots of good shops and some excellent schools. On Saturday nights a few rowdy drunks sometimes start fights in the high street, but no one goes home with more than a bloody nose. Most of the time Mildmay is calm and peaceful. If you were looking for a quiet place to raise a family, you couldn't pick a better spot.

That day I walked round Mildmay for an entire afternoon, searching for something that Pip might have seen.

I wasn't expecting miracles. Four hundred years is a long time. I was sure that no trace of the Smiths' cottage would have survived, but I hoped I might be able to find something, anything, that would have been there when Pip was.

After I had walked for more than three hours, searching street after street, I began to think that my search was pointless. Everything looked so shiny and new.

Over the past few decades, since the arrival of cars, the landscape of England has been completely changed. Roads and houses have smothered the countryside. Where there were once fields and woods, there is now concrete and tarmac.

My searches weren't utterly hopeless. I saw a few gnarled, ancient, crooked trees which might have been saplings when Pip lived here. Down by the river there was a moss-covered wall made from great lumps of old stone. Pip might have watched a farmer rolling them out of his field, clearing a path for his plough and his horses. And then I found St John's.

I had already seen Mildmay's main church, a large Victorian building which hadn't been at all interesting. Late in the afternoon, just as I was beginning to think about going back to the station, I was walking through a quiet part of town, a long way from the shops or the main roads. Tucked away at the end of a residential street there was a small church, surrounded by an overgrown graveyard.

St John's had the solid shape of English churches which have squatted in the same spot for the past seven or eight hundred years. I wanted to go inside and see if the vicar had written a little pamphlet describing its history, as vicars often do, but the big wooden door was locked. In the summer St John's probably saw a few marriages, and the odd funeral in the winter, but I couldn't imagine that many people worshipped there regularly.

I wandered through the graveyard, trying to make out the names and dates carved into the ancient stones. Most of them were illegible. Years of neglect had almost wiped them clean. But that didn't really matter. I had found what I was looking for. I could see Pip strolling through the churchyard on a Sunday morning, walking just behind Isobel and Samuel, making faces at the other kids from the village.

If you do ever to Mildmay, you should definitely have a look at St John's. It's a nice little church with a peaceful graveyard and some pretty yew trees. You can do what I did. Stand near the entrance. Listen to the birdsong. Feel the breeze on your face. You can tell yourself that you're standing exactly where Pip stood and doing exactly what he did, every Sunday, four hundred years ago.

5

On Monday morning, like every other Monday morning, Pip worked alongside Samuel, following his stepfather's orders. He wiped blades, tidied the workshop and kept the fire roaring. But that Monday, unlike any other Monday, they didn't work in the afternoon. That Monday was different.

When Pip woke up in the morning he lay in bed for a few minutes, listening to the sound of voices in the other room. Reluctantly, knowing he would get in trouble if he lazed around much longer, he rolled out of the warmth and pulled on his clothes.

In the workshop, Samuel was sitting on the floor, entertaining the girls, doing tricks with a wooden top. Bridget giggled and clapped her hands. Susannah said, "My turn! My turn! It's my turn now!"

"Morning," said Pip.

The girls looked up briefly and smiled at their brother, then returned their attention to the spinning top. Samuel said, "Morning, Pip. Sleep well?"

"Yes, thanks," said Pip.

"No more nightmares?"

"No."

"Good. We'll have breakfast in a minute."

Susannah tugged her father's sleeve, asking him to spin the top again. Pip walked outside. He had a pee in the woods, then hunched over a barrel of rainwater to wash his face. The cold water shocked him fully awake.

Pip liked his stepfather, but couldn't help feeling a bit contemptuous of him. Although Samuel Smith had fought in a few battles, he'd never actually killed a man.

Barely out of his teens, Samuel had been plucked from the village by a band of roving recruiters, enlisted into the Queen's army and shipped across the sea to Ireland, where he stayed for a couple of years. As Samuel himself was happy to admit, he had been a reluctant recruit, always trying to avoid trouble, spending most of his time working in the smithy, reshoeing horses and repairing broken weapons, dreaming about the day that he could return to Mildmay and sleep in his own bed.

If Pip went to war, he'd want to fight. Of course he would. That was the point of a war. He'd try to kill as many men as possible. He often lay awake at night, dreaming about battles, imagining himself striding forward with a sword clasped in his right hand, a shield strapped to his left arm. He saw himself cutting a path through the enemy, swiping with his long blade, lopping limbs from anyone unlucky enough to come near him, leaving a trail of blood and fingers.

What little Samuel had learnt during those two years in the army he had now passed on to his stepson, showing him how to fight with a broadsword, a rapier, a spear, an axe and a knife. Pip learnt fast. Though he was half the size of his stepfather, he usually won their duels. He was more aggressive, more determined and gradually growing more skilful, taking his stepfather's few tricks and turning them against him, developing and improving what he had been taught. Pip was only twelve years old but, according to Samuel, he could already fight like an assassin.

After breakfast – bread and water, just as always – Isobel cleared away the dishes, then took her daughters outside. They would play in the garden while she weeded the vegetables and fed the hens.

Pip thrust some kindling on the fire and fanned the flames until they were blazing fiercely. The heat was astonishing. That's the worst part of being a smith: the constant heat, frying your eyes, scalding your skin, making your hair frizz. If the fire isn't hot enough the metal won't be bendy, and you can't shape it properly, which is why smiths have to keep piling wood on the flames, even on the hottest summer days.

Pip and Samuel spent the morning working together, sharpening some knives and fitting the handle on an old axe.

Just before lunch a tall thin man walked through the door, followed by a short fat man.

Pip stared at the two men and wondered who they were. Strangers didn't often come to the smithy unless they were selling something, and these two didn't look like salesmen. Pedlars usually wore old, dirty clothes, but these men were smartly dressed in clean black jerkins and leather breeches. They didn't have sacks slung over their shoulders. Nor did they start talking as soon as they came through the door, promising a bargain price on a saint's bone or offering a taste of some new herb from the other side of the world, just a penny a leaf. So, if they weren't selling anything, why were they here? What did they want?

One of them, the taller, had a lean body and an even leaner face, with high cheekbones and a cruel mouth. Pip immediately thought of a nickname for him. The Weasel. Yes, that was perfect. He did look like a weasel, thin and vicious, stealing eggs from a bird's nest or sneaking through the grass in pursuit of a mouse.

The other man was short and plump. Piggy little eyes peered out of his fat face. His belly flopped over the leather belt tied round his middle. He had wild hair, a straggly beard and thick, strong arms. Pip tried to think of a nickname for him too. Fatso. Cake-Lover. Lardy. Big Guts. Blubbermouth. They were all good names, but none of them were quite right. *I'll call him Pigface for now*, thought Pip. *Till I can think of something better.*

The Weasel glanced around the workshop, then pointed

his long forefinger at Pip's stepfather. "Are you Samuel Smith?"

"I am," said Samuel. "And who might you be?"

"We've travelled a long way to see you," said the Weasel, as if he hadn't even heard Samuel's question. "We've been told that no one in England makes a short sword with greater skill than yourself."

"Sadly that's not true," said Samuel. "I'm a smith, not a swordmaker. If you're looking for someone to make a sword, I can give you some names. Where do you come from?"

"London," said the Weasel.

Pip looked at the Weasel with more interest. Maybe later, when his stepfather was calculating prices for whatever the men eventually decided to buy, he would have a chance to quiz the Weasel about life in London. He didn't often meet people who had actually been there. He loved hearing their stories.

Samuel said, "You'll find a hundred good swordmakers in London. Better than me. Cheaper, too."

"You don't make swords?"

"The farmers round here don't have much use for modern weaponry. We mostly do knives." Samuel gestured at the blades arranged in a line on the floor. "Some scythes. The occasional plough."

The Weasel reached to his scabbard and pulled out a short sword. "What do you think of this? Is it a good sword?"

"Why are you asking me?"

"I'd like your professional opinion." He offered the sword to Samuel, handle first. "Go on, tell me what you think."

Samuel took the sword. He turned it over, then over again. He sniffed the handle, ran his finger down the blade and swung the sword through the air, back and forth, then handed it to the Weasel. "Not bad," said Samuel.

"Not bad? That cost me ten shillings."

"It's worth two," said Samuel. "Three at the most."

The Weasel laughed. "You see – you do know about swords. He said you did."

"He?"

"You have an excellent reputation, my friend. People were talking about you in the Bear Garden."

"About me?"

"Yes."

"I am surprised to hear that," said Samuel.

"Oh, yes, they told me all about you," said the Weasel. "They said there's a smith who lives in the woods. He makes a lot of money, but he never spends it. Has a bag of gold hidden in the house."

"That's a good story," said Samuel. "It would be even better if it was true."

"What's not true about it?"

"I have no gold."

"I don't believe you."

Samuel shrugged his shoulders. "Believe what you like."

"I will," said the Weasel. He took a step towards Samuel and lifted the sword, pointing the tip of the blade at

Samuel's chest. "I believe you have a bag of gold hidden in this house and I'd like you to give it to me. Right now."

At that moment, Pigface eased his sword from his scabbard and took up a position near the door, his bulky body blocking the exit, preventing anyone from escaping.

Pip stayed very still.

When you're being robbed, the worst thing you can do is make a sudden movement.

Keep calm, Samuel always said. *Don't panic. Wait for them to make a mistake. Don't worry, they will.*

And he was right – they always did.

Robbers came to the workshop every two or three months, attracted by the prospect of a wealthy smith working in the woods, half an hour's walk from the nearest village, out of earshot or eyesight of nosy neighbours. Most of them were just young lads, sixteen or seventeen years old, who had got bored of working in the fields and thought they could make some easy money. It was their first or second robbery. They didn't have a clue what they were doing. They were nervous and aggressive, and usually made their first mistake after a couple of minutes.

"Come on, my friend," said the Weasel. He didn't sound nervous or aggressive and he looked as if he knew exactly what he was doing. "Where's the gold?"

"People tell a lot of tales," said Samuel, shaking his head and smiling as if he hadn't noticed the sharp sword aimed at the middle of his chest. Pip could tell that his stepfather was making a great effort to stay calm. He wondered if the

Weasel could tell that too. "Who's been telling you these crazy stories?"

"A friend of yours," said the Weasel.

"Who?"

"Just a friend."

"I don't have many friends," said Samuel. "What was his name?"

"George Stone."

For a moment, Pip thought the Weasel had said *George Stone*. But that was impossible. His ears must have been tricking him.

Then Pip realized that he must have understood correctly, because Samuel had heard the same words too.

"George Stone is dead," said Samuel. "He died five years ago."

The Weasel smiled. "If he's dead, how did I see him last Friday?"

Pip stared at the Weasel. He could feel a strange sensation racing through his body, somewhere between terror and exhilaration. Could it be true? Could it?

Samuel said, "Maybe you saw a ghost."

"Then he's a ghost who owes me thirty pounds," said the Weasel. "Come on, my friend. Where's the gold?"

"I've told you already," said Samuel. "I have no gold."

The Weasel must be lying, thought Pip. *It's not true. It's not possible*.

For as long as he could remember, his existence had been defined by the death of his father. He was the boy without a dad. That was who he was, how he thought about himself. But if his father was still alive . . . What would that mean?

If his father was still alive, where was he? In the Bear Garden? No, that made no sense. If George Stone was in London, only thirty miles away, wouldn't he have come to Mildmay?

Of course he would. Unless he'd been in prison. Or lost his memory. Or been forced to fight in a private army. Or. . .

No, no. The Weasel must be lying. That was the simplest explanation and therefore the best. He looked like the type of man who lied. He had a liar's eyes, thin and narrow.

The Weasel took another pace towards Samuel. Now the sword's tip was touching Samuel's chest, right above his heart. "Come on, my friend," said the Weasel. "You got his wife. You can pay his debts. Where's the gold?"

Samuel shrugged his shoulders almost sadly. "If I was rich, would I really be living here, mending knives?"

"Don't lie to me, my friend," said the Weasel, nudging the blade into Samuel's chest. "The gold. Where is it?"

Samuel was forty-three years old. He had grey hair and a bald patch on the top of his head. His skin was ruddy and coarse from years of working at the forge, standing over the hot flames. He was no match for two strong young men armed with swords. In a quiet, melancholy voice, he said, "Philip?"

"Yes," said Pip.

"Fetch the box."

"Right now?"

"Yes. Now."

Pip nodded and walked towards the door. He knew exactly what Samuel meant. They had talked about *the box* before.

The Weasel smiled and relaxed his arm, lowering the sword from Samuel's chest.

There, thought Pip. *Finally. He's made his first mistake.*

6

As Pip walked towards the door, Pigface stepped aside to let him pass. He was grinning. Robberies weren't always this easy.

Pip noticed that Pigface and the Weasel had relaxed. They'd stopped giving the robbery their full attention. They were already imagining what they'd do when they got back to London and how they would spend their share of the cash. That was their second mistake.

Pip paused for a moment by the door. He looked to his left.

Propped against the wall there was a slim, smooth piece of wood. It looked like a walking stick or a broom handle. In fact, it was a stave, used by students in place of a sword. When an apprentice was learning new techniques he wouldn't fight with a real sword, not if he wanted to keep all his fingers.

Pigface and the Weasel were so calm and confident that they didn't bother watching Pip very closely. Neither of them noticed him stretching out his right hand and gripping the top of the stave.

Before anyone had time to react Pip twirled round, swinging his arm with great force, and thwacked the stave into the back of the Weasel's knees.

"Aaaah!" cried the Weasel, dropping his sword and falling forward, his face creased with pain.

That's what Samuel had been waiting for. In a movement that was startlingly quick for such a placid-looking middle-aged man, he stepped forward and punched the Weasel in the eye.

"Owwww!" moaned the Weasel, staggering backwards.

Samuel kicked him in the chest. The Weasel fell to the floor and lay there in a heap, clutching his eye with one hand and his chest with the other.

Everything happened so fast, Pigface had no chance to react. He stood there stupidly, blinking at the Weasel's body on the floor, then lifted his head and looked at Pip.

Pip smiled.

In a low voice Pigface said, "You're going to wish you hadn't done that."

Pip didn't stop smiling. He was waiting for Pigface to make the third mistake. And, just as he'd hoped, that was exactly what happened.

Pigface was a fully grown man armed with a sword,

while his opponent, a mere boy, had nothing but a wooden stave. If Pigface had taken time to think, planning his next move rather than acting impulsively, he could have won the fight quickly and easily. Instead, he lifted his sword and ran across the room.

Pip didn't move. Not yet. He didn't want to commit himself too early. He watched the fat man, observing how his belly wobbled, how his heavy legs thumped on the ground, where his eyes were focused, and listened to the sound of his sword whistling through the air.

At the last possible moment, just before Pigface reached him, Pip finally moved. In one continuous flowing action, Pip jumped forward and batted Pigface's sword aside with his stave, then twisted, ducked and kicked Pigface between the legs.

A moment later Pip was standing on the other side of the room, ready for the next attack, and Pigface was doubled over in agony, clutching himself between his legs.

Pigface slowly eased himself upright. His cheeks were red. His eyes were dark. He definitely wasn't going to stop and think now. Yelling at full volume, he swung his sword and charged.

Pip ducked, letting the blade sail over his head, then swung his stave and delivered a cracking blow to Pigface's left knee.

Pigface fell forward, howling.

Pip was just lifting the stave above his head, preparing to smack Pigface's skull with one final blow, when he felt something nudging the back of his neck.

Something cold. Something sharp.

He stayed very still.

A voice said, "Turn round."

Slowly, taking great care not to make any sudden movements, Pip turned to face the doorway.

A man was standing there. He had a scar on his left cheek, running all the way from the corner of his mouth to the tip of his ear. He was holding a long sword outstretched in his right hand, the sharpened point just a few inches from Pip's neck.

"Drop it," said the man with the scar.

Pip glanced across the workshop.

Samuel was standing over the Weasel with an axe.

Tit for tat. If the man with the scar sunk his sword into Pip, Samuel would chop off the Weasel's head. As the Bible said: an eye for an eye, a tooth for a tooth. Both of them would die, Pip and the Weasel, and no one would get what they wanted.

In all his imaginary fights, Pip had never been confronted by a situation like this. He didn't know what to do. Should he surrender? Or should he carry on fighting? He was young and quick. Maybe he could move faster than Scar's arm, ducking before the sword reached his neck. With a bit of luck, he decided, he and his stepfather could still win this fight. He was just about to jump backwards, hurling himself to the ground, when Scar said, "Look."

Pip turned his head and looked.

Outside the door, Isobel and her daughters were

standing beside a fourth man, the final member of the Weasel's gang. In his right hand the man was holding a knife, the blade pressed against Bridget's white throat. Her eyes were wide with terror.

"Go on," said Scar, nodding at the stave in Pip's hand. "Drop it."

Pip had no choice. He dropped it.

7

The Weasel picked himself off the ground, brushed the dust from his clothes, then punched Samuel in the face three times in quick succession. Samuel greeted every punch with a groan, but didn't even try to resist. His arms hung hopelessly by his sides.

Pigface knocked Pip to the floor and kicked him in the stomach, taking revenge for what had happened earlier. *You might have beaten me once*, Pigface seemed to say with every kick, *but I can beat you a hundred times.*

Pip didn't make a sound. He wasn't going to give Pigface that satisfaction. He just rolled into a ball, wrapping his arms around his skull, trying to protect himself.

Scar and the fourth man stood in the doorway with their arms folded, watching the action. The fourth man was smiling. He only had one tooth.

Over by the far wall, Isobel squatted on the floor, hugging her daughters. Bridget sucked her thumb, confused and scared. Susannah was crying.

With another punch the Weasel knocked Samuel to the ground, then stood over him. Blood dribbled from Samuel's nose and his split lips.

"It's your choice," said the Weasel.

"What?" groaned Samuel.

"You can be sensible. Or you can be an idiot."

"I don't understand."

"You can tell me where the money is," said the Weasel. "Or you can watch me kill your wife. And when I've killed your wife, I'll kill your children. And when I've killed your wife and your children, I'll kill you. Or, if you want to be sensible, you can just give me the money right now. Like I said, it's your choice."

Samuel didn't even hesitate. He told the Weasel exactly where to find the money. "Go outside," he said. "Dig in the vegetable patch. You'll find a bag buried beside the onions."

The Weasel sent Scar and the fourth man outside to fetch the bag. They returned after a couple of minutes with a bunch of onions and a ragged leather bag.

The Weasel shook off the loose dirt and peered inside the bag. He tipped the contents on the floor. Dull coins rolled in all directions, followed by a necklace, a bracelet, a little silver bowl and a lump of gold about the size of a broad bean. The Weasel picked through the coins and inspected the jewellery, then shook his head. He had been expecting more. "This won't do," he said.

The room was quiet. Everyone watched the Weasel, waiting to see what he would do next.

The Weasel turned to Samuel. "I thought you were supposed to be rich."

"I don't know where you got that idea," said Samuel.

"From my friend George."

"George Stone is dead," said Samuel.

"George Stone is very much alive," said the Weasel. "And he owes me a lot of money. He said you'd pay his debts for him."

Samuel shook his head. "I've already told you. I'm not rich. And even if I was, I wouldn't pay George Stone's debts."

"Someone has to," said the Weasel. He turned and stared at Pip. "You're George's son, aren't you?"

Pip didn't reply. He tried to keep his face expressionless, wanting to give nothing away, but he must have failed because the Weasel said:

"Don't look so surprised. He's told me about you."

You don't know my father, thought Pip. *You're lying. My father is dead. And even if my father was alive he wouldn't stand in the same room as scum like you.*

"I'd know you anywhere," said Weasel. "You've got his eyes."

That shocked Pip. *No one's ever said that to me*, he thought. *But is it true? Have I really got my dad's eyes?*

The Weasel said, "You're like him, aren't you? I can see it. You're a proper little fighter, just like your father. Right?"

Pip wanted to reply, but he forced himself to stay silent. If he had opened his mouth, a hundred questions about his father would have bubbled out of him. *Where does he live? Is he married? Does he have more children? Why hasn't he come here? Where has he been for the past seven years?*

The Weasel smiled. It was almost as if he could hear what Pip was thinking. "Your father's got himself in a bit of trouble," he said. "Do you want to pay his debts? That's what a good son would do. Do you have some money buried in the garden too?"

At that moment Pip would have liked to leap across the room and hurl himself at the Weasel, but he wasn't going to be fighting anyone for a while, not until his bruised belly had stopped aching. So he stayed very still, staring at the Weasel, refusing to speak.

The Weasel soon got bored of baiting the boy and turned his attention back to Samuel Smith. "Tell me something, my friend. You say you're not rich. If that's true, why would George Stone say you've got a box of gold?"

"I used to have some money," said Samuel.

"When?"

"A few years ago. But it's all gone now."

"What went wrong?"

"Nothing went wrong," said Samuel. "Something went right. I got married. Now I have a wife and three children to feed."

The Weasel shook his head. "I think you're lying."

"Look at my house. Look at our clothes. Do we look rich?"

The Weasel looked around the room. He shook his head. "No, not really."

"So why don't you believe me?"

"It's just my way," said the Weasel. "I never believe anyone." Turning to Isobel and her daughters, he said, "I'm sorry, ladies. I wish I didn't have to do this, but your husband – your father – isn't giving me much choice. Unless you'd like to tell me where I'll find the rest of the money."

He waited a moment, giving them a chance to answer, but none of them said a word. The Weasel shrugged his shoulders, then issued a series of brisk orders to his men.

Scar, Tooth and Pigface ripped the house apart, smashing the furniture and wrecking the workshop. They broke every pot, pan, plate and jug. Although they couldn't find any gold, they did unearth a silver ring, several good swords and a few more coins. The Weasel told his men to grab whatever they fancied. Scar left with a chair. Tooth took the axe that Samuel had just repaired. Pigface wrapped ten knives in a square of cloth and tucked the bundle under his arm. When the Weasel was sure that they'd gathered everything of any value, he ushered them out of the house. Their voices and laughter faded as they walked down the path, and then they were gone.

8

Today, about fifteen thousand people live in Mildmay. In 1601, there were eighty-three. Dogs and cats roamed along the single street. Wooden pens held snuffling hogs. Sheep and cows grazed in the fields. Gangs of chickens ran free, laying their eggs wherever they pleased. The air was quiet. You could hear a thrush singing, the wind rustling in the trees or the footsteps of someone walking behind you.

When Samuel and Isobel walked into the village, followed by their children, a couple of dogs barked and an old man waved, but no one showed much interest. That changed as soon as Samuel told a farmer about the robbery. His niece overheard the conversation. She ran to tell her brothers. Word spread fast. The houses emptied. Men hurried from the fields. Soon, all eighty-three villagers had come to look at the Smiths, peering at their cuts and bruises, asking questions, demanding to know what the robbers looked like and how much they had taken.

Villagers pressed food and possessions on the Smiths. Someone gave them two chickens. Someone else offered them a six-week-old puppy who didn't even have a name yet. "With him in the house, you'll never be robbed again," said the villager. "Once he's a bit bigger, of course."

No one had seen the Weasel or his men. They must have sneaked through the woods, avoiding Mildmay and the fields, joining the London road further south.

Heading home, Isobel clasped Bridget to her hip with her right hand and held two chickens upside down in her left, carrying them by their feet. Pip and Samuel were laden with bowls and blankets, bread and onions, earthenware pots and wooden implements, donated by villagers. Susannah came last, pulling the puppy on a short length of rope, trying to teach him to recognize his new name. "Pepper! Pepper! Come here, Pepper!"

You're probably wondering why Samuel didn't call the police and report the robbery.

I can tell you exactly why. The police hadn't been invented yet. The first policeman wouldn't arrive in Mildmay for another three hundred years.

In London and the larger towns, the authorities hired out-of-work soldiers as watchmen, paying them to wander through the streets at night, arresting anyone who caused a disturbance. In the countryside, people just had to look after themselves.

In 1601, the police weren't the only thing that hadn't yet been invented. There were no photographs. Or fingerprints. No one carried passports, driving licences or identity cards. It was impossible to know who people really were. Thieves could wander through the countryside, inventing different names for themselves wherever they went, changing identity every day, leaving a trail of confusion. One person would say, "Jack Spot stole my knife" and someone else would say, "Peter Poker nicked my kettle", and they wouldn't even know that they were talking about the same bloke.

It was a good time to be a criminal. Unless you got caught.

Getting caught meant getting hanged. Steal a cake or a chicken, even a few pennies, and you'd earn yourself the death penalty. One or two judges liked to impose more peculiar punishments – ordering that a pickpocket's right hand should be chopped off, for instance, or forcing a conman to walk through the streets wearing a big sign saying I AM A CHEAT – but it was usually cheaper, quicker and easier just to hang someone.

You'd be taken to a public place and made to stand on a wooden stool. A crowd always gathered to watch. As the hangman fitted the noose around your neck, people shouted at you.

"Good riddance!"

"Send my love to the devil!"

Your mum might be standing at the front of the crowd, weeping. A few friends might have come to say goodbye.

Or you'd be alone, facing the angry crowd, trying to pretend you weren't scared.

When the time was right, the hangman kicked aside the stool. The crowd cheered, thumping their feet on the ground and throwing their hats in the air. You plummeted. Your weight made the rope go taut. If you were lucky, the drop broke your neck and you died instantly. If you weren't so lucky, you hung there for ten minutes, writhing and kicking, the rope biting into your neck, slowly squeezing the last scraps of breath from your shuddering body.

9

Samuel Smith was a practical man. He didn't see the point of worrying about the past. Better to think about the future. His house might have been smashed to pieces and his hard-earned savings stolen by a gang of thieves, but he didn't waste his energy weeping, cursing or complaining. Instead, he cleared the debris out of the cottage, dividing the family's possessions into two piles – what could be repaired and what couldn't – then walked into the woods with an axe that he'd borrowed from one of the villagers and chopped down several trees. Pip worked alongside him, sorting the damp wood into piles and carrying armfuls of timber back to the cottage. Over the next few days they would build new furniture for the family and a new workshop for the smithy.

When they paused for a rest, Pip said, "We should go to London."

"Why?"

"To get revenge."

Samuel shook his head. "I've already lost my money. I don't want to lose my life too."

Pip knew there was no point arguing. Samuel was too scared to take revenge on his enemies. *Not like my father*, thought Pip. *That's not what he would have done.*

Since the robbery, no one had mentioned George Stone or discussed what the Weasel had said. Pip wanted to quiz his mother, but she always seemed to be busy, hurrying away whenever he tried to talk to her, and he couldn't bring himself to raise the subject with his stepfather. Talking to Samuel about George didn't feel right.

Had the Weasel been telling the truth? If so, Pip's mother had lied to him. Not just once, either. Again and again. Hundreds of times. If George Stone was still alive, then she had been lying every day for the past five years. The whole thing must have been a trick. To get his father out of the house. And bring Samuel in.

Or had the Weasel been lying? Was George Stone dead, just as his mother said?

There was only one way for Pip to find out. Not by talking to his mother. Nor by quizzing his stepfather. Whatever they told him, he wouldn't believe them. No, he had to discover the truth for himself. He had to go to London.

10

In the middle of the night Pip sat up in his bed. He was wide awake. He had made a plan and he was determined to carry it out. There was no time to waste. He rolled out of bed. The room was dark. Feeling his way by fingertip, he grabbed his clothes, got dressed, collected his father's knife and picked up his boots. Barefoot, he padded to the door.

A few embers glowed in the fire, illuminating the room with a pale orangey glow. Samuel and Isobel were sleeping on a pile of blankets, with Bridget and Susannah curled beside them. Pepper was lying at their feet. When he saw Pip, his tail thumped on the blanket.

Pip stood there for a moment, staring at his family, wondering if this was the last time that he'd ever see them.

He thought about writing a note, but decided not to.

He could only read slowly, and wrote even slower, so scrawling a note would waste hours. They'd guess where he had gone. Anyway, he'd be back soon.

He tiptoed through the workshop, carrying his boots, and stepped outside. The air was cool. The crescent moon cast just enough light to silhouette the trees. He walked to the mossy stump of a long-dead oak and sat down, placing his boots on the grass.

And then he stopped. He didn't pull on his boots. Nor did he start walking. He just sat there, paralysed, unable to keep moving.

What was wrong? He'd always planned to go to London and fight at Bartholomew Fair, just like his father had. So why didn't pull on his boots, stand up and start walking?

Because he was scared.

There, he'd admitted the truth to himself. He was terrified of the long walk to London and, even more, what he might find when he got there. Not just the Weasel and his gang but the city itself. He'd never been anywhere except the cottage, the woods and Mildmay. How would he cope with the biggest city in the world?

He knew a few details about London, gleaned from conversations that he'd overheard in the smithy or the village. Pedlars had talked about the sights that you would see if you took a walk through the city: St Paul's Cathedral and the Tower, Cheapside and Eastcheap, the Rose Theatre and Bartholomew Fair, black men and brown men, Frenchmen and Africans, priests and poets, lords and dukes, elephants and dwarfs, parrots and monkeys, and even old Queen Bess herself, all jumbled together inside the tall city walls. Houses were painted with gold. The water was so dirty that you'd get sick from a single sip. The women wore diamonds and emeralds dangling from their ears. You weren't supposed to shake hands with a Londoner; he'd steal your money quicker than you could say "Pleased to meet you."

Pip stared at his boots.

He was a country boy. He knew the rhythms of the seasons and the smells of the fields. He could recognize the songs of twenty different birds, recite the names of a hundred herbs and track a deer through the forest. But how would that help him in London?

If I was brave, thought Pip, *if I was a man like my father, I'd just pull on my boots and start walking. No matter that I'm a country boy. I'd go to London, find the Bear Garden and catch the Weasel.*

Perhaps he would find his own father too, if George Stone was alive, if the Weasel had been telling the truth, if, if, if. . .

I'm a coward, thought Pip.

He was disgusted by himself. But that didn't make him feel any less frightened or confused.

I should go back to sleep, thought Pip. *Forget London. Tomorrow I'll wake up and eat breakfast with Bridget and Susannah, then spend the day working with Samuel.*

That would be his whole life. Every day and every night. Waking up, working, going to sleep, over and over again, till the day he died. He could already see his entire existence stretching ahead of him. Never moving more than a mile from Mildmay. Working as the smith. Inheriting his profession from Samuel. He'd marry a farmer's daughter. They would own chickens and dogs. Their children would marry the children of other villagers. When he died, he would have a stone in the churchyard engraved with his name, and his children's children would visit every Sunday, bringing flowers cut from the fields.

An ordinary life. No better and no worse than most people's.

He had been sitting there for a long time, staring at the stars and the moon, dreaming about the future, when a soft voice said, "What are you doing?"

11

Pip turned round and stared through the gloom. His mother was standing in the doorway. She had closed the door behind her to avoid disturbing the others. "What are you doing?" she repeated.

"Nothing," said Pip.

"Come on, lambkin. Don't fib."

"I'm not doing anything."

"It's the middle of the night and you're sitting outside in the dark. That's not nothing. What are you really doing?"

Pip stared through the gloom. He stood up, clutching his boots, and was surprised to hear himself say, "I'm going to London."

"Why?"

"To get our money back."

"Forget the money," said his mother, taking a couple of steps towards him, keeping her voice low. "The money doesn't matter. We can always earn more money."

"Of course it matters."

She shook her head. "Some things are more important than money."

"They took what's ours." Each word that he spoke made him more confident, more sure of himself. He wasn't scared any more. He was ready. He said, "I have to get it back again."

"Those men are different. They'll kill you."

"Not if I kill them first."

Isobel walked across the grass to her son. She reached out and touched his face with her hand. She whispered, "I know why you want to go to London. But please don't. Not yet."

Pip looked hard at his mother. "I don't know what you mean."

"You think you'll find your father, don't you?"

"You told me he was dead."

"I thought he was."

"Thought?"

"I still think he is."

"So why did they say they'd seen him?"

"They must have been lying."

"Why would they lie about that?"

"I don't know," said Isobel. "I really don't."

As they spoke, the two of them were gradually shuffling away from the house, keeping their voices low, moving further into the woods so they wouldn't wake Samuel or the girls.

Pip said, "Is he dead?"

"I don't know, lambkin."

"Did you see his body? Did you bury him?"

Isobel shook her head. "No, I didn't."

"So what happened? Why do you think he's dead?"

Isobel shivered. She was wearing a thin pale smock which stopped just above her knees. Her legs and feet were bare. "Come inside," she said, wrapping her arms around herself. "We can talk about this in the morning."

"I want to talk about it now," said Pip. Once again, he was surprised by himself. He'd never spoken to his mother like this before. Something had changed between them, he didn't know what, but he could sense that her power over him was ebbing away, leaving him to make his own decisions. He said, "If he's not dead, why did you tell me he was?"

Isobel paused for a moment. Then she must have decided that there was no reason to hide the truth. "Your father just vanished," she said. "One day he was here. The next he wasn't. I didn't know where he'd gone. Or what had happened to him. I didn't know anything. I waited, lambkin. I thought he'd come back again. I waited two years."

"And then?"

"You know what happened."

"No, I don't."

"Samuel came to live here."

"And you had to say my father was dead? So you could get married again?"

"Not exactly."

"Then what did happen?"

"Come back inside. We can talk about this in the morning."

"I want to talk about it now," said Pip. "Is my father alive?"

"I don't know," said Isobel.

"Please, Mother, just tell me the truth."

"That's the truth. I don't know. But if I had to make a guess, I'd say he's probably dead. He's a violent man, your father. Most likely he got drunk, insulted someone and they—"

"I'm going to London," interrupted Pip. He turned his back on his mother and, carrying a boot in each hand, walked away. The grass was cold underfoot, and stones dug into his bare soles, but he kept going, not wanting to hear any more of his mother's opinions about his father. He'd rather discover his father's character for himself.

He had taken ten steps down the path when a voice cut through the murk.

"Pip, wait."

Something about his mother's voice made him stand still. Perhaps he really wanted to be persuaded to stay. Or perhaps things can't really change that quickly between two people. He was still her child, her boy, and he did what he was told.

When Isobel reached him, she held his face between

her hands, forcing him to look at her. "Your father. . ." She sighed. "You'd be happier if you forgot him."

"Why?"

"He's not a good man."

"I'm going," said Pip, trying to pull himself away.

"Wait," whispered Isobel. She took him in her arms and hugged him. "Good luck, Pip. And God bless."

They embraced for a moment. Then Pip broke free and hurried down the path. He was half hoping that she'd call his name, forcing him to stop, but she didn't say a word.

When Pip reached the edge of the clearing, just before he stepped into the dark woods, he paused to put on his boots. He knelt on the ground. Surreptitiously, sure he was being observed, he glanced over his shoulder and looked at the house.

Nothing stirred. No one was watching him. His mother had already gone back inside, shutting the door after her.

Pip pulled on his boots, turned his back on the house and started walking.

12

You might think it's strange that Pip's mother didn't try harder to stop him. Pip was only twelve years old. Just a boy. How could she let him travel to London on his own? Why didn't she pull him back into the house and send him to bed?

I can think of a few reasons. Here's one: Isobel might have suspected that she couldn't stop him even if she wanted to. Like his dad, Pip was stubborn.

Maybe Isobel also had a secret motive of her own: with only one man around, the house would be a more peaceful place.

There was another reason too. Four hundred years ago people grew up faster.

Pip knew other boys in the village, boys his age, who had already gone into the world, seeking their own fortunes. One became an apprentice in Hertford. Another joined the army, attaching himself to a group of soldiers who were travelling from village to village, scooping up recruits. A third just walked out one morning, stealing a spare shirt, a knife and a hunk of cheese from his folks, not bothering to say goodbye. No one knew what had happened to him. He'd never returned to Mildmay or sent any kind of message to his family. He might have got a job, made some money and turned himself into a rich man. Or he might have been robbed on the road and left for dead.

It wasn't just village boys who grew up fast. Everyone did.

A few years before the events that I've been describing, William Shakespeare wrote a play called *Romeo and Juliet.* I'm sure you've heard of it. Maybe you've seen it. Even if you haven't, you probably know the story. Juliet's parents want her to marry one man. She falls in love with another. They run away together. And then. . .

Actually, I won't tell you what happens at the end. You'll have to see the play for yourself. But the important thing is this. Although Romeo and Juliet have become two of the most famous lovers in the world, there is one fact that people often forget about them. Shakespeare was very specific about the age of his heroine. She's only thirteen.

Today, Juliet wouldn't be allowed to drive or vote or buy a bottle of wine. And she certainly wouldn't be allowed to get married.

In 1601, if you were a girl, you could get married as

soon as you were twelve years old. So said the law.

The same law insisted that boys couldn't get married so young. They had to be fourteen.

As I said, people grew up faster four hundred years ago.

13

The sky was grey now, rather than black, but the trees were still shrouded in darkness. Pip walked briskly through the woods.

When he reached Mildmay, not a single person was awake, but two black dogs stood in the middle of the street, watching him approach, their jaws dribbling drool. He greeted them by name and tickled their ears. "Hello, Rook. Good morning, Berry." They were Charlie Baker's hounds.

Rook and Berry ran alongside him to the edge of the village, then let him go on alone.

He glanced back once. The dogs were still watching him. Smoke trickled from one of the houses. Someone was up.

Pip turned his back on Mildmay and started walking

fast, leaping over puddles. The only sounds were birdsong, the wind rustling among the trees and his own footsteps. He marched along the empty road – the road that would lead him to the greatest city in the world.

Throughout that first long, exhausting day, Pip often thought about going home, but whenever he was tempted to retrace his steps, he reminded himself of what his mother had said. "You think you'll find your father." *Of course I do*, he thought. *Now I know he's alive, how could I not want to find him? And how could you tell me he was dead? How could you lie to me about something as important as that?* Thinking about his mother and his stepfather, he felt an emotion that he didn't know well, a bitter fury, and it forced him onward, step by step, mile by mile, driving him away from home and towards the city.

He drank from a stream and gathered a handful of unripe blackberries growing by the roadside, but they hardly dented his hunger. He hurried through villages. The smell of cooking was almost more than he could bear. He didn't have any money to buy food, and he was too proud to beg, so he'd just have to go hungry. When he got to London and retrieved his stepfather's possessions from the Weasel, he'd buy himself a fresh warm loaf and some boiled beef.

By midday, his pride had evaporated, burnt off by hunger. There was nothing wrong with begging, he decided. Anyway, it was better than starving. In the next village he stopped at every cottage, poked his head through each doorway and pleaded with the housewives inside. Some laughed and others cursed, sending him away with nothing, but one gave him a crust of bread and another fished an old bone out of a pot.

He ate as he walked, sucking every scrap of taste from the bone, then spinning it into the undergrowth.

There was no point continuing in darkness – he'd just lose the road and go round in circles – so he stopped at dusk on the outskirts of a village and sneaked into an empty barn. He was so exhausted, and the straw was so comfortable, that oblivion came immediately.

Voices woke him at dawn. He padded out of the barn. Behind him, someone yelled. "Oi! What d'you think you're doing?" Without even turning round to see who was shouting at him, Pip sprinted down the road.

He walked for several hours. His feet hurt. He was hungry and exhausted. Worst of all, he was bored of the thoughts rattling round his head: he worried about his empty stomach, his sore feet, his father and the Weasel, and then he worried about the same things again his stomach, his feet, his father, the Weasel, and then again and again and again, stomach, feet, father, Weasel, stomach, feet, father, Weasel, the same thoughts whirring round his skull until he thought he was going mad.

Just as he was beginning to think he would never reach London, he saw a fuzz on the horizon, a kind of blurring, as if a giant thumb had smudged the land into the sky. The sight gave him energy. He sped up.

The city grew. He could see the roofs of houses, too many to count. The walls of London rose like a curtain, topped with a hundred spires. He passed three windmills, the sails turning slowly in the breeze.

There was a horrible smell. He looked at his boots, wondering if he'd stepped in something, but they were clean. He walked on. Soon the smell grew stronger and he realized it was being brought by the breeze.

The road was busier. Horsemen trotted past. Carts carried wood and wheat. A girl herded a flock of waddling geese. A man laboured under the weight of a dead sheep slung over his shoulders. Women were working in the fields, weeding lines of vegetables. Shepherds whistled at their dogs. No one took any notice of a small boy, staring with wide eyes at the walls of the city.

Here they were. The walls of London. Tall. Built of big stones. Covered with moss. And on the other side. . . That was still hidden. Pip hurried onwards.

Just outside the walls there was a small market. Farmers had come from the countryside, spread blankets across the mud and laid out neat displays of fruit and veg. Chickens squawked as housewives prodded their flesh. Rabbits and piglets squatted in crates. Miserable calves mooed for their mothers. Stallholders shouted advertisements for their products. "Twelve ripe plums for a penny! Get them here! Good sweet plums!"

A man snapped his fingers at Pip. "You! Boy!"

"Yes, sir?" said Pip nervously, wondering what he had done wrong.

"Come here." The man beckoned.

Pip hurried over.

The man leant forward. In a low voice, as if he were

sharing a secret, he said, "Would you like to buy some new shoes?"

"No, thank you, sir," said Pip. "But will you tell me something? Which way is the Bear Garden?"

"You see that gate?" The shoemaker pointed at a large wooden gate built into the stone walls. "That's Bishopsgate. Go through there, head south, cross the river, you'll find yourself at the Bear Garden."

"Thank you, sir," said Pip. "Thank you very much."

He walked to Bishopsgate. A broad-shouldered guard lingered by one of the wooden gateposts, flirting with a pretty girl. Pip was worried that he might be forced to declare his business or explain why he should be allowed into the city, maybe even pay an entrance fee, but when he hurried past, the girl was flicking her long hair away from her face, and the guard didn't even glance at Pip.

14

Pip hadn't taken more than ten paces into London when a white-haired woman lunged towards him, holding something in her right hand. Pip raised his fists and took a step backwards, ready to defend himself, then glanced at her weapon and saw that it was nothing but a strip of pale pinkish flesh. The woman said, "Will you buy some nice smoked eel?"

"Sorry," said Pip. "I've got no money." Smiling at the woman and turning to continue down the street, he collided immediately with a burly man who was hurrying past, carrying a duck under each arm. "Watch where you're going!"

"Sorry, I didn't mean to. . ." said Pip, but the man had already gone.

Pip stumbled onward, dodging through the crowd,

heading deeper into London. People flooded towards him. A chicken ran through his legs. On either side, ramshackle houses drooped over the street, shutters lolling open, windows spilling laundry, spread across the sills to dry in the sun. In the strip of blue sky that was visible above the houses, Pip could see the crisp silhouettes of martins flitting from roof to roof.

An unbelievable stench rose from the gutters. Once, years ago, before he learnt to defend himself, three boys from the village had picked him up and hurled him into a pigsty. They forced him to stay inside, rolling around with two pigs, until his clothes were stained brown and dripping wet, but the pig muck hadn't stunk half as bad as London. The stink on the road – that had been the city itself.

He turned left at a crossroads, hurried across a wide street lined with stalls selling fruit and vegetables, and jumped back to avoid two men brawling in the middle of the road. The smaller of the men reached down to his belt and drew a knife. The taller backed away, lifting his fists and shouting, "Never touch her again! Do you hear me? Don't you ever come near her!" The man with the knife just laughed, swishing the blade from side to side.

Pip circled past, not knowing where he was going, and not caring either. Already he was lost, bewildered by the ever-flowing mass of people and houses, and couldn't have found his way back to Bishopsgate. After a couple of minutes he must have seen more people than he had seen in all the rest of his life added together.

He thought of Mildmay, the eleven houses, the families who all knew one another, the quietness and calm that almost always hung over the village, the feeling that nothing had ever changed and nothing ever would. Everyone in the village knew everyone else's name. A stranger would be noticed, followed, interrogated. An unexpected noise had people hurrying out of their houses, coming to see what had happened. Here in London, Pip had realized already, no one cared.

A group of women stood around a pump with buckets. Pip stopped and asked one of them for a cup of water. She laughed in his face. Pip hurried away, wanting to know what was so funny but not daring to ask.

When he turned the next corner a hand grabbed his sleeve. Pip whirled round to find a red face pressed close to his. His first thought was that he'd caught by the Weasel. But it wasn't the Weasel's voice which hissed: "The day is coming!"

Pip said, "What?"

"The day is coming," repeated the man with the red face. He was a wild-eyed preacher in a long brown smock. A wooden cross was hanging around his neck on a length of withered cord. "Tell me, boy, are you ready to be saved? Will you repent of your sins?"

Pip stammered hopelessly and tried to pull himself away, but the preacher was stronger than he looked, keeping a tight grip on Pip's sleeve. "Unless you turn against Satan and embrace the path of Our Lord, you will burn in hell!"

With a mighty tug, Pip freed himself, then sprinted away, pushing through the crowd. The preacher's shouts pursued him to the end of the street. "Make your choice! The day is coming! The day is upon us!"

Confused and completely lost, Pip stumbled through the city, heading down one street, then another.

"Look out below," shouted a voice.

Pip stopped where he was and looked up.

A bucket of slops dropped from an upstairs window and splashed on to his head.

The fresh, warm filth dribbled down his cheeks, clogging his ears and nostrils. His eyes stung. He spluttered and coughed and spat the slops out of his mouth, blew his nose to clear his nostrils, scrubbed his face with his sleeves and hurried onward.

In the countryside, you used the woods and the fields as your toilet. You squatted behind a tree and wiped your bum on a leaf.

In the city, inside your house, you used a bucket. When the bucket was full, you tipped it out of the window into the street. You shouted first: "Look out below!"

Down in the street, people jumped aside, knowing what was coming.

You heaved the bucket on to the windowsill and tipped it out. A stream of pee and poo poured into the street, cascading on to the road, splashing the legs of anyone unlucky enough to be walking past. Or soaking the head of anyone foolish enough not to jump aside.

An open drain ran down the middle of the street. Debris collected in the drain. Not just pee and poo but bones and fur, grass and twigs, apple cores and onion skins, fish heads and stale bread, all kinds of rubbish, all jumbled together, waiting for a good rainstorm to wash them down the street towards the river.

That was why the city smelt so terrible.

If the wind was right, you could catch a whiff of London from ten miles away. Anyone who lived in the city or one of the neighbouring villages got used to the stench, but posh visitors spent their first few days in London holding scented handkerchiefs over their noses, trying to block out the stink.

Two hundred thousand people lived in London, crammed inside the walls with an army of animals – not just chickens, cows, sheep and goats, but hawks and ravens, rats and roaches, squabbling over every scrap of food. Altogether, this vast mass of creatures belched a symphony of sounds, smells and sights unlike anything that a quiet country boy could have imagined. Pip was hungry and thirsty, and he stank like a cesspit, but the city overwhelmed his senses, crowding out his own physical discomforts, and he found himself walking slower and slower, stopping often to look at things.

Some men were speaking a language that he couldn't understand, so Pip paused for a minute, eavesdropping on their conversation, trying to decide if they could actually understand one another or were just having a laugh, making up the strange sounds as they went along.

They were speaking French, but Pip didn't know that. He'd never heard anything except English.

As he continued through the streets, he heard all kinds of languages, dialects and accents. Just like today, people from all around the world lived in London. The majority of the citizens were English, but there were lots of Scots, Welsh and Irish, plus a few French, Dutch, Spanish and Italians, and a smattering of other nationalities too.

A terrible scream came from a dark doorway. A painted sign hung above the door with three words scrawled in black ink. Letter by letter, Pip read the words to himself: WEE PUL TETH. While he was standing there, another scream echoed from inside the doorway, and he hurried onward.

He passed a dead cat lying in the gutter, a pair of black rats feeding on its bloody entrails. The rats were fearless, taking no notice of the people walking past.

A painted carriage eased through the street, pulled by two horses. Four uniformed men walked in front of the carriage and four more walked behind. Like everyone else, Pip tried to peer inside, but the curtains were drawn. He wondered who might be riding in a carriage like that. A noble lord, perhaps. An elegant lady. Or even the Queen. Now she was nearly seventy she wouldn't want to walk. No, he reminded himself, if Queen Elizabeth was processing through London she would be guarded by more than eight men. Pip had heard stories of the foreign assassins sent from Scotland and Spain, determined to kill the Queen and replace her with a Catholic monarch.

He walked down a street full of bakeries. The smell of warm bread oozed into the air. Shops sold spices that he had never smelt and fruits that he had never seen, taunting his tastebuds. He scoured the ground with his eyes, searching for a discarded scrap of bread or a half-eaten apple, but found nothing.

At every corner, the name of each street had been painted on a wall. The bakers were in Bread Street and the cheesemakers in Milk Street. Candlewick Street housed the candlemakers. Goldsmith's Row was packed with jewellers. Down the length of Threadneedle Street, tailors and weavers hung strips of fine cloth from their windows. Friday Street stank of salt. The fishmongers stood by their stalls, gutting fish. A river of scales, tails and blood ran down the gutter. Two dogs fought over a herring. Pip was tempted to break up the fight and steal the fish for himself, but the dogs looked vicious.

Two men were standing nearby, talking in loud voices. "Sorry to trouble you, sirs," said Pip, interrupting their conversation. "Can you tell me the way to the Bear Garden?"

"Cross the river at the bridge," replied one of the men. "Turn right on the other side. You can't miss it." He turned his back on Pip and continued his conversation.

Pip said, "And sir? Sir?"

The man snapped, "Yes?"

"Then what? When I've crossed the river."

"I told you, turn right."

"And then what?"

"You'll come to a large building. With high white walls. And a flag flying on the roof. That's the Bear Garden."

"And which way is the river?"

The man lifted his arm and pointed. "That way."

"Thank you, sir. Thank you." Pip hurried in the direction that the man had pointed. As he walked, he repeated to himself the description that he had just been given, making sure he didn't forget anything. A large building with high white walls and a flag flying on the roof. That should be easy enough to find.

When Pip had been walking for a long time, pushing through busy streets, stopping every few minutes to ask directions, he found a bucket of water, left unattended outside a house. The water looked brown and dirty, but he was too thirsty to care. He cupped his hands and drank several long sips, then scrubbed himself until the stink of poo had completely gone.

He sprawled on the ground, waiting for his clothes to dry in the sun then kept walking. Every few minutes he stopped and asked directions for the bridge, until someone blinked at him and said, "What? You want the bridge?"

"Yes, sir."

The man pointed at the wooden planks under their feet. "You're standing on it."

15

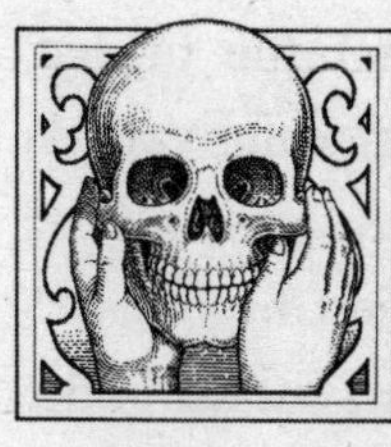

The Romans were the first people to build a wooden bridge across the river at London. At roughly the same time, and about three thousand miles to the east, Jesus was born in Bethlehem.

After a few years, that bridge burnt down. One replacement was washed away in a storm. Another was destroyed by the Vikings. The Saxons built a couple more and so did the Normans. By the time Pip arrived in London, sixteen hundred years after the Romans, ten different bridges had stood on the same spot.

In 1601, London Bridge had shops and houses running along its sides. Walking across was like walking down a street. That was why Pip hadn't realized he was actually standing on the bridge.

He wandered slowly from the north end to the south,

stopping every few paces to inspect a shopkeeper's display – rows of sweet-smelling spices, pairs of fine leather shoes, balls of multicoloured wool – or stare at the crowds. He saw women in long dresses, men with twirly moustaches and a little dog in its own leather coat.

Halfway across, there was a gap in the houses. Pip stood on the edge of the bridge, gripping the handrail. He could see up and down the river. Houses lined each bank. Smoke billowed into the air from hundreds of chimneys. Some of the buildings – St Paul's Cathedral and the Tower of London, for instance – were bigger than any man-made structure that Pip had ever seen. For the first time, he had a real sense of the city's vastness.

A man stood beside him and peed off the bridge, creating a long yellow arc which extended gracefully down to the river. On the water, a boatman steered to avoid the stream of pee, saving his passengers from getting wet.

Pip turned his back on the peeing man and walked to the end of the bridge, then stopped and stared in horror at thirty human heads. They'd been sliced off their bodies and skewered on tall wooden poles. Most looked as if they'd been there for years. The rain had washed them clean, leaving nothing but white bone and brown teeth. A couple were more recent arrivals, still speckled with a few clumps of hair and dangling flaps of skin. A week ago, these two men would have been pacing up and down their cells in the Tower of London, listening out for the sound of the executioner's footsteps in the corridor. Now their eyeballs had been plucked out by ravens and their flesh crawled with maggots.

That was the punishment for betraying Queen Elizabeth. Your head was chopped off, stuck on the end of a pole and left to rot on the south side of London Bridge.

Behave yourself, their skulls reminded every passer-by. Be an honest citizen and a faithful Protestant. Don't betray the Queen. Don't consort with Catholics. Don't spy for the Spanish. Be careful, be obedient, be good. Or your head will be cut from your shoulders and stuck on the end of a sharp pole.

16

The walls of London didn't stretch south of the river. When you crossed from the north bank to the south, you left the main part of the city and entered a suburb called Southwark.

The rich glared down their noses at Southwark. They didn't often venture on to that side of the river, leaving the south side to the poor. Thieves, cheats, conmen, poets, gypsies, clowns and actors – you'd find them all down here in the south, milling through these narrow streets, jostling for position, fighting for crumbs, picking one another's pockets, picking yours too.

Pip stopped several times to ask directions to the Bear Garden, but people were even ruder on this side of the river. They stumbled past without answering or just waved their arms, shouting, "That way! Over there!" He had been walking for a long time, probably going round and round in circles, completely lost, thoroughly confused, unsure where he had come from or which way he should be going when he finally found a tall building with whitewashed walls, just as those two men had said, and a large flag on the roof, billowing in the breeze. People were queuing to go inside. A painted sign hung above the door, a picture of Hercules with the world on his shoulders. Women squatted on the ground, selling cherries, plums and apples from wicker baskets, calling out to passers-by: "Sweet cherries! Sweet English cherries! Ha'pence a handful! Come and get 'em!"

Pip joined the end of the queue. It moved quickly. When he reached the front, a squat man barred his path. Pip stepped past to get a look inside. He just managed to glimpse a big crowd of people when a hand landed on his shoulder, whirling him round. The doorman said, "Where's your penny?"

Pip said, "What penny?"

"This isn't free entertainment, you know. Pay or get lost."

"I am lost."

"Very funny. Come on, boy. Are you going to pay or not?"

"How much?"

"Penny for the pit. Tuppence for the gallery. Thruppence for the gallery with cushions."

"And what do I get for that?"

"You can watch."

"Watch what?"

"Omelette."

Behind Pip, the other men in the queue were getting restless. They shouted at the doorman to be allowed inside. The omelette had already started.

Pip said, "Have I missed the bears?"

"The what?"

"The bears."

"What are you talking about?"

"This is the Bear Garden, isn't it?"

"No, boy," said the doorman. "This is the Globe."

"What's the globe?"

"I told you, *this* is the Globe."

Pip and the man glared at one another, each of them convinced that the other was a complete idiot.

"Make up your mind," said the doorman, snapping his fingers. "If you want to come in, you have to pay."

"I don't have a penny," said Pip.

"Then you're not coming in."

On special occasions, marking one of their birthdays or the sale of some expensive knives, Pip's mother had sometimes cooked an omelette. He could almost taste it in his mouth, runny in the middle and crisp on the outside.

"Please, sir," begged Pip. "I'll pay you later."

"Don't make me laugh," said the doorman.

"I'll come back with a penny, I promise."

"Go away."

"But, sir," said Pip. "Where can I get a penny?"

"You think I care?" The doorman looked over Pip's head. "Who's next?"

"Me." A thin man stepped forward. He had delicate features and long eyelashes. He was wearing a scarlet jacket decorated with gold braid. His leather breeches were covered with dangling silver chains which jingled when he walked. "Thank you, my friend," he said, handing four coins to the doorkeeper.

"This is fourpence," said the doorkeeper, staring at the coins.

"I do realize that, yes."

"But the gallery with cushions is only thruppence."

"Three of those pennies are to pay for myself," said the man in the velvet jacket. He pointed at Pip. "And the fourth is for him."

"Get in, then," said the doorkeeper, stepping aside to let them pass, then looked down the queue. "Come on, come on, who's next?"

Once they were through the door, the man in the extravagant jacket brushed aside Pip's thanks. "Anything to stop you holding up the queue."

Pip said, "What's your name?"

"Why on earth do you wish to know my name?"

"So I can repay your penny, sir. When I'm rich."

The man laughed. "And just when will that be?"

"Soon, sir."

The man laughed again. "Very well, then. My name is Inigo Jones. I look forward to seeing you again, my young friend. With all your wealth."

"And, sir, where will I find you?"

"You won't."

"Why not?"

"Because I'm going to Venice next week and have no intention of returning to this dismal country. So you can forget the penny and I will too." Without waiting for a response, the man turned his back and strode up the stairs that led to the more expensive galleries.

"Thank you, sir," Pip called after him. "Thank you, Mister Jones!"

The man didn't respond. He probably hadn't even heard Pip over the noise of the crowd.

Pip resolved not to forget that name. He didn't like being in anyone's debt, even for a penny. As soon as he had earned some money, he would find Mister Inigo Jones and repay what he owed.

He looked around. He was standing at the back of a large crowd crushed inside a round building which had no roof. He started pushing through the crowd, determined to get as close as possible to the omelette. He wanted to see the eggs being broken.

17

There must have been two thousand people crammed inside the wooden structure, some sitting round the sides in the expensive seats that lined the galleries, the majority standing in the middle. Near the front, they were tightly packed together, pressing forward. Almost everyone was bigger and taller than Pip. There wasn't room to manoeuvre. There was hardly room to breathe. He pushed through the crowd as far as he could, then found a good vantage spot behind two women, the smallest people that he could find. There, he stood on tiptoe and peered over the women's shoulders, staring at the stage.

He was relieved to see that the omelette hadn't been started. There weren't even any signs of cooking apparatus. Several men were just standing at the front of the raised stage, dressed in odd costumes. They spoke in deep, resonant voices which echoed around the galleries, audible to everyone, wherever they were sitting.

They did not talk of eggs. No one mentioned frying pans. And yet, to Pip's surprise, the actions on the stage, and the things that people said, were so fascinating that he soon forgot the gaping emptiness in the bottom of his stomach.

The men spoke to one another in a curious language, something like English, using all kinds of long words, and Pip could only understand half of what they said, often even less. But that was enough.

One of the men spoke more than the others. He was trying to decide whether to believe in ghosts. Pip had often puzzled over exactly the same problem. If the two of them had been alone, he would have mentioned the shadowy white forms that he had twice glimpsed in the forest and the strange sounds that he had often heard in the middle of the night, but he didn't dare say anything in front of so many people.

The man who talked a lot was thin and handsome. He had a neatly trimmed, pointed beard which accentuated the angles of his long, lean face. His clothes were black and a rapier hung from his belt. When he was alone on the stage, he walked to the front and discussed his troubles with the crowd.

People shouted back, telling him what they thought of his problems, giving advice, making suggestions.

Slowly, Pip understood what was going on. He was

watching a play. The men and boys on the stage were actors. He'd heard of plays, although there had never been an opportunity to see one in Mildmay. Actors often toured their theatrical productions around England, taking to the road when plague or political problems closed the theatres in London, but they would stick to the larger towns where audiences were bigger, not wasting their time in obscure little villages. However, pedlars had gossiped about the strange behaviour of Londoners, describing how people paid good money to watch men tell stories in big houses called theatres. *That's where I must be now*, Pip realized. *This must be a theatre and the Globe must be its name.*

He'd missed the beginning of the play but, by concentrating on what the actors were saying, he soon picked up the threads and learnt the names of the characters. The man in black was called Hamlet and he was the prince of Denmark. Until recently, Hamlet's father had been the king, but he was now dead.

The ghost of Hamlet's father appeared to Hamlet wearing a suit of armour, painted white, which clanked with every step that he took. The ghost revealed the truth behind his own death: he had been poisoned by his own brother, Hamlet's uncle. Now the brother, the murderer, had married Hamlet's mother and become king of Denmark.

Hamlet paced up and down the stage. He talked to himself, chatted to the crowd or his best friend, Horatio. He went over his options, sorting right from wrong, trying to decide what to do. He knew that he should take revenge and kill the new king, but something stopped him.

While Hamlet wavered, people yelled advice at him. "Stop talking so much!" "Don't be a mouse! Be a man!" A woman threw a cake. Hamlet caught it, took a bite, and threw it back again.

Hamlet had several chances to kill his stepfather, but he just couldn't do the deed. Pip didn't really understand why not. If he'd been in Hamlet's situation, he would have challenged his stepfather to a duel. One against one. A sword each. The best man wins. Instead, Hamlet accepted a job from his stepfather, carrying a letter to England.

Pip was furious. It was just cowardice! He couldn't believe an intelligent man like Hamlet could be such a coward. The audience shared his feelings. People jeered and booed, begging Hamlet to run his rapier through his stepfather's body.

Hamlet took no notice. He boarded a ship and sailed from Denmark to England. But he had only been gone two days when pirates attacked his ship.

The actors didn't actually show this on the stage. Horatio received a letter from Hamlet, explaining what had happened. In the letter, Hamlet asked Horatio to come and meet him so they could return to the court together.

Pip was desperate for Hamlet to do the right thing. *Kill your stepfather*, he wanted to shout. *Kill him!* He wanted to see a fight between them, a duel with rapiers, culminating in the king's death. He could already imagine the satisfying squelch as Hamlet's blade slid between the old man's ribs. *If you can't kill your stepfather*, Pip wanted to say to Hamlet, *I'll do it for you. Let me help. I'll show you exactly what to do.*

But before Hamlet had a chance to reach the court and confront the king, two men arrived with spades and everything went crazy.

18

The two men walked to the front of the stage and pretended to dig a hole. They were gravediggers, Pip realized, doing their job in a churchyard.

Of course, they couldn't really dig through the stage. It was made of wood. People walked on it. And yet, like magic, one of the gravediggers reached down into the floor, as if he were putting his arm into a hole, and pulled out a white skull.

A few people applauded the trick. The gravedigger nodded, thanking them, then tossed the skull in the air and caught it.

Most of the actors were tall and handsome, but the gravedigger was short, plump and startlingly ugly. He had a bald head, bushy eyebrows and a shiny red nose. Just looking at him made Pip want to laugh.

The gravedigger held the skull at the same height as his face and chatted to it as if he were talking to an old friend. He had only spoken a few words when an apple flew through the air and smacked into his forehead.

For a moment the gravedigger was too surprised to do anything. Then he turned his head slowly and stared at the audience. He said, "Who did that?"

No one answered.

"Come on," said the gravedigger. "Who did that?"

The crowd was quiet.

"It'll be better for everyone if you just tell me," said the gravedigger. "Who threw that apple?"

Someone shouted, "Who cares?"

"Not me," yelled someone else.

"I do," said the gravedigger. "I'm an actor, a serious actor; you can't throw fruit at me. Come on, own up, who threw the apple?"

People in the galleries started slow-clapping. Jeers, whistles and catcalls went round the Globe. Someone shouted, "Do your job! Say something funny!"

The gravedigger wasn't in the mood for jokes. He was furious. Holding the skull in his right hand, he picked up the apple in his left and said, "I'm asking you for the last time. Who threw this?"

"Me!" shouted a voice.

"No, me!" shouted another voice.

From all around the Globe, more and more voices joined in.

"Me!"

"It was me!"

"No, me!"

"Me!"

"I threw it!"

"Over here! Me!"

The gravedigger stared at the crowd, his anger intensified by his confusion. He wavered, turning his head from side to side, unsure what to do, until the decision was made for him: another apple flew through the air and hit him on the nose, exploding with a loud crack that could be heard all around the Globe.

Yelling with pain and fury, the gravedigger turned and, using all his strength, but without aiming or even really looking, hurled the skull into the audience.

The skull whirled through the air, heading directly towards a red-faced, broad-shouldered man in a white shirt. His name was Dominick Cleaver and he was one of the best butchers in London.

Once a week, Dominick Cleaver left his butcher's shop in the hands of his apprentice, exchanged his bloody apron for a clean white shirt, and went to the theatre. He had never been to another country – in fact, he had never ventured more than a few miles from London, and then only to visit the farmers who provided his chicken, beef and mutton – but, over the years, actors had transported him to Italy, Russia and dozens of other countries that he would never have a chance to visit himself. He had seen births, battles, weddings and massacres. He had followed the careers of kings and generals. He had eavesdropped on an argument between two Venetian merchants, witnessed the fury of a Turkish emperor and followed a rabble running riot through the streets of Rome. But he had never been hit on the head with a human skull.

Until today.

The skull bounced off Dominick Cleaver's face. A couple of teeth flew through the air. One belonged to Dominick Cleaver and the other belonged to the skull, but neither was ever seen again; the two teeth dropped to the ground and were lost in the mud.

Up to that moment Dominick Cleaver had simply been enjoying the play. He hadn't thrown an apple. He didn't even shout. But this was different. He turned round and punched whoever was unlucky enough to be standing next to him.

Within seconds, fights had broken out in every part of the Globe. Men pulled daggers from their belts. Steel flashed in the sunlight. Fists flew. Voices screamed. Actors jumped off the stage and joined in.

Pip would have been happy to fight a duel with anyone who had insulted him or his family, but he didn't want to hurt someone who'd never done him any harm. So he stayed as calm and quiet as possible, avoiding fists and feet, leaving his knife in its scabbard, standing in one place and waiting for the fight to finish.

His patience didn't last long. When an elbow smacked into the side of his head, swiftly followed by a boot that thudded into his shin, he decided that he'd had enough. It's no fun standing still while people hit you. He pushed through the crowd, protecting his head with his hands, and tried to find a way out.

Instead, he found an empty nook under the galleries, just big enough to fit a bag of costumes, a box of props or a small boy. There he took shelter from the fight. No one followed him inside or even noticed where he'd gone. They were all too busy slapping, punching and kicking one another. Footsore, half starved and completely exhausted, Pip lay down, closed his eyes and drifted into a deep, dreamless sleep.

19

While Pip is asleep, I'll tell you a little more about the Globe.

A couple of years earlier, on the spot where the theatre now stood, there had been nothing but an empty patch of marshy ground, grazed by sheep. Watercress grew there. You'd often see old men hunched over the mud, searching for debris that had been washed ashore, hoping to find a grubby coin. Criminals were sometimes chained to a post for a day or two, forced to endure the tide as it swept ashore, half drowning them.

One chilly afternoon in December, in the year of Our Lord one thousand five hundred and ninety-eight, a huge pile of wood was lugged across the river in barges and dumped on the mud. In January, men started digging foundations, breaking their spades on the frozen soil. Soon, everyone in Southwark knew what was happening: the Burbage brothers had leased this patch of land to build a new theatre. The walls went up quickly, but the galleries and stage took longer, and the Globe wasn't ready to open until the summer of 1599. For their first show, the Burbages chose to perform *Julius Caesar*, a play by their most successful writer, William Shakespeare.

That performance had been a triumph. In the two years since then, the Globe had become the best theatre in London.

If you ever visit London, you can still see a play there. The Globe itself looks almost exactly the same as the theatre that Pip saw. It's not, though. Shakespeare's Globe burnt to the ground on 29 June 1613, twelve years after Pip first walked through the door.

The fire started during a performance of *Henry VIII*. Someone had the brilliant idea of using a real cannon to liven up the battle scenes.

While the actors were charging up and down the stage, one of the technicians lit the fuse. The cannon exploded with a realistic roar. Sparks shot in all directions. Flames licked the theatre's thatched roof.

The audience started cheering and applauding, impressed that the fire looked so real. Then they started screaming and running.

The flames weren't part of the play. The theatre was burning down.

Smoke billowed into the blue sky. People pushed and

shoved, fighting to reach the exits, trampling over anyone who had the bad luck to fall down.

In the end, only one person was badly hurt. His trousers caught fire and he got a burnt bum. Luckily, someone threw a pint of beer over him and put out the flames, so he got a wet burnt bum.

The Globe itself wasn't so lucky. It burnt to the ground.

A year later the theatre was rebuilt and reopened.

The second Globe stayed standing for thirty years. And then, in 1642, the Puritans closed its doors, forbidding the performances of any more plays.

As you probably know, the Puritans were a bunch of grumpy people who hated fun. They didn't like having fun themselves and they didn't like the idea of anyone else having fun either.

They particularly hated theatres. Lots of people crowding together in one place and having fun together – it was the Puritans' idea of hell.

In 1642 the Puritans stopped all fun in London. They closed down the theatres. They banned dancing, fighting, bullfights and acting.

They locked the doors of the Globe. Two years later they arrived with hammers and axes and demolished the theatre, building some houses on the site.

After a few years, Londoners kicked out the Puritans and brought back fun. People danced in the streets and the theatres reopened. But the Globe wasn't rebuilt for another three hundred and fifty years.

A replica has been built beside the Thames, about two

minutes' walk from the place where the Globe originally stood.

There's a little museum and a café. You can wander round the stage and the seats. Or, even better, you can watch a play. Throughout the summer, from May to October, actors perform in the Globe, doing plays by Shakespeare and a few other writers. If you're ever in London, you should definitely go.

20

When Pip opened his eyes, he was lying in a tangled heap on the floor, tucked inside the nook. He rolled over, sat up and looked around.

The sun had dipped behind the roof, casting the Globe into shadow. The crowds had gone. A few people were walking along the galleries, picking up rubbish and stacking the cushions.

The play must have finished. Hamlet had made his decision. But what had he decided? Did he do the right thing and kill his stepfather? Or did he remain a coward, unable to draw his sword, incapable of taking revenge? Pip looked around the theatre, searching for someone to ask.

He noticed two men standing at the front of the stage, engaged in an earnest discussion. Pip couldn't hear what they were saying, but he recognized them as actors who had appeared in the play, one playing the gravedigger and the other playing Hamlet. *Perfect*, thought Pip. *They'll know how the story ended.* He hurried across the pit and stood at the foot of the stage. The two men were so involved in their conversation that they didn't even notice him.

During the play, Hamlet had worn black clothes and looked quite mad, pacing from one side of the stage to the other, waving his arms, shouting and wailing, veering wildly from glee to despair, passivity to violence. Now, dressed in brightly coloured clothes, he was speaking in a cold, clear tone, looking like a man who never lost control of his emotions. He was wearing a blue shirt which reached almost to his knees, a lush purple velvet jacket and leather trousers decorated with dangling tassles. A gold hoop hung from his left ear. His long face, high forehead and neatly trimmed beard made him look extremely distinguished; if you hadn't known he was an actor, you might have imagined he was a nobleman of great power and wealth, a duke or an earl, one of Queen Elizabeth's most favoured courtiers.

"Don't you understand?" he was saying. "When they throw things at you, or shout at you, or interrupt your lines, they're just testing you, because you're new. They want to see how strong you are. If you allow yourself to be upset, then you have done exactly what they want."

"I know, I know," said the man who had played the gravedigger. Close up, he looked even uglier than he had done during the play. "I promise it won't happen again."

"That's what you said last time. And the time before." Hamlet shook his head and sighed. "Have I made a mistake?"

"What's that supposed to mean?"

"I had clowns queuing round the block for this job. I chose you because I thought you could bring the Globe to life."

"I can," said the gravedigger. "And I will."

"Maybe you should take a few days off."

"No, no. I don't need a holiday. I want to work."

"Everyone needs a holiday," said Hamlet. "Take the wife and kids somewhere nice."

"I'm not married."

"Even better. Go on your own. Head to Highgate for a couple of nights. The views are fantastic at this time of year. While you're gone, we'll give a chance to one of those other clowns."

"I want to keep working," said the gravedigger. "This is my life. This is what I do. I'm an actor! I have to work! Trust me, I don't need a holiday."

Hamlet didn't reply. He just sighed, crossed his arms and stared at the gravedigger, trying to reach a decision.

Pip took advantage of the silence to interrupt. He put his hands on the edge of the stage and called up to Hamlet, "Did you kill him?"

The actor who played Hamlet was not used to being interrupted. He was an important man. A respected man. Who would dare interrupt his conversation? Slowly he turned his head and peered over the edge of the stage to see who had shouted at him. To his astonishment he saw a small boy with a grubby face and the clothes of a peasant. He said, "Do I know you?"

"No, sir," said Pip.

"What are you doing in my theatre?"

"I want to ask you a question, sir."

"If you want a job, you've come to the wrong place."

"I don't want a job, sir."

"That's something, I suppose. Go on, then. Ask your question. What is it?"

For the second time, Pip said, "Did you kill him?"

"As far as I know, young man, I have never killed anyone."

"In the play, sir. In the play. Did you kill the king?"

"Oh, I see. The play's the thing, is it? Well, if you want to know the answer to that particular question, you'd better come back in a fortnight."

"Why?"

"Because that's the next time we'll be performing *The Tragedy of Hamlet, Prince of Denmark*, a new play by William Shakespeare, the greatest poet that the world has ever seen. Only a penny for the best show in town, tuppence for the gallery, thruppence for the gallery with cushions. Same time, same place, two weeks from now. See you then, my young friend."

"I can't come back in two weeks," said Pip. "I don't even live in London."

"Then you'll never know what happened," said Hamlet. He smiled without warmth or humour, then turned his attention back to his employee. "Very well, Robert, you can keep your job, but this is your last chance. You have two more weeks. If things aren't better when we next perform *Hamlet*, then you're out on your ear. And, please, Robert, if that happens, don't say I didn't warn you."

"Things will be better," said the gravedigger. "I promise."

"I hope so," said Hamlet. "For your own sake. Right, I have to go. I have a thousand and one things to do." He turned his back and, without even glancing at Pip, walked briskly away.

The gravedigger put his hands on his hips and sighed as if all the sorrows of the world were pressing down on his shoulders.

Pip gestured at Hamlet, who was walking through a door at the back of the stage, and whispered, "What's he so upset about?"

The gravedigger waited until the door had safely swung shut, then said, "Don't worry about him. All bark and no bite. He just likes to take himself a bit too seriously, that's all."

"Who is he?"

"His name's Burbage. He owns this theatre. Part-owns it, I should say, with his brother. There are two of them, Cuthbert and Richard."

"Which one was that?"

"Richard."

"Richard Burbage," said Pip, trying out the name on his tongue. "And he's an actor?"

"Yes, yes, he acted in the play that you've just been watching. *If* you were watching."

"I was," said Pip. "But I didn't see the end. Please, sir, could you tell me what happened at the end? Did Hamlet kill the king?"

Rather than answering Pip's question, the gravedigger leant forward and asked one of his own. "I want your honest opinion," he said. "And I mean honest. Can you do that?"

"Yes, sir."

"Whatever you do, please don't flatter me. Don't tell me what you think I want to hear. I'd prefer the truth, even if it hurts. So – what did you think?"

"Of what?"

"The play. Did you like it?"

"I liked it very much," said Pip. "But what happened at the end? Did he kill him?"

"Answer me honestly," said the gravedigger. "Did you really like it?"

"Yes, sir."

"You promise?"

"Yes, sir. Really. I think it was probably the best thing I've ever seen."

"Excellent, excellent." The gravedigger smiled. "And was there anything that you enjoyed particularly? About my performance, for instance. Were you struck by anything particular in the way that I interpreted the part?"

"I liked all your stuff with the skull. That was so funny. And the singing!" At the memory of it, Pip started laughing. "I think it was the funniest thing I've ever seen in my life."

"I am delighted to hear that." The gravedigger leant down and held out his hand. "My name is Robert Armin. And you are?"

"Pip, sir."

"Pip? Interesting name."

"My name is Philip Stone, sir, but everyone calls me Pip. When I was learning to speak, sir, I couldn't pronounce Philip. I used to call myself Pip. And it stuck."

"An excellent justification for an excellent name," said Robert Armin. "It's a pleasure to meet you, Pip."

"And you, Mister Armin, sir."

"Call me Robert."

They shook hands.

"Thank you so much for your kind words," said Robert. "You don't know what it means to hear from a real fan. Sometimes, we actors have the sense that our performances are simply thrown into the void. The words are taken away as soon as they're spoken and just disappear, as if we're whistling on the wind." Robert hauled himself to his feet. "Well, Pip, it's been very nice to meet you. We're doing *The Merchant of Venice* tomorrow. Have you seen it?"

"No, sir," said Pip.

"Let me tell you, it's wonderful show. Full of good jokes. My Launcelot Gobbo has, if I may say so myself, been a triumph. Come back, if you can. Only a penny. The best bargain in town. Goodbye, Pip, and good luck, and thank you again for your kind words." With a broad smile, Robert bowed his head, turned and walked away.

Pip pulled himself on to the stage and hurried after Robert Armin. "Sir? Sir? Please, sir? Will you help me?"

"I don't know if I can," said Robert, stopping just before he reached the doorway.

"Which way is the Bear Garden?"

"Just round the corner," said Robert. "Is that where you're going?"

"Yes, sir."

"Then I'll take you there myself."

21

Had he known the way, Pip could have walked from the Globe to the Bear Garden in a couple of minutes, but Robert Armin paused every few paces to chat with people in the street, and their journey took almost half an hour. Robert dropped a couple of coins into a beggar's outstretched hand, gossiped with a woman selling bundles of lucky heather and had an earnest discussion about the war in Ireland with an old blind man.

Robert stopped at a fruit stall and bought six small apples. "Here," he said as they walked on. "Try these."

"Thank you, sir," said Pip. The first bite of crisp white flesh reminded him that he hadn't eaten all day. He chomped through apple after apple, stopping only when he realized that he'd eaten five of the half-dozen.

Suddenly ashamed of himself he passed the sixth back to Robert, who refused it, telling him to keep it for later.

They reached a circular building with high walls and no windows. This was the Bear Garden. On the top of the wall, a large flag fluttered in the wind. Robert explained that this flag, just like the one on top of the Globe, could be seen from the other bank of the Thames. If for any reason the day's performances had to be cancelled, the flags didn't fly, warning people not to make the trip across the river.

Several horses were tethered to a wooden pole beside the entrance and a couple of boys stood nearby, watching over them. When the owners came out of the play, they'd tip the boys a penny for guarding their horses from thieves. Women were sitting on the grass, selling fruit, drinks and snacks. At the gate, men were taking money from anyone who wanted to see the show.

"I'm sorry, sir," said Pip to Robert. "Could you lend me a penny? I'll pay you back, I promise."

Robert laughed. "You're still hungry? Well, what do you want? Cherries? Almonds? More apples?"

"No, sir. I just want to pay my way into the Bear Garden."

"Oh, we don't need to pay here. They know me." Robert glanced at the sky, trying to judge the time from the position of the sun. "I'll come inside for one fight, just one. Then I have to go home and practise my lines for tomorrow. Come on."

He led Pip through the crowd and headed to the gate. When the two doormen saw Robert, they jumped to their feet and slapped him on the back. "Hey, clown," said one of them. "How are you?"

"Pretty good, thanks."

The other doorman said, "Going to tell some jokes for us?"

"You can't expect me to be funny when I'm not working," said Robert.

"Fair enough. In you go." The doorman gestured at Pip. "He's with you, is he?"

"Indeed he is."

"Go on, then," said the doorman, slapping Pip on his back so hard that he stumbled. "Get inside. Last fight is just about to start."

This isn't much of a garden, thought Pip. *No trees. No herbs. No flowers. Nothing but mud.*

Like the Globe, the Bear Garden had no roof. The circular arena was open to the skies. In the rain, everyone got wet.

Unlike the Globe, the Bear Garden had neither a stage nor galleries, just a low wall separating the audience from the action. People stood or sat on benches to watch the show.

Three brown, furry creatures were squatting in the centre of the circle. They looked like enormous moles. Those were the bears.

Pip didn't give them more than a brief glance. Peering round the mob of faces, he searched for familiar features, but couldn't see the Weasel, Scar, Tooth or Pigface.

What about George Stone?

If the Weasel was telling the truth, thought Pip, *this is where he met my father.*

Pip wondered whether, after seven years' separation, he and George Stone would even recognize one another. Probably not. Just about any one of these men might have been his dad and he wouldn't even know it.

As they pushed through the crowd, searching for empty seats, Robert explained that the day's performance had almost finished. They had missed the jugglers, the fire-eaters, the drummers, the pipers, the fencers, the wrestlers and the bull-baiting, but they were just in time for the main attraction. The bears.

"Let's sit here," said Robert, leading Pip to a small empty patch of wooden bench between a group of raucous women and some melancholy preachers. As soon as they sat down, one of the women poked her finger into Robert's shoulder. "Don't I know you?"

"I don't think so," said Robert.

"I know you, I know I do."

"I think not, ma'am."

"Oh yes I do. What's your name? Where have I seen you before?"

"Do you ever go to the Globe?"

"All the time. We love the Globe. Don't we, girls?"

There was a chorus of giggling and agreement from the other women.

"Then perhaps you've seen one of my roles," said Robert. "My Launcelot Gobbo, for instance, in *The Merchant of Venice.*"

The women were thrilled. They were sitting next to a

celebrity! An actor from the Globe! They crowded round Robert, quizzing him for gossip, asking him all kinds of questions about life in the theatre and the private lives of the other actors.

Pip wasn't interested in their conversation. He leant on the low wall that separated the audience from the ring and took a longer look at the bears. All three had silver rings through their nostrils and leather collars round their necks. Thick ropes tethered them to wooden posts buried in the ground. Although their brown fur reminded him of moles or mice, and their muscular thighs and shoulders made him think of badgers, he'd never seen anything quite like them. Apart from anything else, they were huge. As big as him. Maybe even bigger. It was hard to tell right now, because the three bears were squatting or lying down, having a rest before the battle began.

One of the bears, the biggest, was sprawled on the ground and looked more like an enormous fur coat than a living creature. Another was snuffling in the mud, digging a hole with its nose and front paws. The third, the smallest and skinniest of the trio, was sitting like a baby, legs outstretched, arms raised, wiping its face with its paws. Every now and then the bear lifted its head and looked around the stadium, staring at the crowd, watching its watchers. Pip stared back, hoping to make eye contact, but the bear didn't seem at all interested in him.

A man in a long blue cloak put a trumpet to his lips and blew a long blast. Shouts echoed around the crowd.

"Last chance to bet."

"Dead dog gets you sixpence!"

"Who'll give me two to one on Bruno?"

Bruno was the biggest bear, explained Robert. He didn't know the names of the other two.

Men ran round the rim of the arena, jingling coins in their cupped hands, offering bets on the dogs and the bears. A short man with curly black hair stopped beside Pip and Robert. "Which bear will die? You tell me, sir."

Robert said, "The baby."

"Which one, sir? Point him out."

Robert pointed at the smallest of the three bears. "That one."

"That's a good choice, sir. You obviously know your bears. I'll give you sixpence if you're right. Just pay tuppence now."

"No, thank you," said Robert. "I don't bet."

"Just tuppence, sir. Tuppence gets sixpence."

"Haven't you heard that gambling is a sin?"

"This isn't gambling, sir. This is just a bit of fun."

"Haven't you heard the Puritans preaching in the yard of St Paul's? They say that fun is a sin."

"I couldn't go along with that, sir. If you ask me, there's nothing wrong with a bit of fun."

"I agree. But I'm still not going to give you tuppence."

"Your loss, sir. Not mine." The man glanced at Pip, saw immediately from his clothes that he wasn't the type of person who could spare tuppence, and hurried onward, calling out his wagers. "Tuppence gets sixpence! Come on, ladies, have a bet with me. Afternoon, gents. What do you reckon, sir? Which bear will die?"

The man in the blue cloak lifted the trumpet to his lips again. He blew another long blast. The gamblers made their final bets. People clapped and cheered.

At the back of the Bear Garden a pair of double doors swung open. A man stepped through the doorway and walked across the mud, surrounded by a crowd of ten dogs, their tails wagging, their heads turning from side to side, sniffing the air.

The three bears pulled themselves to their feet, squatting on all fours, raising their heavy heads and warily watching the dogs.

It was time for the fight to begin.

22

Two years earlier that bear – the small, skinny one – had been roaming happily through the forests of the desolate north.

Four of them travelled together, a mother and three cubs, padding across the carpet of pine needles, weaving between the trees. The father had long gone, leaving the mother to nurture her babies alone. Now the three cubs were a few months old. Small and chubby, they had sleek fur, rounded ears and sharp, inquisitive eyes. They played together, wrestling, rolling about, pushing and shoving, cuffing one another with their paws, always keeping their long claws sheathed.

As the family moved through the forest, the mother raised her head every few moments, looking around, sniffing for food and checking for predators, always wary of potential threats.

It was late summer. The sun was still warm, but the leaves were already turning brown. The bears were getting fat, although they weren't nearly as fat as they needed to be to hibernate. Over the next few weeks they would have to eat almost constantly, absorbing protein, layering their bodies with the blubber that would keep them alive through the long winter snooze. Next year, they would wake in the spring and begin the whole process again.

The bears rambled throughout the forests and the mountains, treating the land as their own personal empire, often travelling ten or twenty miles in a day. They chomped herbs and mushrooms, plucked berries from the bushes and scooped honey out of hives, licked caterpillars from branches and grabbed moths out of the air, snatched fish from the streams, chased squirrels up trees and sprinted across the grass in pursuit of rabbits and deer.

Bears were the biggest animals in the forest and few predators dared attack them, but cubs were vulnerable, having not yet learnt how to defend themselves. A pack of wolves wouldn't attack a healthy adult bear, but they might try their luck with a cub, isolating him from the others then overpowering him. The mother bear remained vigilant, keeping her eyes open and her ears raised.

Over the past few months the mother bear had protected her cubs from all kinds of dangers, teaching them how to survive in the forest, but this time she wasn't cunning or careful enough. It was her last mistake.

Five hunters were hiding in the trees, big men armed with spears and axes. As the bears approached, the hunters crowded round, yelling and screaming, raising their spears. The mother fought bravely but she wasn't strong enough. If the cubs had been able to fight they might have won, but the three of them huddled backwards, blinking and terrified, watching their mother thrash and roar as the spears pierced her flesh.

The hunters camped near the scene of the slaughter. They skinned the mother's carcass. That night they held a banquet. They built a fire and stuffed themselves on bear meat. The three cubs were tied to a tree within sight of the feast, hungry and confused, straining on the ropes.

For the next few days the men hunted in the woods, catching rabbits, trapping birds and searching for more bears, but finding none.

Each night, they returned to the camp and feasted on the bear, roasting different bits of her body. When they had eaten they lolled around the cooling embers and discussed what to do with the three cubs, whether to kill them or transport them back to the town. Bears were worth much more alive than dead – but would these three little cubs survive the journey?

One of the hunters suggested killing the smallest. "It wouldn't survive anyway," he said. "We can keep the skin, eat the meat, and save ourselves the bother of lugging another animal back to the town."

All but one of the others disagreed, preferring to take the risk. Three against two – the runt survived.

When the hunters had collected two big bundles of skins they loaded their horses, strapped down the bundles and started on the long trek back. They tied ropes round the necks of the three cubs and dragged them behind the horses. The cubs stumbled through the forest, moaning piteously, missing their mother.

One cub died on the journey. To the hunters' surprise it wasn't the runt, but the biggest of the three.

They reached the town. In the market an Englishman bought both bears, took them aboard his ship and sailed for London.

The Englishman was a merchant. He had filled most of his allotted space on the ship with furs, amber, timber and salted fish. The two little bears were a bonus. With any luck, he thought, he should be able to sell them to an actor or a gypsy.

The sailors had carried all kinds of strange cargo, but never a bear. They asked the Englishman to do some tricks with his bears – *make them dance*, begged the sailors, *make them fight* – but he refused. "Bears can't do tricks until they've been trained," he said, "and I don't know how to train them."

On the voyage a second cub died, driven mad by seasickness, perhaps, or simply starved. Only one was left. The runt.

In London the ship moored at Rotherhithe. Traders hurried aboard. The sailors laid out their cargo on the deck. When the Englishman had sold most of his goods he walked through the streets of Rotherhithe and Southwark, leading the cub on a rope, ignoring the stream of jokes and comments that followed them. He went to the Bear Garden, found the bearkeeper and asked if he would like to buy a new bear, freshly imported from the forests of the desolate north.

"I'd love to buy another bear," said the bearkeeper. "But not that one."

"Why not?" said the merchant.

"Because that bear's too small. Who's going to pay an honest English penny to watch a bear like that?"

A big bear, an aggressive bear, a bear that loved to fight – that might be worth five pounds, although you would sometimes be able to buy one for as little as fifteen shillings. During the autumn, when the Russian ships docked in Rotherhithe once a week, you could pick up some pretty nice bears for a pound or two. But a small, calm, quiet bear like this one, with its dribbly nose and soft paws, was worthless. Even if he fattened it up, said the bearkeeper, its fur wouldn't make more than a couple of hats. The bearkeeper offered a derisory price and allowed himself to be bargained upwards a little.

The Englishman strolled back to his ship, jangling a few coins in his pocket. *Better than nothing*, he thought. *But not much better*. Next time, he wouldn't waste his time or money on bears.

When the Englishman had gone, the bearkeeper fetched his tools. He strapped down the bear with thick ropes, then laid out his instruments on the floor: a saw, a pair of tongs, knives, files and hoops.

The bearkeeper filed down the bear's teeth, flattening

the sharp points. He'd have pulled out a bigger bear's teeth, but this one was so small, he didn't bother. The claws were next. The bearkeeper snapped them off. The left paw: one, two, three, four, five. Having performed these procedures often, he worked fast, but the bear still suffered appalling pain. The right paw: one, two, three, four, five. Moaning and whining, the bear struggled desperately, trying to break the ropes, but they were tied too tight. Finally the bearkeeper forced the metal hoop into one of the bear's nostrils and out the other, smashing through the soft cartilage in between.

With a hoop through its nose, the bear had been tamed. When the bearkeeper untied the ropes the bear didn't even try to escape or attack, meekly allowing itself to be ushered into a cage.

Every day since then, the bear had sat inside that cage, staring at the wooden bars. In two years, the cub should have grown into a broad, muscular bear, afraid of nothing. Instead, fragile from lack of food and exercise, the bear was small, skinny and always nervous.

23

The bearkeeper strolled round the edge of the Bear Garden, showing off his dogs and chatting to the audience, exchanging a few words with old friends, joking with regular customers. He was a tall man with strong arms, broad shoulders and a shaven head. He must have seen more than his fair share of violence: not only did he walk with a limp, but a long scar ran the length of his forehead and his mashed-up nose must have been broken many, many times.

The dogs looked even more battle-hardened than their owner. The bearkeeper owned three different varieties: six sturdy mastiffs, three lean, long-limbed hounds and a single spaniel with droopy ears. Several were missing ears or tails. Their flanks were covered in welts and scars, some hardly healed. As the bearkeeper paraded around the ring a few people tossed a leftover crust or a sliver of cold meat to the dogs, who rolled in the mud, growling and yapping, fighting one another for the scraps.

When the bearkeeper had made a full circuit of the Bear Garden, displaying his dogs to every section of the crowd, he leant down, unclasped the lead from each one's collar and ushered his ten dogs towards the three bears, forcing them forward with his boots and his whip. The dogs weren't keen. They'd rather have begged for more titbits. But the bearkeeper kicked them and lashed them, urging them onward, forcing them to fight. "Yaaahhh!" he shouted. "Go on, Snapper! Go on, Blackie! Go on, Pumpkin! Go on! Yaaahhh!"

Standing on his hind legs, the biggest bear, Bruno, drew himself up to his full height and raised his huge arms, trying to intimidate the approaching dogs with his size. He stood as tall and broad as any man that Pip had ever seen.

The dogs darted at the big bear's ankles, lunging and snapping, their teeth snagging his shaggy fur. The six mastiffs were fighting dogs with strong shoulders and tough jaws, so they had no qualms about attacking a bear, but the other four animals, the hounds and the spaniel, showed less enthusiasm for the fight. If the bearkeeper hadn't driven them onward they would have turned and fled.

Bruno couldn't possibly fight all ten dogs at once, but he did what he could to push them away. He stamped his feet, opened his mouth and roared with rage, baring the blunt white stumps of his teeth. When the dogs kept coming, refusing to be awed by his display, he leant down and swept his right paw along the ground, thumping into the nearest dog, a small white bitch. She spun across the mud, somersaulting three times before coming to rest in a heap, each leg pointing in a different direction. She'd only lain there for a moment, licking her wounds, before the bearkeeper kicked her back into battle.

Another dog sprang on to the bear's back, burying its teeth into his flesh and clinging on. The bear roared again, infuriated, and shook himself hard, swinging his body from side to side. The dog was wrenched one way, then the other, then back again, before finally being dislodged, flying through the air and landing in the mud with a splash. The bear whirled round, reached down and grabbed the dog with both paws, hauling it off the ground.

The dog wriggled desperately, yelping and growling and snapping, trying to get free. The bearkeeper hurried forward, cracking his whip, knowing what would happen next, but he wasn't quick enough. In a sudden movement, the bear wrenched his paws apart and tore the dog in half. Blood splashed into the air. Innards dribbled to the ground. The bear threw each half of the dead dog in a different direction – the head to the left, the tail to the right – and turned on the others with a roar.

All around the Bear Garden people cheered and whistled, stamping their feet and shouting their appreciation.

All of them, that is, except one.

Pip wasn't sentimental about animals. The idea of being a vegetarian, for instance, would have seemed ridiculous to him. Like everyone else that he had ever encountered, he ate meat whenever he could and was perfectly happy killing an animal for food. If he caught a rabbit, he'd slit its throat with his knife. He shot pigeons with his sling. He gutted fish. He wrung the necks of chickens. But watching a bear rip a dog in half – what was the fun in that? He sat with his head in his hands, staring at the dogs and the bears, horrified by what he was seeing.

If the people around him had shared his horror he might have felt better, but their enthusiasm made him even more depressed. They screeched encouragement to the dogs, urging the bearkeeper to drive them onward, and cheered every drop of blood. For the first time in his life Pip felt ashamed to be human.

You might not know it, or even believe it, but there are still some people who pay good money to watch dogs and bears ripping one another to pieces.

Most governments have banned bear fights, but that doesn't matter. Not everyone obeys the law.

Bear fights today are pretty much the same as bear fights were four hundred years ago. Crowds gather. Every spectator pays an admission fee. They place bets on which dog will be torn apart or which bear will die, then clap and cheer as the bears fight for their lives.

Actually, bears aren't the only animals that suffer like this. Bulls do too. And dogs. Even chickens. All around the world you'll find men and women paying to watch cock fights, dog fights and bull fights. It's difficult to find a good word to say about such people.

When Bruno staggered backwards and slumped on to all fours, exhausted by his efforts, the bearkeeper yelled and cracked his whip, turning his dogs' attentions to the other two bears.

These were easier targets. The dogs crowded round them, barking and biting, jumping up, snapping at ears and muzzles. These bears' teeth and claws had been removed, just like Bruno's, but they lacked his strength, making them just about defenceless. They could do nothing but endure attack after attack, hunching their shoulders, spinning on the spot, thumping the earth with their paws, trying to shake themselves free of the dogs' teeth. Soon blood was dribbling down their bodies, spilling both from fresh wounds and old scars that had reopened under the onslaught. Clumps of fur lifted on the breeze, blowing across the stadium like scraps of blossom shaken from a cherry tree.

Pip hunched on the bench, repulsed and horrified, but unable to stop watching. He wanted to close his eyes or turn away, but the urge to see what happened was even stronger. One bear in particular held his attention – the little one, the one that Robert had guessed would die today. It was the smallest, weakest and most pathetic of the three bears, a little broader than Pip himself but no taller, and it seemed to know that it had no chance against the dogs. They sensed that too, crowding round, snarling and barking, snapping at the bear's ankles, biting its outstretched paws. As the dogs lunged, the skinny, scared bear ambled backwards, trying to escape, but it couldn't go any further than the length of the rope tethered to its collar. Recognizing weakness, the dogs attacked more fiercely, grazing the bear's legs with their teeth, leaping on to its back and belly, grabbing fur and biting flesh.

When the small bear was exhausted and almost defeated, swaying on its feet, just about to collapse, the bearkeeper whistled, calling his dogs off. He didn't want to kill any of his bears, not until he had lined up a replacement, or he'd be left one short for the next show. The dogs retreated, spitting out mouthfuls of fur and gobbets of foamy blood, and the bear sank to the ground.

24

People gathered their belongings and stood up. The show was over.

The bearkeeper fastened leads to his dogs' collars and led them towards the double doors at the back of the Bear Garden.

Men wandered around the arena, delivering cash to people who had won bets, commiserating with the losers.

"The bears lived to fight another day. Better luck next time."

"One dog died. There's your sixpence."

"Goodnight, sir. Goodnight, madam. Goodnight."

Pip leant on the low wall, resting his chin on his hands and stared at the smallest, skinniest bear. It was slumped on the ground, covered in mud and blood, licking its wounds. He had a sudden urge to run across the mud and commiserate with the bear in some way. Tickle its ears, perhaps. Stroke its fur. Or say something, although he wasn't sure what he'd say. "Sorry about us," perhaps. "Sorry about humans." Best of all, he'd offer it some food. A chicken wing or a piece of cheese. He remembered the apple in his pocket. Did bears like apples? If he'd been alone in the Bear Garden he would have jumped over the wall and found out, but he didn't want to walk across the arena in front of all these people. He didn't want to be spotted by the Weasel or any of his men. If they were here Pip wanted to see them before they saw him.

The raucous women were trying to persuade Robert Armin to go to the pub with them.

"I'd love to," said Robert. "But I have to go home."

"Doesn't matter if you're married," said one of the women. "So are we."

"I'm not married," said Robert. "I'm not the marrying type."

"So what's stopping you?"

"Maybe next time." He gave the women one of his most charming smiles then turned his back on them and reverted his attention to Pip. "How are you doing, Pip?"

"Fine," said Pip, although he didn't feel fine at all.

"Did you enjoy the show?"

"No. It was horrible."

Robert laughed. "What was horrible about it?"

"I've never seen anything so disgusting in my whole life. What's wrong with people? Why would anyone want to watch a bear being bitten by a dog? Don't they understand how much it must hurt?"

"Oh, don't worry," said Robert. "Bears aren't like us."

"What do you mean?"

"They can't think. They can't speak. They don't even feel pain in the same way as us."

"How do you know?"

"Everyone knows that. It's just a fact."

Pip stared at the bears. Was Robert Armin right? Couldn't the bears think? Or feel pain? Pip wasn't so sure. Looking at them, he thought he could see creatures who were pretty much like himself, capable of thinking and feeling pain and maybe even speaking. Not English, of course. But they probably had a language of their own. Like those Frenchmen that he'd seen earlier.

"It's been a pleasure to meet you, Pip," said Robert Armin. "I'd love to stay here all day chatting. But I've got lines to learn for tomorrow. So I'll say goodbye. I hope you find whatever you're looking for."

"Thanks," muttered Pip.

"Goodbye then," said Robert. "And good luck." He patted Pip on the shoulder, blew a kiss to the group of women and hurried away.

The Bear Garden emptied fast as the audience flooded towards the exit, chattering and laughing, pushing and jostling, trying to get out first. Pip watched them, searching for the Weasel, Scar, Tooth or Pigface, but he couldn't see any of them. And, although he saw innumerable men who could have been George Stone, he had no way of knowing if any of them actually were him.

The bearkeeper returned to fetch his bears. He looped ropes through the silver hoops in their noses, Bruno first, then the middle one, and finally the skinniest.

Pip watched how he did it, wondering why the bears didn't resist. With a single slap of their heavy paws they could have knocked him to the ground.

Bruno shook his head from side to side, and the middle bear padded backwards, trying to avoid the rope, but the smallest, skinniest bear didn't even protest. As the bearkeeper slipped the rope through the hoop in its nose, it just stood there, head bowed, paws flat on the ground, waiting patiently, as if offering itself up for sacrifice. When the bearkeeper tugged the rope, the bear trotted meekly towards him.

Holding all three ropes in his left hand and a whip in his right, the bearkeeper led the bears towards the wide wooden doors at the back of the Bear Garden.

Each tug of that rope must have been agony, the hoops tearing at their nostrils, digging into their soft flesh, forcing them to go wherever they were led. But they had no chance to complain. If any of them ever showed the slightest sign of wanting to stop or change direction, the bearkeeper cracked his whip, lashing at their ankles, reminding them who was boss.

Pip decided to give his apple to the small, skinny one. It wouldn't be much of an apology, but it was better than nothing.

He looked around the Bear Garden once more. Most of the audience had gone now. Of those who remained, no one resembled the Weasel or his gang. They weren't here. He could safely leave.

He vaulted over the low wall, landed in the mud with a splash, and hurried after the bears.

25

Pip pushed through the big wooden doors, stepped outside and found himself at the back of the Bear Garden. Pedestrians hurried past. A black pig snuffled along the ground, searching for food. Three ravens flew overhead. There was no sign of the bearkeeper, his dogs or his bears.

Pip looked down at his feet. In the mud he could see some scraps of fur and a few drops of blood. He followed them.

The trail of blood and fur led across the grass, through some trees and down a dark alleyway. The alley narrowed between two ramshackle buildings; here the trail stopped at a heavy wooden door.

Pip turned the latch and gave the door a soft nudge, easing it open an inch or two, just enough of a gap to see a muddy floor, some hay and a bucket. He waited for a few seconds, prepared to turn and run, but no one shouted at him, demanding to know what he wanted. Maybe the bearkeeper had gone. Maybe he was asleep. Only one way to find out. Pip glanced left, then right, then left again, making sure that the alley was empty and no one was watching, before swinging the door fully open and stepping inside.

He found himself in a low-roofed building like a cattle shed. The air stank. Puddles of brown water spread across the muddy floor. Taking care to make no noise, Pip closed the door behind him and padded quietly into the middle of the room, hopping over the puddles, turning his head constantly from side to side, looking and listening for the bearkeeper.

A doorway in the far wall led into the rest of the building; it was covered by a thick woollen cloth, oatmeal-coloured, put there to keep out draughts. Six large cages stood against the near wall, built from wooden staves and lashed together with rope. Three cages were empty and three contained bears.

Pip walked along the line of cages, glancing first at Bruno, then the middle bear, but not stopping until he reached the smallest and skinniest of the bears. It was lying on the ground, curled in a heap, and showed no interest in him.

Pip wrapped his hands around the bars of the cage and made a low whistle, so quiet that he could hardly hear it himself.

The bear didn't even lift its head.

Standing so close, Pip could clearly see the splotches of dried blood on the bear's flanks, matting together clumps of fur, and the flies buzzing round its wounds. A thick leather collar, covered with scratches, was tied around its neck.

Pip whistled again, a little louder, but there was still no response. So he whispered, "What's your name?" He wasn't expecting a reply, knowing quite well that bears can't speak, but hoped the bear might at least raise its head or look at him.

His efforts were wasted. The bear stayed exactly where it was, slumped in the straw, its eyes averted, licking its wounds with its heavy pink tongue.

With his left arm Pip reached into his pocket, taking great care not to scare the bear with any sudden movements, grabbed the apple and passed it through the bars.

The bear lifted its head and stared at the apple. Its nostrils twitched. Its mouth opened. A long sliver of saliva dribbled down from its lower jaw and dangled towards the ground. The bear struggled to its feet and, like a weary old woman, hobbled across the floor.

Pip was scared but he tried not to show it – he breathed calmly, not flinching, not even moving, just leaving his hand there, outstretched, clutching the apple.

With both paws the bear plucked the apple from Pip's hands and, without even glancing at Pip, retreated to the back of the cage. The bear checked the apple from every angle, turning it over and over in its paws. Satisfied, the bear put the apple in its mouth and ate it in two quick gulps, then lolloped forward again.

Pip was still feeling nervous and was tempted to jump backwards, out of the bear's range, but he forced himself to stay exactly where he was, even when, gripping the bars of the cage with both paws, the bear hauled itself to its full height. The bear might have been shockingly small and skinny for a bear, but it was still much broader than Pip.

The bear's mouth opened, revealing a long pink tongue and the brownish stumps of several teeth.

Pip was almost too scared to breathe. If the bear felt vicious it could chomp off Pip's fingers or rip his arm right out of its socket.

But the bear wasn't feeling vicious. Slowly, playfully, the bear stretched its right paw through the bars, placed it in the middle of Pip's chest, and gave him a push.

Pip staggered backwards, tripped over his own feet and fell to the ground, landing in a puddle.

Bears don't laugh but Pip saw an expression on the bear's face which looked to him like a smile.

Pip got up, walked back to the cage and slid his right arm through the bars. He knew he might be doing something very stupid, something that he might regret for many years to come, but it seemed a risk worth taking: he stretched his arm forward until he touched the bear's flank. Slowly, carefully, he touched the bear's muzzle with the tips of his fingers, then stroked the bear's thick neck, feeling the layers of fat and fur.

The boy and the bear looked at one another.

There was a strange expression in the bear's big black eyes, something like sadness.

They were more like the eyes of an owl than a fox or a dog; huge and dark, although lacking the serenity that an owl has.

Sadness wasn't the only expression that Pip could see in the bear's eyes. He could see fear too. And something else, something more surprising. Intelligence. The bear's eyes were searching and inquisitive, trying to make sense of a mysterious world.

Have you ever met someone for the first time and, before you'd exchanged more than a couple of words, before you've even had a chance to look at one another properly, known instinctively that you could become best friends?

It's a good feeling, isn't it?

That had never happened to Pip. He'd never had a real friend, a best friend, someone to whom he could confess everything, even his innermost secrets. But now, staring into the bear's eyes, he saw someone who could be his friend. He didn't know why, and he certainly didn't know how, but he wanted to be friends with this small skinny bear.

A dog barked. The bear shambled backwards. Another dog barked, and another, and then many more. Pip dropped his arm and turned round, just in time to see several dogs pushing past the oatmeal-coloured curtain and rushing straight towards him. He backed against the wall, holding his hands in the air. "Good dog," he said.

"Please don't bite me."

The dogs surrounded him, baring their sharp white teeth. Saliva dribbled from their jaws. If they attacked, they'd have ripped him apart, but they just pinned Pip against the wall, growling softly, waiting for their master.

And there he was. The bearkeeper. He stood in the doorway, his clothes looking as if they hadn't been changed for a year, and pointed his whip at Pip. "Who are you?"

Pip's throat was dry. He couldn't speak or move. He was so scared of the dogs and the whip and their owner, his voice had left him. He could only open his mouth and blink his eyes like an idiot.

The bearkeeper advanced into the room. His breath stank of booze. Up close he looked less vicious and more of a mess. He said, "Come on, boy. Talk to me. What are you doing here?"

"Nothing," said Pip in a small voice. "I just. . ." And then his voice died again.

"Lost, are you? Just wandered in? And you were about to wander out again, no doubt, taking a few of my possessions. You dirty little thief." The bearkeeper raised his whip. The dogs growled. "What have you taken? Come on, confess. Out with it! Empty your pockets."

"I'm not a thief," said Pip.

"Then what are you doing here?"

"I'm just. . . Just looking at the bears."

"Why?"

"I like them."

The bearkeeper laughed, his expression changing from fury to jolliness. "Fair enough," he said in a kindly voice. "I like them too." He lowered his whip to the ground. Following their master's cue, the dogs backed off.

The two of them stood side by side for a moment, the man and the boy as if there was a kind of secret bond between them, a shared fascination for bears.

Pip didn't want to break the silence but he was so eager for information that he couldn't hold back his own questions. He pointed at the smallest, skinniest bear and said, "I like that one best. What's his name?"

"Her," said the bearkeeper.

"What?"

"Her name. Not his name."

Pip stared through the bars at the bear, who was huddling at the back of the cage. "She's a girl?"

"Of course she's a girl," said the bearkeeper. "If she was a boy, do you really think she'd fight so badly? Useless scrap of a bear. Teach me never to buy another girl. But she was cheap, I'll say that much."

"What's wrong with her?"

"Look at her! Look! What's not wrong with her? She's too small. No fire, no aggression. She can't fight to save her life. As soon as we have another delivery, a few more bears, we'll clear her right out."

Pip stared at the bear. For some reason, although he didn't know why, he was amazed that she was a girl. He didn't know many girls, just his sisters and a few farmers' daughters in the village, but the bear looked very different to them. He said, "When you get another delivery, what will you do with her?"

"What we do with all the old bears."

"And what's that?"

"Feed the flesh to the dogs and make a nice hat from the fur." The bearkeeper touched his shaven head. "I could use a new hat. I lost my last one. More likely some thief nicked it. One of your mates maybe."

Pip said, "When are you getting another delivery?"

"Not sure. Could be tomorrow. Should be a shipment from Russia any day now. But that's what they've been saying for months. Ruddy useless, those Russians."

"And what's her name?"

"That runt doesn't have a name."

"Why not?"

"Bears don't have much use for names. They can't talk, can they?"

"Bruno has a name."

"He's different."

"What's different about him?"

The bearkeeper didn't have an answer to that question, so he said, "Didn't I tell you to go away? I've don't have time for chitchat. I'm a busy man. What are you doing here, anyway?"

Pip wasn't sure what to say. What *was* he doing in the bearkeeper's home? *I'm looking for the Weasel*, he could have said. But the bearkeeper wouldn't know what he was talking about.

I could tell him that I've just arrived in London, thought

Pip. *And I'm looking for someone.*

No, I don't even need to say that. I'll just tell him that I'm new to the city. Maybe he knows where I can stay.

He might offer me some bread. Even a piece of cheese.

Perhaps the bearkeeper needed an apprentice. Perhaps he'd give two meals a day to a boy who carried buckets and scrubbed floors and washed bears.

Yes, thought Pip. *That's a fine plan.*

While searching for the Weasel and his father he could stay here and tend the bears, feeding them, washing them, stroking their soft fur and tickling their ears, protecting them from the horrors of London. He said, "Please, sir, will you teach me to be a bearkeeper? Will you take me as your apprentice?"

"This isn't a job for a boy," said the bearkeeper. "Bears are vicious creatures. Dogs too. You need strength."

"I'm stronger than I look."

"Even so. You're not half as strong as them." The bearkeeper jerked his thumb towards the bears. "Even the smallest is stronger than you. Stronger than me too. Give them a chance and one of those bears will knock your head off in a second."

"I don't mind."

"You will when you don't have a head."

"I'm a good worker," insisted Pip. "I get up early. Go on, sir, give me a chance."

The bearkeeper shook his head. "Sorry, boy. I'm sure you can work hard but I like being alone. I don't want an apprentice."

"But I can—"

"Go home," interrupted the bearkeeper. "You'll find a job somewhere else. Bright boy like you, ask around, you'll find work."

"But I—"

"Go home," said the bearkeeper again. "I have things to do."

"Please, sir, can't you—"

"Are you deaf? I said go home!"

Pip tried to argue his case, showing off his hands and muscles, promising to work for nothing more than board and lodging, begging to be given a chance, even if only for a day or two, but the bearkeeper wasn't interested. He cracked his whip. Pip yelped and grabbed his ankle. The bearkeeper took a step forward and flexed his whip. Pip hopped backwards and said, "Can I come back and visit the bear?"

"Visit? Why?"

"I like her." Pip glanced at the bear. She was crouching by the bars of her cage, watching him. Their eyes met for a moment. He turned back to the bearkeeper and said, "Please, sir. Let me come and see her. I won't do any harm, I promise. I'll just talk to her. Bring her apples."

"If you want to see the bear, you know what you can do?"

"No, sir."

"You can pay a penny and watch her fight my dogs. That's what everyone else has to do."

"Couldn't I just come here and—"

"You're never coming here again," interrupted the

bearkeeper. "This is my home. If I catch you in here, I'll kill you. That's a promise." He raised his whip. "Now get out."

Pip realized there was no point arguing. Not unless he wanted bleeding ankles. He would have liked to stroke the bear's fur again and say a proper goodbye but the bearkeeper was already cracking his whip. Just in time, Pip sprang backwards and sprinted out of the shed.

26

Darkness embraced the city. The streets turned black. People hurried home. No one wanted to be outside. After sunset, sensible people shuttered their windows, bolted the front door and stayed inside till sunrise.

Pip walked slowly, keeping to the shadows, looking around all the time, watching for danger. He glanced anxiously at other people in the streets, keeping his hands near his belt, prepared to pull out his father's knife and protect himself. They glanced back at him, saw a shifty-looking boy with dirty clothes and suspicious eyes, and crossed to the other side of the road to avoid him.

While Pip was keeping his eyes on potential thieves and murderers, he was searching for something else too. Food. Apart from those five apples he hadn't eaten all day and his stomach felt tight with hunger. Maybe, he thought, giving his last apple to the bear had been a mistake. And then he realized that it hadn't. He'd had five; she got one. If he'd kept it for himself he would have felt too guilty to eat it.

He peered into the gutters, hoping to catch a glimpse of some discarded scrap of someone else's dinner – a old loaf, a pork chop, a half-eaten turnip, anything would have done – but saw nothing worth eating, just piles of stinking, rotten rubbish.

Eventually hunger overcame his squeamishness and he stopped at the junction of two streets where several drains collided, bringing garbage from different neighbourhoods. Tomorrow someone would come and unblock the main gutter, allowing the rubbish to flow unimpeded through the streets and empty into the river. For now a huge heap had collected, wet and dark and evil-smelling.

Can you imagine keeping all the rubbish that your family produced for an entire month? Every little bit. Cherry stones. Apple cores. Potato peelings. Toenail clippings. Hair. Paper. Bones. Gristle. Bath water. And, on top of it all, everything that went into the toilet too. A month of pee. A month of poo. Imagine all that heaped into a huge pile. And then you'll have some idea of where Pip searched for his supper.

He crouched on the ground beside this enormous heap of stinking garbage, shooing aside his competitors – a family of black rats and two squawking ravens – before rolling up his sleeves and thrusting his hands inside the pile, scooping aside handfuls of onion skins and soggy crusts and twigs and leaves and all kinds of unidentifiable nastiness, digging for his dinner. The rats fled, but the ravens just hopped angrily aside, flapping their wings, and stood there, watching him resentfully, waiting for him to go away.

The rats and ravens needn't have been so bothered. They'd already taken all the good stuff. Pip found nothing edible but half a carrot, two squishy onions and an egg, which must have been laid there by a lost hen. He washed them in a puddle, then hurried away. Cawing after him, warning him never to return, the ravens pecked over the new rubbish that he'd exposed.

Have you ever eaten a raw egg? No? Until that day neither had Pip. But he was so hungry he would have eaten just about anything. In a gloomy, deserted alleyway which went nowhere he squatted in the shadows, hidden from passers-by, cracked open the egg and forced himself to gulp down the wobbly yolk and dribbly white. He swallowed the last dregs, then licked out the shell.

When he'd eaten the egg, the carrot and the onions he slid further into the shadows, trying to make himself invisible, and wrapped his arms around himself. He was cold, lonely and miserable.

I'm an idiot, thought Pip. *I came to London thinking I'd just bump into the Weasel. But London isn't a village. You don't bump into people here. You could walk the streets for a week, day and night, and you wouldn't find who you were looking for.*

He'd never find the Weasel. He'd never get the money back. Worst of all, he'd never discover the truth about his dad.

So what was he going to do? Go home?

No. Never. Not after what he'd discovered about his mother.

He'd stay in London. If he lived here long enough he'd have to bump into the Weasel eventually. It might take weeks, months or even years, but that didn't matter. He wasn't in a hurry.

To stay here, he'd find some work. Enough to pay for food and a bed. If he couldn't work as a bearkeeper, he knew what he could do. From all he had learnt with his stepfather, Pip knew he was already a skilled smith. Someone would give him a job mending knives and sharpening swords.

He knew where to go too. Every year Bartholomew Fair was held in a place called Smithfield. The field of smiths. That was where they must work. Tomorrow he would go there and find a smith to take him as an apprentice.

He just had to survive tonight without being murdered.

His back pressed against the wall, he muttered a quick prayer. "Please God," he whispered, "let me live through tonight. Save me from the murderers. And then, tomorrow, help me get a job. Help me find the Weasel. And my father. If you do, I'll be good, I promise."

The preachers said God was everywhere. If so, he must be here too, hidden in this alleyway.

The sound of his own voice was strangely comforting, as was the thought that God could hear what he was saying, so Pip whispered one more prayer, the words that he said every week in church. *Our Father, which art in heaven, hallowed be thy name.* The familiar phrases sounded good, so he spoke them aloud. If a thief or a murderer had been lurking nearby, hunting for easy prey, they would have known exactly where to look, but he didn't care. God would be protect him. "Thy kingdom come," he said, his voice resounding through the darkness. "Thy will be done, on earth as it is in heaven. Give us this day our daily bread. And forgive us our trespasses, as we forgive them that trespass against us. And lead us not into temptation. But deliver us from evil. Amen."

When the prayer was finished Pip felt better. God was in this alleyway, he was sure of that now, and would protect him against the city's horrors. He pulled his clothes around himself, trying to keep warm, and closed his eyes.

He didn't go to sleep immediately. He lay there for a long time, thinking through the events of the past two days, remembering what he'd seen. His thoughts returned again and again to the bear, and he tried to decide which of them was worse off, him or her.

She had a few advantages over him. Some food. Clean water. Somewhere to sleep. A roof over her head and walls to keep out the draughts. But she couldn't walk more than a few paces in any direction before bashing into the bars of her cage. He might be lost, lonely, hungry, cold and penniless, but at least he was free. Given the choice between her life and his, Pip had no doubt which he would choose. It was always better to be free.

27

Pip woke with an empty stomach and a dry throat. To his surprise, the sun was high in the sky. He must have slept for a long time.

He stood up, shaking his limbs to get some warmth back into his body, then walked back the way that he had come last night, wandering alongside the Thames. He didn't yet know his way around London but he recognized some landmarks – the distinctive steeples of the tallest churches, the silhouette of London Bridge, the flags flying over the Bear Garden and the Globe.

He remembered Robert Armin, the one person who he knew in London. What about asking him for a job?

It's worth trying, thought Pip. *And if he says no, I'll cross the river, find Smithfield and beg the smiths for work.*

Pip thought about the play that he'd seen. Acting looked easy. You just stood on a stage and spoke some words. Who couldn't do that?

The Globe would make a good base. Near the Bear Garden. Always packed with people. The perfect place to watch out for the Weasel.

He headed towards the flag. The streets were full of people but no one took any notice of him. He was just another scruffy boy with mud on his clothes. The city was packed with kids like him, runaways and outcasts, stealing or scavenging whatever they could. Some of them died after a few days. Others lived on the streets for the rest of their lives. And a few earned enough to start a business, buying a horse or hiring a shop, and slowly turned themselves into ordinary citizens.

He reached the Globe. People were hurrying in and out of the entrance, carrying costumes and props. Some actors lay on the grass outside, chatting. Pip recognized them from the play. This morning, stripped of their costumes, they looked unimpressive and ordinary. Looking at them, you'd have thought that anyone could be an actor.

Even me, thought Pip.

He imagined himself standing on the stage of the Globe, entertaining a big crowd. They'd laugh at his jokes. Applaud his wisdom. Cheer as he drew his sword and slaughtered his enemies. Pretty soon he would become the most famous actor in London. People would queue for hours to see him. One afternoon, a few months from now, he would be standing on the stage, speaking the lines of a play, and he would look down and see a familiar face in the crowd. He wouldn't be like Hamlet. Oh, no, not Pip. He would never waver or hesitate. He would jump off the stage, holding his sword, and run the blade straight through the Weasel's chest.

He strode towards the Globe, already imagining how the Weasel would look as he staggered backwards, blood spilling down his front, and collapsed in a heap.

As he walked through the main entrance a man grabbed his arm and pulled him round. "Where do you think you're going?"

"Inside," said Pip, shaking off the man's hand.

"Not now, you're not. The show doesn't start till this afternoon."

"I'm meeting someone."

"Yeah? Who?"

"Mister Robert Armin," said Pip.

"Does he know you?"

"Of course he knows me."

"Oh. Come on then." The man stood aside, letting Pip through the door. "Sorry for shouting at you, but we get people sneaking in here all the time. Even at this time of the afternoon. Crazy, innit? They'll do anything to avoid paying for a ticket."

"I'll just be five minutes," said Pip.

"No problem. Take your time. He's over there." The man pointed to a group of three men who were standing on the stage.

Pip thanked the doorman and hurried into the Globe.

The theatre was packed with people. Actors were sitting in the galleries, discussing their hangovers. Soon they would be called to the stage and asked to rehearse their entrances and exits for today's performance. Carpenters and stagehands were already building the scenery. Since the Globe staged a different play every day, the scenery had to be constructed every morning and dismantled every evening.

Pip walked across the pit and ran up the stairs that led on to the stage. He felt nervous as he approached the group. Robert Armin was arguing with two other men. Pip recognized both of them from the play. One had played the king. The other, a boy of Pip's own age, had played a girl, disguising his sex under a long white dress and a blonde wig. Today, dressed in leather breeches and a bright-blue shirt, he looked like any other swaggering boy, cheeky and full of confidence.

Pip tugged Robert's sleeve. "Begging your pardon, Mister Armin, could I have a word?"

Robert broke off whatever he was saying and turned around. "Oh, hello. It's Pip, right?"

"That's right."

"What are you doing here?"

"I have to ask you something," said Pip.

"Go on then. Ask."

"It's private."

"This is a theatre," said Robert. "Nothing is private here."

The other two actors laughed.

Pip said, "I'd rather speak in private, sir."

"These men are my friends. I have no secrets from them. Go on, spit it out. What do you want to say?"

"I want to be an actor," said Pip.

Robert smiled and shook his head. The other man grinned. The boy burst out laughing.

Pip felt embarrassed and furious. He glared at the three actors. What was so funny?

Robert was wearing different clothes to yesterday. That marked him as a rich man. In Mildmay most people wore the same clothes for at least a month. The other man, the actor who had played the king, must have been handsome a few years ago, but now he had a pot belly and deep wrinkles around his eyes. But it was the boy, the one who had played a girl, who held Pip's attention.

He was probably about eleven, although he could have been just about any age between ten and sixteen. He had soft cheeks and a boy's face, but he held himself like a grown man, looking at the world with the poise and self-confidence of someone who had seen it all before. His hair was blond and cleaner than Pip's had ever been. He had blue eyes, freckles and a straight nose. He was wearing expensive clothes and carrying a leather purse strapped to his belt, the coins chinking whenever he moved.

Standing beside these three sophisticated men, Pip felt like a country bumpkin. He was conscious of his dirty face and smelly breeches. He remembered that his last meal had been pulled from a heap of rubbish and his last bed had been an alleyway and, only yesterday, someone had tipped a bucket of poo on his head.

It had been a stupid idea, he now realized, to come back to the Globe. He was a country boy, a villager, a peasant, a smith. He knew how to fight, how to forge metal, how to milk a cow, which herbs cured a headache and where to find wild garlic, but he didn't know the first thing about acting. He should have stuck to what he knew. He was just about to turn his back on the three actors, walk out of the theatre and make his way to Smithfield when Robert Armin said, "Why?"

Pip said, "What?"

"Why do you want to be an actor?"

Pip could have answered: *I need a job so I can stay in London and find the Weasel. And I want to find Scar, Tooth and Pigface too. And kill all four of them in revenge for what they did. And then I want to find my father*. But he was pretty sure that Robert Armin wouldn't have the patience to listen to a lengthy explanation and wouldn't be interested either. What would interest him? Praise. Robert Armin was vain. Yesterday he'd sucked up compliments from Pip, people in the street and those women in the Bear Garden. Pip said: "I want to be an actor because of what I saw yesterday. That play was the best thing I've ever seen in my life. What you did – I want to do that too."

The three actors smiled.

"Well, it wasn't bad," said the man who had played the king. "Shakespeare is definitely getting better. If you think of the nonsense he used to knock out. . ."

Robert Armin nodded. "Remember *The Comedy of Errors*? What twaddle that was! Rotten gags and not a single decent song."

"I still think *Romeo and Juliet* is his best," said the boy. "More action. More love interest."

"More lines for you."

"That too." The boy grinned. In a high voice, he started reciting his lines: "Farewell! God knows when we shall meet again." He fluttered his eyelashes like a woman and put his hand over his heart. "I have a faint cold fear thrills through my veins, that almost freezes up the heat of life."

"We've all seen your Juliet," interrupted Robert. "No need to do it all again."

"*He* hasn't," said the boy, pointing at Pip.

"Lucky him."

As the boy started to protest Robert turned to Pip. "I'm sorry, my young friend, but I can't help you. If you want my advice, learn a trade. Why don't you become a carpenter? Everyone needs carpenters. The money's good and you're always sure of a job. Any day now the Puritans are going to shut the theatres. If by some miracle we manage to stop them, the plague will close us instead. The actors, the musicians, the writers – we'll be unemployed. But the carpenters, they'll still be putting up shelves and building doors, earning a decent wage."

Pip's shoulders slumped. The bearkeeper didn't want to employ him. Nor did the actors. What if the smiths didn't either? What would he do then? Starve?

The boy stared at Pip. Perhaps he felt some sort of connection to him – they were both the same age, after all, and might have been friends if their circumstances were different – because he said, "Why can't he have a chance?

We all had to start somewhere. Go on, Armin. Give him a chance."

Pip looked up, full of hope.

"No," said Robert Armin.

"Why not?" said the boy.

"We're busy. What would happen if we gave a chance to every kid who walked in here, wanting to be an actor?"

"It won't take more than two minutes," said the boy. "You know Richard. If he likes someone he says so after two minutes."

"I can tell you now," said Robert, "he's not going to like him."

"Then we've all wasted two minutes of our lives. So what?"

"Oh, very well," said Robert. He cupped his hands around his mouth and shouted across the Globe to a tall, thin man who had his back to them. "Richard! RICHARD!!!"

The tall, thin man turned round. Pip recognized him. It was Richard Burbage, the man who had played Hamlet. "There's no need to shout. I'm right here."

"Do you have two minutes?"

"If it's extremely important," said Richard Burbage. "What's the problem?"

Robert gestured at Pip. "This pup wants an audition."

28

Pip had been attacked by mad dogs. He had been charged by a wild boar. He had been woken in the middle of the night by burglars. But nothing had ever terrified him as much as this.

He was standing at the front of the stage, looking around the theatre, staring at the pit and the galleries, trying to remember the words that he had just been taught.

His mind was empty. His palms were sweaty. He had an almost irresistible urge to turn round and run through one of the doors at the back of the stage. Why had he even imagined that he could be an actor?

About twenty men were watching him. They were dotted around the Globe, standing in the pit or sitting in the galleries, enjoying this unexpected diversion from their work. Everyone liked auditions. It was always fun to see some idiot making a fool of himself, strutting across the stage, imagining he had what it took to be an actor.

Pip cleared his throat. The noise echoed around the Globe. He remembered what the boy had said. *You know how Richard works. If he likes someone he says so after two minutes*. Pip wondered how many minutes had passed. He couldn't have been standing here for two minutes already, could he? He'd better start right now or else his time would be gone before he'd even started. *Come on*, he told himself. *Time to start. I'm thinking too much. I shouldn't be thinking, I should be talking. I should be speaking the words that Nathan taught me.*

The boy's name was Nathan Field. While Richard Burbage was finishing a few bits of urgent business before the audition, Nathan had introduced himself and given Pip some tips on acting. "Stand at the front of the stage," he had said. "Speak loudly. Turn your head from side to side. You shouldn't always look at the same person. Now, what are you going to speak?"

"Speak?"

"What lines? Which play?"

"I don't know any lines," said Pip. "I've only ever seen one play and that was yesterday."

Nathan shook his head. "Then you'd better learn some now. We'll do something easy. Repeat after me." Nathan spoke a few lines, saying them again and again until Pip could repeat them back again with pausing or getting anything wrong.

But now he couldn't say a word. He just stared at the men in the pit and galleries. There was Robert Armin. And Richard Burbage. And there, standing alone, was Nathan Field. When their eyes met, Nathan lifted his right hand and gave a thumbs-up.

Pip cleared his throat again and started speaking. What came out was a meek little whisper.

"Oh Romeo."

His voice was so quiet that even he could hardly hear it. He cleared his throat and started again.

"Oh Romeo! Romeo!"

He was still too quiet. He started once more.

"Oh Romeo! Romeo! Wherefore art thou Romeo?"

That was better. With each word he spoke, Pip gained a little more confidence. He spoke louder. He made bigger gestures with his arms. He looked men directly in the eye and spoke straight at them. He said:

"Deny thy father and refuse thy name;
Or, if thou wilt not, be but sworn my love,
And I'll no longer be a Capulet."

Pip was beginning to enjoy himself. He liked the sound of his own voice echoing around the Globe. He took a deep breath and started on the next line.

"'Tis but thy name that is my enemy;
Thou art thyself, though not—"

At that moment, although Pip was halfway through his sentence, speaking in a loud clear voice and gesturing towards the galleries with both hands, a voice interrupted him.

"Stop."

The voice was quiet, but it still echoed around the whole theatre. Richard Burbage had one of those voices that booms across any space, demanding to be heard, however quietly he spoke.

Pip stopped speaking and stood there with his mouth open. Like everyone else he stared at Richard Burbage, waiting to hear what he would say next.

Richard Burbage shook his head and said, "He's a no."

All around the Globe, as soon as they heard those words, people hurried to resume their work, preparing for the afternoon's performance. Within seconds, noise and movement resounded from every corner of the theatre. Pip had been forgotten already.

29

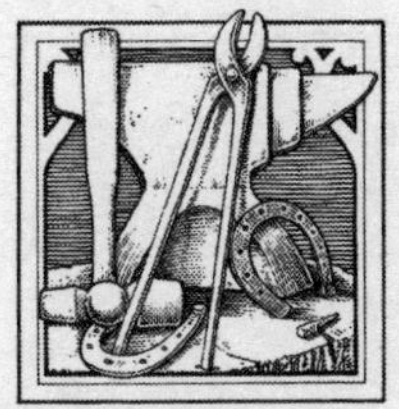

A carpenter hammered a nail into the scenery, fixing a painted tree against the back wall. Two boys ran across the pit, carrying armfuls of hats and swords. Someone shouted, "Who nicked my knickers?" Someone else shouted, "Who's seen the plot? Has anyone seen the plot?"

The plot was a sheet of paper on which the stage manager wrote all the entrances and exits that actors had to make. During the play, if an actor forgot his lines or couldn't remember when he came on next, he hurried round to the back of the stage and read the plot. If the plot went missing, the more forgetful actors wouldn't know when to make their entrances, and the play would descend into chaos.

In the middle of the pit Richard Burbage was giving orders to a trio of burly men. They listened to him, nodded, and ran in three different directions. When they had gone, Richard Burbage started walking briskly towards the stage. Then he stopped.

A small boy was blocking his path. "Can I ask you a question?"

"This isn't a good moment," said Richard Burbage. "Come back later."

Richard Burbage tried to step to the left of Pip, then to the right, but he couldn't get past. Whichever way he went, Pip went there first, blocking his path.

"Please, sir," said Pip. "Just a quick question."

"I'm sorry you didn't get much time," said Richard Burbage, who was beginning to get irritated. "But this is a tough business. And to be honest, you'd be better off out of it. Now, I don't want to be rude, but I'm very busy."

Again he tried to continue walking. And again Pip blocked his path. "Just one question," said Pip.

Richard Burbage sighed. "Fine. One question. But only one. And then I have to get back to work. What is it?"

Pip said, "What did I do wrong?"

"Nothing," said Richard Burbage.

"Then why did you stop me?"

"Because you're not an actor. And you never will be."

"Why not?"

"Because you either have it or you don't. And you don't. Now, you've just asked three questions, which is two more than we agreed. So, if you'll please excuse me, I have a theatre to run."

Again, Richard Burbage tried to step past, and again,

Pip stopped him.

Pip said, "What's 'it'?"

"'It' is 'it'," said Richard Burbage.

"I don't understand."

"Nor do I. If I did, I'd be rich."

Pip stared at the older, taller man. "Now I really don't understand."

"All I can tell you is this. A few people have it. Most people don't. And no one, absolutely no one, knows exactly what it is."

"Maybe I do have it," said Pip. "Maybe I just can't find it."

Richard Burbage shook his head. "You don't have it."

"How do you know?"

"Because I can tell."

"How?"

"I can see it. I can feel it. Listen, my child, you don't have to crucify yourself. You just don't have it."

"Will you teach me?"

"No, no, it can't be taught."

"Why not?"

"Haven't you heard a word I said? You either have it or you don't. And you don't have it. Simple as that."

"But why not?"

"I told you," said Richard Burbage. "I don't know." He sighed. "I'll say this once more and then I'm going back to work. You either have it or you don't. For some reason, who knows why, I have it." He turned and, one by one, pointed at several of the other actors who were dotted around the Globe. "Robert Armin has it. Augustine Philips has it.

Thomas Pope has it. William Shakespeare has it. Wentworth Smith has it. Nathan Field has it." Then he pointed at Pip. "But you – you, my friend – you most certainly do not have it. You can't learn it. You can't buy it. You can't steal it. And if you don't have it now, then you're never going to have it."

"But I want to be an actor," said Pip.

"I'm sorry, but you'll never be an actor. And trying will only make you unhappy. Find something else to do with your life."

"Like what?"

"I don't know, that's up to you. It's your life. You'll find something. You know my brother?"

"No," said Pip.

"There he is." Richard Burbage pointed across the pit to a dreary-looking man in a pair of cheap brown breeches and a white shirt. "That's my brother, Cuthbert."

As he stared at the man, Pip noticed his resemblance to Richard Burbage. At first glance you wouldn't have imagined that the two were related. Richard wore garish jewellery, brightly coloured clothes and a constant smile. If he walked into a room, everyone would immediately look up. Cuthbert, on the other hand, would hardly attract your attention even if he was the only other person in the room. His clothes were cheap. His hair was cropped short. He wore no jewellery. But the Burbages both had the same long face, the same high forehead and the same keen, curious eyes. It made sense that they were brothers.

"He and I share just about everything," said Richard Burbage. "We always have done. We had the same parents, obviously, and he's only a year older than me, so we grew up together. We went to the same school. We ate the same food. We played the same games. We've lived in the same houses. Our lives have followed the same path. We're almost the same person. But I have it and he doesn't. No one knows why. If he ever steps on stage, they'll laugh him off again before he even opens his mouth. So he does the books. And he does them brilliantly. Without him, the Globe would never even open. We depend on him. Each of us has a talent, child. You'll find yours. It might take some time, but you'll find it."

Pip said, "How?"

"Keep your eyes open. Try things out." Richard Burbage glanced upwards, staring at the position of the sun in the sky, guessing the time. "Now, I'm sorry, but I really do have to go. Stick around if you want. See the show for free. Goodbye."

As Richard Burbage turned to go, Pip ran after him. "Mister Burbage?"

"No, no, no. Not another question; I've had enough."

"Please," said Pip, grabbing his arm. "Just one."

Richard Burbage shook himself free. "Absolutely not," he said. "You've taken up enough of my time. Now leave me alone."

He tried to keep walking, but Pip blocked his path. "Please, sir. Just one question. Please."

Richard Burbage sighed. "You really are very irritating."

"Sorry, sir."

"Go on, then. Let's hear your question."

Pip said, "Can I have a job?"

30

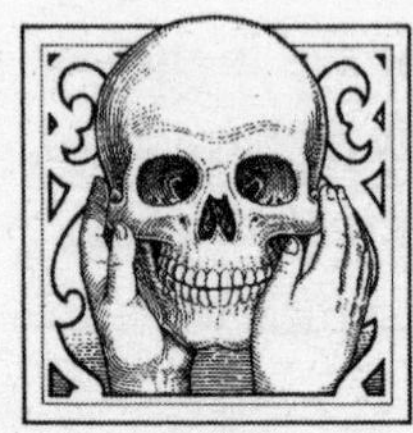

Out of little more than admiration for Pip's persistence, Richard Burbage agreed to employ him as one of the theatre's boys. He would be a stagehand, a cleaner, a dogsbody and a jack-of-all-trades, given the tasks that no one else had the time, energy or inclination to do. His only specific duty was clearing up the Globe, sweeping the floor before every performance and again afterwards. He would be paid a penny a day and he could watch the shows for free.

Pip started work immediately. He swept the stage, then scrubbed the wooden planks with a wet cloth. The work was boring but curiously satisfying. He hunched over spots of dirt which had been embedded in the wood for weeks, if not years. Soon the blond timber was glistening in the midday sun.

Nathan came to congratulate him. They chatted for a few minutes. Nathan pointed out a few of the important men in the company, describing their roles, then went to prepare for the play.

In the afternoon people started flowing into the Globe, paying their pennies at the door and taking their places. Pip stood at the back, watching the audience. He searched their faces, looking for the Weasel or Pigface or Scar or Tooth, seeing none of them. He kept a lookout for Inigo Jones, hoping to repay his debt, but Mister Jones was nowhere to be seen. Maybe he'd taken an early boat to Venice. Finally, Pip looked for his father, but that felt like the most hopeless of his quests. Hundreds of men came into the Globe and just about any of them might have been his father. He hoped that if he did actually see George Stone a sudden shock of recognition would pass between them, a mutual understanding that the same blood ran through their veins, but it never happened. Perhaps his dad was a thousand miles away. Perhaps he was six feet under the ground. Or perhaps he was here, mingling with the crowd, and they simply hadn't recognized one another.

As more and more people flooded into the Globe, Pip found himself distracted by the variety of faces and bodies, and gradually forgot to look out for his enemies and his dad. There was too much else to see.

When the play was just about to start Pip pushed through the pit and made his way to the front, standing just under the rim of the stage. If he'd stood anywhere else in the pit he would hardly have been able to see a thing, because he was so much shorter than most of the men and women in the theatre.

Tomorrow, he decided, he would sneak into the gallery and watch from there. He wouldn't need a cushion. He would be happy to sit anywhere. But he would like to look down on the play rather than standing on tiptoe at the front of the crowd, squashed between two men, smelling their armpits and garlicky breath.

He looked up and recognized one of them. It was the writer. Nathan had pointed him out. Pip tugged his sleeve and said, "Excuse me, Mister Shakespeare? Excuse me?"

Shakespeare glanced down at Pip. "Yes?"

"Could you move your arm, please? You're hurting my ear."

Without a word, Shakespeare moved his arm.

"Thank you, sir," said Pip.

"You're the new boy, aren't you?"

"Yes, sir."

"Good luck."

Shakespeare didn't address another word to him, but Pip didn't care. *Good luck*. The company's writer had wished him luck! Feeling very pleased with himself, Pip turned his attention to the play.

Today the company performed an Italian comedy. Rich merchants paced up and down the stage, discussing love, money and boats. They wore velvet breeches and leather jackets with fur collars. Rapiers hung from their belts. *That's a good sign*, thought Pip. *There might be a fight later*.

When the men finished their conversation and left the

stage, a door opened at the back and two tall, glamorous women emerged. They had blonde hair, pale skin and scarlet lips. Their dresses were covered with rubies, glistening in the sunlight, and long chains of pearls hung around their necks.

As these two beauties strolled towards the front of the stage, someone in the crowd put his fingers to his lips and wolf-whistled.

The women smiled at the whistler. One of them, the prettier of the two, swayed her hips and fluttered her eyelashes.

The whistler shouted out: "I love you!"

The pretty woman lifted her long white fingers to her lips and blew him a kiss.

The whistler yelled, "Come here and do that!"

"Maybe later," said the pretty woman, giving him another flutter of her long eyelashes. She turned to her companion and said, "By my troth, Nerissa, my little body is aweary of this great world."

"You would be, sweet madam," replied the other woman, "if your miseries were in the same abundance as your good fortunes are."

As the two women talked, they paced slowly up and down the front of the stage, showing off their sexy bodies and elegantly tailored dresses. Both of them had small breasts and delicate feet, but nothing was as attractive as their faces. In the clear sunlight they looked like angels. Pip had been watching them for a few minutes when, to his astonishment, he realized that one of them, the prettier, was Nathan Field.

Pip became even more confused later in the play when Nathan's character – a rich heiress named Portia – disguised herself as a man so she could get a job as a lawyer. So Nathan was a boy pretending to be a girl pretending to be boy. Thinking about it made Pip's head hurt.

That wasn't the only complicated part of the play. Pip found himself bewildered by most of the words that people spoke. They always used ten when two would do and deliberately picked vocabulary which only a schoolteacher would understand, rarely speaking in the plain way that ordinary people spoke.

Things improved when Robert Armin sauntered on to the stage. He sang several songs and told a string of rude jokes which had Pip doubled over with laughter.

Richard Burbage played a Jew who was owed money by a Christian. Pip had never met a Jew, so he was interested to see what they looked like. Richard Burbage wore a big false nose and a long red beard. *If all Jews look like that*, Pip thought, *they must be easy to recognize*. He decided to try and spot one in the streets of London.

The audience hissed and booed whenever the Jew spoke. At the end, when the Christian took revenge on the Jew, grabbing his money and his daughter, cheers broke out all around the theatre.

The actors lined up at the front of the stage and bowed. Richard Burbage whipped off his false nose and hurled it into the audience for some lucky person to keep as a souvenir.

31

When the play had finished and the audience had gone, Pip collected rubbish from the galleries, then swept the pit.

It was amazing what people left behind. He found a leather glove, a sprig of lavender, a half-eaten bun, some sugared almonds and, best of all, about thirty raisins, scattered in the mud. He picked them carefully into the palm of his hand, ate a few and saved the rest for later.

This time yesterday he'd been sitting in the Bear Garden, watching the small, skinny bear try to defend herself against ten dogs. Right now she'd probably be doing the same thing again. Pip hoped she was winning.

He remembered her moist black eyes and her soft fur. He wanted to tickle her ears and push raisins or almonds or the half-eaten bun through the bars of her cage and watch her pleasure as she scoffed them down. Often, as he worked, he dreamt about doing exactly that. Less often, and with more difficulty, he admitted to himself why he didn't. It was very simple. He was scared of the bearkeeper. The whip was certainly a good reason for staying away – it had cracked with a terrifying noise and hurt a lot when it snagged his ankle – but what really frightened Pip was the man himself. His strong arms. The long scar that crossed his forehead. His mashed-up nose. And, most of all, the expression in his eyes. He'd killed people. You could see that just by looking at him. If the bearkeeper hadn't been so frightening Pip would have returned to the cottage and happily spent hours befriending the small skinny bear, winning her affections with apples or tickling or cheese or whatever bears liked best. But he didn't dare.

Anyway, he told himself, he was too busy to make friends with bears. As soon as he finished one job and paused for a rest, an actor, a carpenter or the wardrobe mistress summoned him to a different part of the theatre and gave him another.

Every pub in London catered to a different crowd. Butchers drank in The Black Pig. Fishmongers drowned their sorrows in The Elephant. In The Albion, pickpockets spent what they'd stolen and plotted their next theft. For actors, The White Swan in Southwark was the place to be.

It was long past the bedtime of any sensible citizen, but The White Swan was packed. Between the hours of sunset and sunrise the citizens of London were supposed to be tucked up in bed, and you could be arrested just for walking through the streets at night, but the actors didn't care. They were still partying.

If you were a regular theatre-goer, you'd have recognized many of their faces. Over there – you see those two men playing dice? – that's Ben Jonson and William Shakespeare, who many say are the two best writers in the world. And there's Richard Burbage! Can you see his brother, Cuthbert? No, me neither. Maybe he's at home, counting his pennies.

That's William Kemp, the famous clown, playing a jazzy tune on a lute. And that's Robert Armin, the not-quite-so-famous clown, who took Kemp's job at the Globe. They hate one another now.

And that man – the one whispering in that skinny girl's ear, giggling as she blushes – that's Tom Dekker. And there's John Marston and Nathan Field and Robert Gough and Augustine Philips and dozens of other actors and writers.

Women weren't allowed to act, but that didn't stop them working in the theatre or drinking in the pubs. There's Joan Alleyn, Ned's wife. And that's Judith Shakespeare, the playwright's sister. You see the short, fat woman with the big smile? That's Molly Plunkett, the wardrobe mistress.

There are even a couple of babies, somehow managing to sleep through the roar of conversation and laughter and flirting and gossip and argument that fills the narrow, sweaty, low-ceilinged pub.

Some of the stagehands are sitting at a table together,

sipping beer and giggling, but none of them look like Pip. There's a boy asleep under a table, but that's not Pip either. He's not here. It might be the end of his first day working at the Globe, but he hasn't followed the rest of the company to the pub.

A light rain was falling. Clouds covered the sky. There was no moon. The Globe was shrouded in darkness. The few remaining people carried candles as they locked valuables into wooden chests and closed all the doors. Most of the actors had left hours ago. The last stagehands called "Goodnight! God bless!" to one another and made their way to the street.

When they had gone, nothing moved.

The silence and stillness lasted for a few minutes. Then a small dark shape scampered across the stage and turned its head from side to side, sniffing the air. Another tiny shape took a few steps into the pit. The mice grew more confident, venturing into the middle of the pit and running along the balconies, searching for dropped scraps.

They were joined by a few other creatures, also hunting for food. Rats ran round the pit. Bats dodged through the gloom. A marmalade cat stalked along the galleries. On the roof a big old owl squatted, motionless and silent, his wide eyes staring into the darkness, waiting for the perfect moment to swoop down and plant his claws on the back of some unwary mouse's neck. But none of them had to worry about human interference. At night the Globe belonged to animals and birds.

Actually, that's not quite true. There was a human being in the theatre. Just one. But he was hidden from sight. If you stood on the stage or walked around the pit, you wouldn't have seen him. Only if you had climbed two flights of stairs to the top gallery, high above the stage, and walked to the furthest end, would you have noticed a lump tucked in the corner, half hidden under a bench. Even then, you probably wouldn't have bothered to investigate any further. You'd have assumed that the lump was a roll of carpet or a pile of cushions, left there by the cleaners. But if you had leant down and pulled aside the cloth you'd have discovered a small boy, wrapped in a blanket, lost in the deep sleep of someone who has been working all day.

32

In the morning, when Cuthbert Burbage arrived at the Globe, bringing a bag of coins and his accounts book, several people had already started preparing for that afternoon's performance. The wardrobe mistress was sewing costumes, a carpenter was building a ship's prow, a bleary-eyed writer was making some last-minute corrections to the prompt book and a small boy was kneeling in the centre of the stage, scrubbing the wooden planks. Cuthbert greeted each of them in turn, saying, "Good morning, Molly" to the wardrobe mistress, "Good morning, Christopher" to the carpenter, "Good morning, Mister Dekker" to the writer, and "Good morning, boy" to the boy scrubbing the stage.

"Good morning, Mister Burbage," replied the boy.

Cuthbert recognized him as the boy who had

auditioned yesterday. Last night, over dinner, his brother Richard had mentioned how, partly out of pity and partly through an intuition that the boy might be a hard worker, he had offered him a job. Cuthbert said, "What's your name, boy?"

"I was christened Philip, sir. But people call me Pip."

"Philip what?"

"Philip Stone, sir."

"It's nice to meet you, Philip Stone. I'm Cuthbert Burbage."

"I know you are, sir."

"Tell me something, Philip. Do you think it's going to rain?"

"No, sir."

"I hope you're right."

Without another word Cuthbert walked back to the galleries, took a seat and started working on his accounts, pausing every few minutes to glance at the sky and check the state of the clouds. He certainly hoped that the boy was right. Rain caused problems for the theatre. In the more expensive seats, up in the galleries, sheltered by the roof, the audience might manage to stay mostly dry, but the groundlings, the people who paid a penny to stand in the pit, had no protection from the weather. They were baked in the sun and drenched by the rain. On wet days, or days that looked like they would turn wet, most of them stayed at home rather than risk a soaking. Without their pennies the Globe – and the Burbage brothers – lost money on every performance.

It never occurred to Cuthbert that Pip might have spent the entire night in the theatre, sleeping in one of the galleries. He simply assumed that the boy had come to work as early as possible on his first real day, determined to make a good impression.

Every few minutes Cuthbert lifted his head from his books, keeping a mental note of who arrived late, who looked drunk and who sneaked upstairs for a quick snooze when he should have been rehearsing. He knew what actors were like. They needed a firm hand. Otherwise they'd just laze around all day, doing nothing. Even the most hard-working actors really only worked for two hours a day, wasting the rest of their lives in gambling, gossip and drink.

If Cuthbert had been an actor himself, perhaps he would have felt differently, but his very few experiences of stepping on a stage in front of a paying audience had always ended in boos, laughter and soft fruit flying through the air in his direction.

That day one person did gain Cuthbert's approval. Other boys spent half their time giggling, chatting or playing the fool, but not Philip Stone. He was always to be seen waiting patiently for orders, then fulfilling them without complaint or question.

In the afternoon, after the play had finished, Cuthbert found Pip, paid him an extra penny and promised to find him more interesting tasks. "You've worked hard," said Cuthbert. "Well done. Have you enjoyed your first day?"

"Very much, sir."

"Good lad. See you tomorrow." Carrying his bag of coins and his accounts book, Cuthbert headed out of the theatre and went home, not giving the boy another thought.

33

As soon as the other stagehands discovered Pip's talent with weapons, and learnt that he had spent practically his entire life apprenticed to a smith, they started bringing him anything metal which needed repairs. Word spread fast. Cuthbert arranged for him to use a local forge. Molly Plunkett found a pair of tongs and a hammer which had been bought for a performance of Tamburlaine. Soon people treated Pip as if he'd never been anything except the theatre's smith. Only a couple of weeks after he arrived at the Globe he'd become a fixture, several little tasks always awaiting his attention: a chipped sword, a shield with a snapped strap or a spear that had lost its head.

Today he was sitting on the edge of the stage, making his way through a pile of belt buckles which needed to be hammered back into shape. Robert Armin was sitting beside him. It was about midday, a couple of hours before the performance was due to start.

"This is my last chance," said Robert in a melancholy voice. "My very last chance. And then it's over."

Pip said, "What is?"

"My career."

"Why?"

"Because if I screw this up the Burbages are going to fire me."

Today the company was performing one of that season's most popular plays: *The Tragedy of Hamlet, Prince of Denmark.*

It was the performance that Pip had been waiting for. He still didn't know what happened at the end. Did Hamlet kill his stepfather? Did he take revenge for his father's murder? Or did he decide to forgive and forget? Pip could have asked one of the actors to tell him the ending but he'd chosen not to, wanting to see it for himself.

It was also the last day of Robert's probation period. Tonight, after the show, the Burbage brothers would make their decision. Either they would keep Robert as the company's clown or they would fire him and find a new funny man. Until now they hadn't given him any hint of their decision, refusing to discuss the matter in advance.

"You won't get fired," said Pip. "You're really good."

Robert sighed. "If only that was true."

"It is true. You're much funnier than anyone else."

"You're too kind, my young friend."

"I'm not being kind," said Pip. "I'm telling the truth. Everyone loves you."

"I should have stayed a goldsmith," said Robert.

"A what?"

"I was a goldsmith for years. Didn't you know that? My father sent me to be apprenticed at the Royal Mint. If only I'd stuck to an honest trade I'd be rich by now. I'd probably even have my own shop."

"Don't talk rubbish," said Pip. "You're a brilliant actor. You should never have done anything else."

"That's nice of you to say so."

"If anyone's got it, you have."

Robert lifted his head and looked at Pip. "Got what?"

"It."

"What's 'it'?"

"'It'," said Pip, "is that mysterious ingredient which some people have and others don't. Actors have to have it, otherwise they can't act. Richard Burbage has it. William Shakespeare has it. Nathan Field has it. And you do too."

"Do I?"

"Yes. You do."

"How do you know?"

"Because I can tell," said Pip. "That's why you're funny. That's why you're an actor. Because you've got it."

"I hope you're right," said Robert.

"I am right," said Pip.

Robert grinned. He pushed himself to his feet. "I'd better go. Wish me luck."

"Good luck," said Pip.

"Thanks, kid." With a wave, Robert hurried away to change into his costume. There was a new-found swagger in his walk, as if his veins had been injected with a sudden surge of self-confidence. If he didn't have "it" a minute ago, he certainly did now.

34

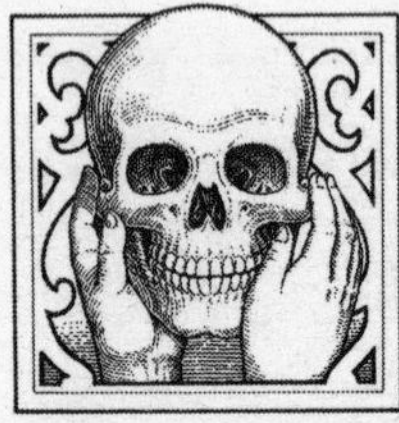

That afternoon Pip was determined not to miss a line of Hamlet. He stood at the front of the pit, bagging himself a good spot before the audience arrived.

Gradually the theatre filled up. In the galleries every seat was taken. More and more people crammed into the pit.

At two o'clock Cuthbert Burbage nodded to one of the stagehands, who darted round the back of the gallery, disappeared through a dark doorway and whispered a message to the stage manager. He alerted the actors. They took their places. The play began.

Two men walked on to the stage, one from either side. Despite the mid-afternoon sunshine, each of them was holding a blazing torch in his right hand and using its glare to illuminate the view as they peered at the pit and the galleries. From the angles of their bodies and the expressions on their faces, you could tell that, in the world of the play, it was the middle of the night and they were staring into the darkness, trying to distinguish shapes in the murk.

Pip knew both of them. The young man on the left was called Tom Phipps and the old man on the right was called Dogbreath. That probably wasn't his real name, but it suited him perfectly and no one ever called him anything else.

Dogbreath called across the stage in a loud voice, "Who's there?"

"Nay, answer me," replied Tom Phipps. "Stand, and unfold yourself."

Half the audience hadn't yet noticed that the play had begun, or didn't care, and continued chattering. On one side of Pip, people were discussing the latest news from France; on the other, two men were debating whether adding a raw egg to beer really makes you get drunk faster. A married couple argued loudly about the cost of a week's meals, their voices carrying across the theatre, letting everyone hear the details of their domestic arrangements. A woman wove through the crowd, selling fruit and handkerchiefs, calling out the prices of her wares. "Only a farthing for a nice roast onion! Spiced with nutmeg! Get them while they're hot!"

"Long live the king!" shouted Dogbreath, trying to be heard over the noise of the audience, but no one took much notice.

In the play, he and Tom Phipps were watchmen, pacing

up and down the battlements of a castle on the coast of Denmark. They wore military uniforms and carried spears. Two more men arrived, then a ghost dressed in cumbersome armour, painted white, which clanked with every step that he took. Although the ghost was wearing a heavy helmet which hid his face, Pip knew who was inside: William Shakespeare.

Even the presence of the ghost didn't quieten the audience. Every sentence that the actors spoke was accompanied by a continuous low-level muttering. Pip didn't care. He could hear what was being said. He stared at the stage, absorbed in the words and the action.

He was surprised to discover that he remembered most of the action. This time he also recognized all the actors – not just Shakespeare as the ghost but Richard Burbage as Hamlet and Nathan Field as Ophelia, Hamlet's sweetheart, and all the others too. And this time when Robert Armin pulled a skull out of the stage Pip wasn't amazed, because he knew how the trick was done. There was a trapdoor in the stage. Robert reached down into the hole and a stagehand passed the skull up to him. When the company next performed *Hamlet*, Pip might be down there himself.

Richard Burbage and Robert Armin, Hamlet and the gravedigger, stood in the middle of the stage, fiddling with the skull's teeth as if they'd belonged to a goat rather than a man. While Hamlet was speaking, the gravedigger glanced down at the pit and saw Pip. Their eyes met for a moment. And then Robert Armin was back in the play, responding to

Hamlet, being the gravedigger rather than himself.

The king and queen arrived, followed by several courtiers. The king declared that Hamlet and Laertes, the prince and his girlfriend's brother, would fight a duel. A servant arrived with six Italian rapiers. While Hamlet and Laertes were choosing their swords, the king described the rules of the competition. They would play the best of three. The winner would be allowed to drink a sip of wine. There was one more thing that he didn't tell them: he had tipped a deadly poison into the wine and rubbed it on to the tips of the rapiers. This was a duel to the death.

The king retreated, followed by the other actors, and stood at the back of the stage, leaving an open space for the two duellists.

Hamlet and Laertes stepped forward. They raised their swords.

"Come on, sir," said Hamlet.

"Come, my lord," said Laertes.

They darted forward. Their swords clashed. The noise echoed around the theatre. By now no one was chattering. The audience watched the action in rapt silence.

Although Hamlet was scratched by a rapier, letting the poison into his blood, the king's plan backfired: the queen took a sip of the poisoned wine. She gurgled horribly and dropped to the ground, groaning. Others died too. Hamlet stood in the middle of the stage, surrounded by bodies, holding his sword in his right hand.

This was his last chance. If he was going to kill his

stepfather he had to do it now. In a few moments the poison would have worked through his blood, reached his heart and killed him.

The Globe was still and quiet. Everyone was watching Hamlet, waiting to see what he would do.

These were the last seconds of Hamlet's life. How would he choose to die? Like a girl? Or like a man?

Would he allow his stepfather to survive him? Or, with the last action of his life, would he kill the man who had murdered his father?

"Do it," whispered Pip so quietly that, even in the silence, he could hardly hear his own voice. His fists were clenched. He wanted to clamber on to the stage, grab Hamlet's sword and kill the old man himself. But he couldn't. This wasn't his fight.

Every man has his own destiny and this was Hamlet's.

"Do it," Pip whispered once more, begging Hamlet to make the right choice, to act, to kill, to take revenge.

And then, finally, Hamlet raised his sword.

Pip was so tense, he couldn't even breathe.

Holding his sword outstretched at the end of his arm, Hamlet ran across the stage and plunged the blade into the middle of his stepfather's chest.

The treacherous king stumbled backwards, crying out in terrible agony. A great gush of scarlet blood spurted from his clothes and poured down his front. He sank to his knees, then fell forward on to the stage.

Around him, Pip heard people discussing the trick. "Red paint," suggested one know-it-all.

"Beetroot juice," whispered another.

"No, no, no," said a third. "They use a bladder filled with sheep's blood. His sword cuts it open and the blood pours out. I've seen it done a hundred times."

Shhh, Pip wanted to say, *I'm watching; don't distract me.*

The poison took effect on Hamlet himself. He staggered, clutching his belly, then sank to his knees. He spoke a few final breathless words to his friend Horatio, uttered a long moan and fell backwards, then sat up suddenly and stared at the audience. In a deep melancholy voice, he said, "The rest is silence." His eyes widened. He slumped, gasped and lay still.

Horatio wiped away a tear and spoke a few words, looking down at his friend's corpse.

That wasn't quite the end. There was music and the entrance of a soldier in armour and yet more words. Four men lifted Hamlet and carried him away. A fifth fired a shot into the sky. And then it was over.

The actors sprang to their feet and hurried to the front of the stage. The audience roared their approval, none more so than Pip, standing right at the front of the pit, cheering at the top of his voice.

Robert Armin looked down at Pip and winked once. He knew already that the performance had been a success. His job was safe.

35

Today everyone has heard of William Shakespeare. Thousands of books have been written about him. His plays have been translated into just about every language on the planet. Tourists visit the house where he was born. Professors pick over every word that he wrote, arguing about exactly what he meant. Every hour of every day someone, somewhere, is watching or performing one of his plays. He's probably the most famous writer in the world.

The other people who worked at the Globe haven't been so lucky. Over the past four hundred years they've been just about forgotten. Today, not many people have heard of Augustine Philips, Thomas Pope, John Hemming, Richard Burbage or Cuthbert Burbage. But in 1601 they were as famous as Shakespeare. He wrote the plays, but they acted in them, played music in them, paid for them and, most importantly, provided the theatre where they were performed.

With the help of Nathan Field, an excellent source of information, Pip learnt who held power in the theatre and who had none, who should always be obeyed and who could be ignored. He discovered that the Globe had six owners. The Burbage brothers held the largest share, which amounted to half the theatre. The remainder of the shares were divided equally between four men: Shakespeare, Philips, Pope and Hemming. If one of those six men shouted, "Boy! Come here!", Pip dropped whatever he was carrying and sprinted towards them, arriving breathless and eager.

Pip was well rewarded for his hard work. He was earning a penny a day, sometimes two or even three, and saving most of what he earned, handing his money to Molly Plunkett, the wardrobe mistress, who was keeping his pennies safe until he needed them.

Cuthbert Burbage promised to double his wages after a month. Augustine Philips gave him a penny as a tip for carrying his costume. John Hemming gave him another when he fetched eight tankards of beer from the nearest pub. Twice Pip found a penny on the ground while he was sweeping rubbish. He'd never possessed such wealth. Even better, he saved it all, because he never needed to spend anything. Food and lodging were free. It was amazing how much people discarded during the performances, leaving apples and pears on their seats, dropping bread rolls and lumps of cheese in the pit, all perfectly tasty and quite clean if you cut off the corners. Once Pip even found three cold lamb chops tucked inside a leather pouch.

Although the money was good, working gave him a different and much more important feeling of satisfaction. He felt useful. Nothing made him happier than being thanked by Richard Burbage or William Shakespeare, complimented on the good job that he'd done.

His old life seemed like a dream, fading every day. He would have liked to see his mother and his sisters, but he never missed them.

He never once went to the Bear Garden and hardly even thought about the bear. He was too occupied with his own life to worry about anyone else's.

Does that sound cruel? Or even heartless? Perhaps it does. But don't be too quick to judge Pip. You might be just the same. If you're busy, and having fun, your brain simply doesn't have very much room to care about anything or anyone else.

Pip knew that several weeks must have passed since he first arrived at the Globe, but he had no idea how many. There hadn't been time to count. So much had happened, he never seemed to have a chance to stop and think.

He'd got into a routine. At night he hid in the theatre until everyone else had gone home. When nothing was stirring except the mice and the bats, he emerged and strode around the Globe as if he were the third Burbage brother. The theatre was his home, his fortress and his playground. He paced along the balconies like a tightrope walker and got to know each creaky floorboard.

Every morning he took care that no one should catch him asleep. By the time anyone arrived he was already cleaning the stage or clearing last night's props into a corner, checking them off: sixteen arrows, four wooden snakes, three gold boxes, two crowns, a boar's head, a lion's skin, a wooden leg, a bay tree and the back half of a dragon.

Between eight and nine o'clock a stack of posters would arrive from the printer. Pip would be sent into the streets with a couple of other boys, carrying the posters, a pot of glue and a paintbrush. They scurried through Southwark, crossed London Bridge and rushed through the streets, plastering walls and doors, letting people know which play would be performed today. The posters shouted in big letters:

FOR ONE DAIE ONLIE

Under the headline there was usually a picture or two and below that, in smaller letters, the title and a couple of sentences about the plot, promising violent murders for a tragedy or outrageous jokes for a comedy. At the bottom, more big letters proclaimed:

PRICE BUT ONE PENNIE

After a few days of postering, following shortcuts through the back alleys, visiting every church and pub, Pip learnt how the city fitted together. He could recite the names of the seven main gates in the city's walls – Ludgate, Newgate, Aldersgate, Cripplegate, Moorgate, Bishopsgate and Aldgate – and knew which was which. He never got confused between St Mary Overie and St Andrew by the Wardrobe. If you'd asked him to find his own way from Hog Lane to Blackfriars he might have got lost once or twice, but he'd have arrived only a little after anyone who had been born in London.

Whether he was hurrying down dark deserted alleyways or pushing through a crowded market, he searched the face of every man who passed him, but he never saw the Weasel, Scar, Tooth or Pigface. As for George Stone – well, Pip had pretty much accepted that he wouldn't recognize his own father even if they passed one another in the street. His only clue to his father's appearance was one casual comment that had slipped out of the Weasel's mouth. "You have your father's eyes." As he walked through the streets he stared into other men's eyes, hoping he might have an experience like looking in a mirror, seeing his own eyes staring back at him, but he never did.

By the time that he finished postering and returned to the Globe, the stage would be frantic with activity, everyone preparing for that afternoon's performance, the actors rehearsing their words, the musicians practising their tunes, the carpenters building the set and Molly Plunkett hunched over the costume cupboard, trying to find a bishop's hat or a pair of green stockings suitable for an Italian villain. Pip would stand in the middle of the pit, waiting to be given orders. He never stood there for more than a minute before someone shouted at him. "Boy! Yes, you! Come here! Hold this!" He'd work like a demon until the play began; then he could relax for a couple of hours.

While he watched the play, he watched the audience too, hoping to spot one of his enemies, but there was no sign of them. As the summer wore on he began to worry that he'd chosen the wrong place to work. Perhaps the Weasel never went to the theatre.

And then one sunny afternoon a thin man came to the Globe and paid for seven seats with cushions in the top gallery.

36

Over the course of the summer the actors of the Globe probably performed forty plays, rotating premieres and old favourites. Every year William Shakespeare wrote two or three new ones, which were usually the company's biggest successes, but the company hired several other writers too.

Today the company was putting on a premiere – a new and previously unperformed comedy, *The Blind Beggar of Bethnal Green*. It had been written by a pair of bright young things, Henry Chettle and John Day, who some said would soon be the most famous writers in London, and others said wouldn't last longer than a jug of milk on a sunny morning. No one knew whether the play would be a triumph or a disaster. Nevertheless, the theatre was packed. People paid a penny and took a chance, hoping they would see the first performance of a play which went on to become famous. If not, and the play was boring, they could always chat to their friends or throw things at the actors.

Just as *The Blind Beggar of Bethnal Green* was about to begin, a fat man hurried down the staircase from the top gallery and pushed through the crowd, heading for the exit. He shoved people out of his way, ignoring their angry complaints, and finally reached the door where Pip was standing.

"'Scuse me," said the fat man, pushing past Pip. "Gotta pee."

Pip's heart raced as he recognized Pigface. Without thinking, he reached down to his belt and put his hand on his father's knife, then realized it would be better to wait. If Pigface was here, maybe the Weasel was too. And the Weasel was the one that Pip wanted.

The fat man was halfway through the doorway, neither in nor out, when a sudden thought struck him. He turned and stared at Pip. He knew that boy's face from somewhere, he was sure he did. He pointed his pudgy finger at the boy and said, "Don't I know you?"

"No," said Pip, shaking his head.

"I think I do."

"I think you don't."

The fat man stared at Pip. He frowned. "I'm sure I've seen you somewhere before."

"Maybe here, sir."

"What do you mean?"

"Haven't you been to the Globe before?"

"Of course I have," said the fat man. "I come here all the time."

"Then you've probably seen me here, sir. I've been working here for the past two years."

"For two years? Really?"

"Yes, sir."

The fat man peered closely at Pip, then grunted. "That must be it then."

He stumbled out of the Globe, opened the fly of his breeches and had a long, loud pee against the back wall.

When he came back into the theatre, determined to have another look at the boy, the doorway was empty. He was looking around, hoping to spot him, when a roar of laughter came from the pit. The play had started. The fat man hurried up the stairs, heading for the top gallery, not wanting to miss another second.

The Blind Beggar of Bethnal Green was a triumph. It was the funniest show that anyone had seen for years. People laughed so much, you could hear them on the other side of the river.

Only one person wasn't laughing.

Pip stood at the back of the pit, hidden in the shadows, never even glancing at the play. His attention was focused somewhere else entirely.

Sitting in the front row of the topmost gallery, there was a party of four men and three women. The man in the middle had a lean face and a cruel mouth. He stared at the stage, smirking and chuckling. He never noticed a face in the shadows, lifted to look at him. The Weasel had no idea that he was being watched.

37

The end of the play was greeted by wild applause. A line of actors stood at the front of the stage, bowing to the audience. All around the Globe, people stood up, cheering and whooping. They threw things into the air – hats and coins and apples and herrings and even a little white kitten who had sneaked into the theatre during the play, searching for food, a mistake that she would never make again.

Up in the top gallery the Weasel clapped his hands together two or three times, then stood up. He didn't like hanging around at the end of a performance. Followed by his party, he headed for the staircase. The rest of the audience were still enjoying the show – milking the applause, Robert Armin had started dancing a jig – so the Weasel knew he'd be able to get out quickly before the crowds blocked the exit.

*

Cuthbert Burbage hated comedies. He was irritated by songs, bored by jokes and depressed by a happy ending. That was why he hadn't bothered watching *The Blind Beggar of Bethnal Green*.

Cuthbert liked tragedies. Three or four juicy murders – that was what he called a good afternoon at the theatre. Amputations were OK. Torture was better. And there was always something to be said for a mother eating her own children, particularly in a pie.

But during a comedy Cuthbert waited by the door of the Globe, taking money from latecomers, and spent a useful couple of hours reading through his accounts book, checking for errors.

When one of the stagehands, that new boy called Pip, emerged through the doorway Cuthbert put down his leather-bound book and gave him a stern look. "Where do you think you're going?"

"To fetch some beer," said Pip. "For Mister Armin."

Cuthbert nodded. He might have doubted one of the other boys, but Pip was a good lad. Cuthbert reached into his purse and pulled out a penny. "Buy one for me too, will you?"

"Yes, Mister Burbage," said Pip, pocketing the penny.

"And keep the change."

"Thank you, sir. Thank you very much."

At that moment a piercing scream echoed from inside the Globe.

"Oh, turnips," said Cuthbert. "What have they done

now?" He tucked his accounts book under his arm, stepped through the door and peered over the top of the crowd, trying to see what was happening.

When Cuthbert's back was turned, Pip hurried towards the nearest group of trees and hid behind a large oak.

He didn't have long to wait. Before the crowds started to leave the theatre, the Weasel and Pigface walked out of the Globe and strode into Southwark, heading towards London Bridge. Scar and Tooth stumbled after them. The three women hurried behind, picking up their skirts to avoid the thick mud.

Pip followed at a safe distance, darting between trees and doorways, keeping in the shadows, never letting himself be seen and never losing sight of the Weasel.

38

The gang's destination was a large house in a cramped street. Tall buildings loomed on either side, blocking out the sky.

The Weasel reached inside his shirt. A metal key was hanging around his neck on a grubby string. He unlocked the door. The gang followed him into the house.

Pip stood in a doorway at the end of the street and waited. He could have gone closer and tried to peek through the windows, but he was too nervous. He didn't want to get caught.

I'll stay here, he decided. *Hidden in the shadows. After dark, I'll go and look through the windows.*

And then what?

He didn't have a clue. Despite all the time that he'd been chasing the Weasel, he hadn't ever decided what to do when he actually caught him. *I'd better just wait*, he thought. *Take my time.* The most important thing was not getting caught. Alone, armed with nothing but his father's knife, he wouldn't have a chance against four grown men.

After no more than a few minutes, the Weasel emerged from the house and marched along the street at a brisk pace, followed by Scar, Tooth and a slightly breathless Pigface. The three women must have stayed inside.

Pip followed them.

They crossed London Bridge, going north, turned down Eastcheap and hurried past St Paul's. Just before they reached Fleet Street, they dodged through a dark alleyway and stopped at a small, ramshackle cottage. Broken shutters hung from the windows. Weeds dangled down from the roof. The Weasel slammed his fist against the wooden door three times.

An old woman opened the door, demanding to know what all the fuss was about. When she saw the Weasel the words faded in her throat. She darted backwards and tried to slam the door, but the Weasel was too quick for her, thrusting her aside and plunging into the house. Pigface followed his boss inside, while Scar and Tooth stayed in the street, guarding the doorway.

Pip waited at the end of the alley, watching the house, wondering what was happening inside. Was the Weasel robbing the woman? But she knew him. That was obvious from her reaction. So who was she? His wife? His sister? A friend? An enemy? What was going on?

After two or three minutes the Weasel emerged from the house, jangling some coins in his palm. He muttered something to his men. They laughed and followed him to the other end of the alley.

Pip hurried after them.

They crossed the city. At another house, alongside the walls at Moorgate, the Weasel rapped on the front door and barged inside, followed by Pigface. A moment later a man sprinted out of the door and charged down the street.

He didn't get far. The Weasel's gang were blocking the road. The man tried to dodge past, but Scar and Tooth were too quick for him. They threw him to the ground, then stood on his wrists and ankles to stop him getting away.

The Weasel came out of the house and looked down at the man. He said, "I'd quite like to kill you."

"I'm sorry, I'm sorry," begged the man. "I've had a bad month."

"But if I killed you," continued the Weasel as if he hadn't even heard the sound of the man's voice, "who would pay me?"

"You'll have it by Tuesday, I promise."

"Hmmm," said the Weasel, staring down at the man writhing on the ground. "Maybe I should cut off some of your fingers."

"On my mother's life, I promise I'll get the money by Tuesday."

"You'd better." The Weasel nodded to his men. "Let's go."

They strolled away, leaving the man in the middle of the

road, rubbing his bruised ankles. Pip would have liked to go and help him, or question him, but there wasn't time. He'd lose sight of the Weasel. He hurried after the gang and followed them through the streets.

As the same routine was repeated at three different houses on the north side of the river and two more on the south, Pip began to get an idea of what was happening. The Weasel was collecting debts. At every house that he visited, he rapped on the door and barged inside, brushing past anyone who tried to stop him, emerging a few minutes later with a smile on his face and some coins in his hand.

It all made sense. That was why the Weasel had come to Mildmay. George Stone owed him money too. Pip remembered how the Weasel had turned to him and asked if he'd like to pay his father's debts.

The memory of that day made him furious. He reached down to his belt and touched his father's knife. *Not yet*, he told himself. *Be patient*. Soon enough, he'd get a chance to use it.

The Weasel and his men made their way through the streets of Southwark. Round the back of the Bear Garden, they crossed a lawn and ducked down a dark alleyway between two buildings.

Pip recognized the route. He had taken it himself. This was the way to the bearkeeper's cottage. He hurried after them, dodging from tree to tree, doorway to doorway, never letting the gang leave his sight.

The Weasel stopped at the bearkeeper's heavy wooden door. Without bothering to knock or announce his presence, the Weasel shoved the door open and went inside, followed by his three men.

The door swung shut behind them.

Pip hurried down the alleyway and pressed his ear against the wooden door. Through the thick planks he couldn't hear a thing.

Why was the gang inside? What was the connection between the Weasel and the bearkeeper? What brought them together? The answers to all these questions were waiting for him on the other side of the door. All he had to do was push. . .

Pip put his hands on the door, but couldn't persuade himself to open it. He was too scared. He hated admitting it to himself, but it was true. He was terrified.

On the other side of the door, they would be waiting for him. The Weasel and the bearkeeper. The two most frightening men that he'd ever encountered.

No one would know if he didn't go inside the cottage. Why not just walk away?

It would be so easy go back to the Globe and sweep the pit and pick up the rubbish in the galleries, pretending to himself that he'd never even seen the Weasel.

No. He wasn't going to run away. Not when he was this close.

I have to do it, Pip thought. *I have to.*

He eased the wooden door open. Just a jot. And waited. But nothing happened. No one shouted at him. No sword swished through the air towards his head. No whip cracked at his ankles.

He pushed the door a little more and looked inside. He could see six cages and three bears, but no people.

He stepped into the cottage.

39

The three bears lifted their heads and stared at Pip.

The two biggest lost interest immediately, slumping back into their usual state of depressed inactivity. Years of captivity had robbed them of curiosity. Only the third bear, the smallest, felt differently. As she stared at the boy, her eyes widened and her nostrils wrinkled. Maybe she recognized his face or his smell. More likely she remembered that his pocket had once produced a crisp, delicious apple. Rolling over and raising herself on to all fours, she shuffled forward, pressing her thick muzzle against the bars of her cage and peering at Pip.

Pip stared back. He wanted to go to her. Tickle her ears. Pat her nose. But he didn't have time. From the next room he could hear the sound of an angry argument. Two voices were batting back and forth. He wanted to know what they were saying.

The thick oatmeal-coloured blanket hung across the doorway between the two rooms. Pip turned his back on the bear and tiptoed towards the blanket. Although the cloth muffled sound, Pip could just make out what was being said on the other side.

"I don't care if you're a mess," a man's voice was saying. "It's your life. Mess it up however you want. But why do you have to get me involved in your mess? Huh?"

"I'm sorry," said a second voice.

"Sorry isn't good enough. Sorry doesn't pay my bills." With each word that the voice spoke Pip felt more certain that it belonged to the Weasel.

"I don't know what else I can say." That was the second voice again, which Pip felt sure belonged to the bearkeeper. He sounded different now. Not scary. More scared.

"You could stop wasting my time. And get my money."

"I have been trying. You know I have."

"Trying? Hah! You call that trying?"

"Yes, I do."

"I went sixty miles. Thirty there. Thirty back. And for what? A few quid and a cheap bracelet."

"I'm sorry. He used to be rich."

No, thought Pip. *It can't be true*.

Not the bearkeeper.

There was only one way to find out. He had to get closer. To see what was actually happening. Very gently, he pushed aside the curtain and peered through the gap.

This is what Pip saw.

The bearkeeper was sitting on a stool, his arms by his sides. Blood trickled from a cut on his lower lip. His dogs were huddled against the walls, cringing and scared. Scar, Tooth and Pigface were standing behind the bearkeeper. The Weasel was pacing up and down the room, his hands curled into fists.

The Weasel spoke in a low voice: "If you don't get the money, I'm going to have to kill you. Not because I want to. I like you. But I have a reputation and I'm not going to lose it. Come on, make it easier for both of us. Pay me what you owe me."

"I can't," said the bearkeeper.

"Then you shouldn't have borrowed it in the first place."

"I know I shouldn't." The bearkeeper shook his head. "I'd pay you if I could. But I can't."

"Get my money or I'll have to kill you," said the Weasel. "It's as simple as that."

"Give me a month."

"No."

"Two weeks. Give me two weeks. I'll have your money in a fortnight."

"No," said the Weasel. "I need that money now."

"I understand, but I can't—"

"If you were anyone else," said the Weasel, "I'd want the money right now. But you're an old friend. I'll give you two days."

"It's impossible. How do you expect me to—"

"Two days," said the Weasel. "If you don't have the money by then. . ." He ran his finger along his own throat.

The bearkeeper tried to argue, begging for more time, but the Weasel was already heading for the door.

Pip dropped the edge of the curtain and sprang backwards, sure that he was going to be caught. He turned on the spot, then sprinted across the room. Would they hear his footsteps? He'd have to take that risk. He hurled himself into the corner and curled in a heap against the wall beside the small bear's cage, trying to merge into the shadows, praying that they wouldn't look in his direction.

The bear glanced at Pip. She seemed confused. She opened her mouth, showing off her big wet tongue and her filed-down teeth, as if she were just about to roar a furious warning.

Please, thought Pip, staring at the bear, *don't give me away. Don't make a sound. Don't let them know I'm here.*

The Weasel thrust the curtain aside and walked through the room, heading straight outside, looking neither right nor left. He was followed by his three men. The door swung shut. And then they were gone.

The bear hadn't make a sound.

Pip waited till he was certain that they weren't coming back. Then he pushed himself to his feet and whispered to the bear, "Thank you."

She was watching at him with a strange expression, half curious, half aggressive, as if she wasn't sure whether to trust him or lunge at him.

Pip didn't know much about bears, but he knew how to

make friends with dogs and foxes: you let them smell you. With any luck, bears were the same. He put his hand through the bars of the cage. The bear wrinkled her nostrils and sniffed his fingers.

"Sorry," whispered Pip. "Got no food."

The bear put her head on one side and looked at him with an expression which seemed to say: if you don't have any more apples, why did you bother coming here?

"I'll get you something soon," whispered Pip. "Some more apples. Cherries, plums, whatever you like. I'll bring them next time, I promise."

He couldn't tell if the bear believed him. Or understood him. Or even cared.

She just stared at him. Her moist black eyes were calm and reassuring. Somehow they made Pip feel stronger.

"I'll be back in a minute," he whispered. He walked across the room and pushed aside the curtain.

40

A couple of the dogs glanced at Pip, but none growled, barked or made any move towards him. They were more interested in the meat in their master's hands. All nine dogs were clustered at the bearkeeper's feet, long lines of saliva dangling from their jaws, waiting to see where he'd throw the next piece of beef.

Pip said, "Sir?"

The bearkeeper jumped. He hadn't even noticed Pip coming into the room. There were streaks of blood on his shirt, which might have dripped from the meat in his hands or his own wounds. Angrily, he said, "Who are you? What are you doing here?"

Pip said, "Don't you recognize me?"

The bearkeeper stared into Pip's face for a moment, then nodded. "Oh, yes," he said. "Of course I remember you."

"You do?"

"Yes, you're the boy who was here before. Asking dumb questions. And I'd rather you didn't ask any more."

"So you don't know who I am?"

"I just told you, I know exactly who you are. And I told you already, I don't need an apprentice." He waved Pip away. "Go on, boy. Get out. I have work to do."

"I want to talk to you."

"Well, I don't want to talk to you."

The bearkeeper threw the rest of the meat to his dogs. They raged and tussled, taking bites out of the meat and one another. Pip stood nearby, watching the dogs. He'd initially assumed it was nothing more than fear that attached the dogs to the bearkeeper, but he could now see something else too, a stronger bond. Respect, perhaps, or even affection.

The bearkeeper turned to face Pip, wiping his bloody hands on his breeches. He said, "Didn't I tell you to go away?"

"I have to talk to you," said Pip.

"I work alone. And even if I needed someone to help me, I wouldn't have any money for wages."

"It's not about that," repeated Pip.

The bearkeeper stared at him. "Then what is it about?"

Rather than answering, Pip reached down to his belt and pulled his knife from its leather scabbard.

Seeing the blade, the bearkeeper stepped backwards. He said, "Don't you dare!"

Pip didn't say anything. He felt very calm. There was no

hurry. He held the knife in his right hand, stood his ground, and waited to see what would happen next.

"You've come to the wrong place," said the bearkeeper. "I don't have any money. I've got nothing."

Pip just stood there, very still, holding the knife, neither moving nor speaking.

The bearkeeper raised his fists. Maybe he couldn't stop four thugs, but he could defend himself perfectly well against a boy. He said, "You'll do yourself a favour if you put that knife away and walk out of here. I won't come after you. Even if I see you in the street, I won't touch you. We'll just forget this happened. Put it down, boy. Walk away."

Without a word, Pip turned the knife around and offered it to the bearkeeper, handle first.

The bearkeeper glanced at the knife, then at Pip. He said, "What does this mean?"

Pip didn't say anything.

The bearkeeper was confused. He looked down at the knife, then slowly reached out and held it with both hands. He ran his fingers over the handle, feeling the five-pointed star carved into the wood.

Something changed in his face.

He looked up.

He said, "Who are you?"

Pip said, "Don't you know?"

The bearkeeper shook his head. "I don't believe it." He looked down at the knife, turning it over in his hand, then up again. "You're not."

"I am."

"It's not possible. You don't look anything like him. How old are you?"

"Twelve."

"No, no, no. This is some kind of trick, isn't it? Who are you? Who sent you?"

"You know who I am," said Pip. "I'm your son."

41

Pip and George Stone could have embraced or shaken hands, but neither of them made any move towards the other, nor did they say a word. They just stood there in silence, the past seven years separating them like a physical barrier.

It's funny, thought Pip. *For seven years, I would have given anything to see my father. And now I've found him I can't think of anything to say.*

George Stone turned the knife over and over in his hands, staring at the blade and the five-fingered star carved into the handle. Finally, he lifted his head and looked at Pip. "That's a good knife."

"I know."

"I'm glad you still have it." He handed the knife back to Pip, handle first. "Look after it."

"I will." Pip took the knife and slid it into its scabbard.

George Stone smiled, but didn't say another word.

Staring at the dishevelled middle-aged man who stood before him, Pip wondered whether he would look like that one day. Would his chin be covered with scabs and stubble? And his nose broken in ten different places? Would he have bloodshot eyes and bad breath? Pip hoped not. He searched his father's face, trying to see some resemblance to himself, something that suggested a bond between them, but he couldn't find anything. Did his eyes really look like that? He hoped not. He certainly couldn't see himself in them. If he hadn't known the bearkeeper and George Stone were the same person – his father – he'd never have guessed.

George suddenly said, "Are you hungry?"

"No."

"You look thin. Doesn't your mother feed you properly?"

"Of course she does."

"Let's have something to eat. Sit down. I'll get some food."

Pip wasn't hungry but he had no wish to quarrel with his father about something so trivial, so he righted an upturned stool and sat down at the table. George fetched a loaf of bread, a jug of beer and a muslin bag holding a soft white cheese. He drank a gulp from the jug and handed it to Pip, apologizing for the lack of cups. Pip took a sip. The warm beer had a bitter taste.

George squatted by a bucket of water and washed his face, cleaning off the dried blood, then joined Pip at the table. He broke the bread and opened the muslin bag, flopping the soft cheese on to the table.

They ate in silence.

For years Pip had puzzled over an impossible conundrum: how might his life have been different if his father hadn't died? How would he himself be different? Would he be stronger or braver? Would he have more friends? Would he be happier? He had often walked through the woods, imagining how much better things would have been if only his father were there too. Together they would have made traps for rabbits, tracked deer, watched birds, picked blackberries, discussed everything. Over and over again, Pip had imagined all the questions he would ask, the secrets he would share, the intimate conversations that they would have, father and son, best friends. And now he had the feeling that, if his father had stayed rather than left, his life would have been much worse. Imagine spending every day with this man. Waking to find him in the house, eating opposite him every night. Looking at the scar on his forehead. Staring into his bloodshot eyes. And, worst of all, sitting for hours in silence, no one knowing what to say.

For the first time in weeks Pip felt a sudden stab of nostalgia for his home. He wondered how his mother had been. He missed his sisters. He even wanted to see Samuel.

Well, he would soon. He'd go back there. Just for a day or two. He'd take a holiday from the Globe and go to Mildmay.

He looked across the table at his father. George Stone lifted his head, met Pip's eyes for a moment, then returned his attention to his food. Neither of them said a word.

Pip remembered the threats that the Weasel had made. Were they real? Would the Weasel really come back in two days' time and kill George Stone?

If this was the last time that he ever saw his father, was there anything that he wanted to say? Or ask?

He thought through the hundreds of questions that he'd once wanted to ask his father, but none of them seemed important any more. Only one question really mattered. So he asked it. He said: "Why did you leave?"

George wiped his mouth with the back of his hand. "Leave where?"

"Home."

"That was a long time ago. I can't remember."

"You must be able to remember," said Pip. "What happened? Were you really working?"

"Working? No. Your mother and I had an argument, that's all. Yet another argument. I said I was leaving. She said nothing would make her happier. I gave her the knife, told her to give it to you, and walked out. She didn't try to stop me. I came straight to London. Did the walk in a day and a half. I could walk fast in those days. Didn't have this." He slapped his leg, the one that made him limp.

Pip said, "And then what happened? Why didn't you come back?"

"Come back where?"

"Home. To see me."

"When?"

"Anytime. You've been gone for seven years. Mum told me you were dead. Why didn't you come back? I was there. You knew I was. Why didn't you come and see me?"

"Because I was in France." When he arrived in London, George explained, he tried to get a job as a soldier or a bodyguard, but no one would take him. He was too old and unfit, having not fought in a war for several years. People thought he'd gone soft. "So I left the country. I travelled round Europe for three years, maybe four, working as a mercenary, hiring myself out to different armies in different countries, but things didn't go well. I'd lost my touch. It's a young man's game, killing people for money."

Returning to London, he had searched for work for several weeks without any success, then finally managed to talk himself into a job at the Bear Garden. The owners, Philip Henslowe and Edward Alleyn, remembered him as a honest fighter. When he was a soldier, during the empty weeks between campaigns, he had appeared at several London theatres as a performer, battling a bear or wrestling other unemployed soldiers. Although he was too old for that now, Henslowe and Alleyn agreed to employ him as a bearkeeper.

They didn't pay much, explained George, and he had expensive tastes, which was how he had managed to get himself in trouble with some bad people. "I was stupid enough to try and gamble myself out of debt. But each bet just dug me in a deeper hole. Now I owe someone a lot of money and he wants it back."

"The Weasel?"

"Who?"

Pip explained why he had chosen the nickname.

George grinned. "His real name's Andrew Nashe. But 'the Weasel' suits him much better. I owe him a lot of money and I don't have any way to get it back again."

"And that's why you sent him to rob us?"

George looked surprised. "You know that?"

Pip nodded.

"I'm sorry," said George. "It was a stupid thing to do, but I was desperate. If I don't pay this money to the Weasel he's going to kill me."

"So you sent him to kill us?"

"No," said George. "It wasn't like that. He'd never have killed you. He was just going to take the smith's money, that's all. Unfortunately, the smith didn't have any money. Andrew – sorry, the Weasel – got a few quid, which kept him quiet for a while. But now he wants the rest."

Pip was sure his father was lying. He remembered the chilling cruelty in the Weasel's face as he stood over Samuel Smith. Even worse, he remembered looking through the open doorway and seeing Tooth pressing a knife against Bridget's white throat. The memory of that sight – Bridget's eyes wide with terror – made him furious. He said, "How could you do that?"

"I didn't have any choice," said George.

"Of course you did."

"I didn't, Pip. You have to understand, if I could have done anything else, I would have. You can be sure of that."

Coming here had been a mistake, thought Pip. The worst mistake of his life. What had he learnt? That his father was a liar, a cheat, a gambler, a mercenary and, worst of all, willing to sacrifice other people's lives to save himself a few pounds.

I wish I'd stayed in the Globe, thought Pip. *I wish I'd never found my father. I wish today had never happened.*

If only he'd done what his mother suggested years ago, and accepted Samuel Smith as his new father.

He was going to walk out now and never return, never even think about his father again. From today he didn't even have a father. If people asked him, he'd say his father was dead.

There was just one more thing he had to do before he left. He wanted a proper answer to his question. If he asked it again, his father would probably just dodge it again. Or lie. But he had to try. He craved an answer which would explain why he had gone seven years without a father. He said, "I still don't understand. You still haven't explained it. Why did you leave us?"

George paused for a long time before answering, as if he was searching for the right words; then he just shrugged his shoulders and said, "I don't know."

"You must know."

"I suppose. . ." George sighed, as if Pip were pestering him with completely unjustified questions, the sort of things that no one had any right to ask. "Your mother and I. . . We weren't having fun."

"Fun?"

"That's right."

"*Fun?*"

"You'll understand when you're older."

"I want to understand now. What do you mean, you weren't having fun?"

George sighed again. "I was bored."

"Bored of what?"

"Country life didn't suit me," said George. "I'm a soldier. A drinker. A gambler. I like having fun."

Fun, thought Pip. *Fun? What does that mean?*

He remembered all the time that he'd spent in the woods, wandering alone for hours, trying to understand what it meant to grow up without a father. All those hours had been wasted. They were pointless, meaningless. All that time, his father had been alive. Working as a soldier, travelling around Europe, having fun.

Because he'd been bored of living in the countryside with his wife and his son.

Pip said, "Why couldn't you have fun with us?"

"I just couldn't. Not as much fun as I had on my own. And that, I suppose, is why I left."

"You mean you're selfish?"

George thought for a moment. Then he nodded. "Yes, I suppose that's exactly what I mean." He lifted his head and looked at his son, staring him down, willing him to look away first. There was a new expression in George's face, defiant, even proud. "I had to live my life. In that little house with you and your mother – I was dying of boredom. It doesn't sound very nice, Pip, but it's true. It's a simple fact. You have to live your own life. Maybe that means hurting other people. Maybe that means being selfish. But you only get one life. It's yours. No one else's. You have to live it your own way."

Pip said, "I'm never going to be like you."

"Wait and see," said George Stone. "Just wait and see."

Pip wanted to be somewhere else. He didn't know or particularly care where, but he was absolutely sure that he didn't want to be here. He pushed back his chair and stood. "I'm going," he said. Without another word he turned and walked towards the door.

Just as Pip lifted the curtain in the doorway, George sprang up from the table, darted across the room with surprising speed and stopped him. "Wait. Don't go. Not yet. There's something I want to give you."

"I'm not interested," said Pip.

"Don't you want to see what it is first?"

"No."

"Yes, you do," said George, grabbing his son's elbow and pulling him. "Come on. This way."

Pip tried to free himself, shaking his elbow and pulling away, but his father was much stronger than him. There was no point struggling.

He allowed himself to be led under the curtain, into the other room and down the line of cages.

42

George picked up his whip and opened the skinny bear's cage.

The bear shuffled back against the wall, squatting on all fours. She stared at the bearkeeper and the boy, warily watching their movements, waiting to see if they were planning to hurt her.

George cracked the whip. "Come on! Yah!"

The bear sniffed the air uncertainly. She didn't want to go anywhere. Being inside was bad, but outside was worse. She'd rather stay here, safe in her cage, protected from the world by a row of bars.

"Come on!" George cracked his whip again and yelled at the bear. "Yah! Yah!"

The bear cringed, raising her paws to protect herself, and let out a low growl.

Keeping the whip raised, threatening her, George stepped into the cage and looped a short rope through her leather collar. He tied a knot, then walked backwards out of the cage and tugged the rope. As if she realized that there was no point struggling, the bear meekly followed him.

When the bear emerged from the cage, George did something which took Pip completely by surprise. He handed the end of the rope to him. "There you go," he said. "She's yours now."

Pip took the rope. He said stupidly, "Mine?"

"You like her, don't you? That's what you said when you were here before."

Pip nodded. "Yes, I like her."

"Then keep her. She'll be a good companion. If you're ever short of money you can dance her or fight her, and you'll earn a decent living. Here, take this too." George handed the whip to his son. "You'll need it."

Pip held the whip in one hand, the rope in the other. He looked at the bear. He wanted to take her. Of course he did. But he didn't know what he'd do with her. Where they'd sleep. How they'd live. And, much more importantly, he didn't want to be indebted to his father in any way. He'd rather just walk out of the cottage and have nothing to do with George Stone ever again.

He offered the whip and the rope back at his father. "I don't think I should take her."

"Of course you can." George pushed Pip's hands away. "You want her. Don't you?"

"Yes, but—"

"Then take her." George nodded at the bear. "She likes you."

"How do you know?"

"Because I understand bears. When you've spent a few days with her, you'll start to understand them too."

"How?"

"You just will."

"But how?"

"Listen to her. Look at her. She'll tell you how she's feeling."

"How? She can't speak, can she?"

"Not in words," said George. "But she speaks in other ways. Look into her eyes. They'll tell you what you need to know. And if they don't, watch her ears. And watch her mouth. Listen to the noises that she makes. She's pretty good at saying what she wants, this one. You'll just have to learn how to understand her. It won't take long, I promise. Not for a bright boy like you. Give it a few days and you'll be able to tell exactly when she's happy, when she's sad, when she's tired. And you'll definitely know when she's hungry. I have to warn you, though; she'll be hungry just about all the time."

George smiled and, for the first time that day, Pip saw an unexpected expression in his father's eyes: affection, tenderness, perhaps even love. But not for him; for the bear.

"Take her," said George. "Please."

"Why do you want me to?"

"Because you'll look after her. And you're my son and, apart from that knife, I've never given you anything. And, most important of all, you want to."

"I don't know about that," said Pip.

"Yes, you do," said George. "Go on, Pip. Just take her."

43

They walked slowly and tentatively down the street, Pip holding the rope, the bear following, neither daring to catch the other's eye.

Pip wondered which of them was more scared. Both about the same, probably. Both terrified. He wanted to reassure the bear that he wasn't going to hurt her, but didn't know how. *We aren't going to the Bear Garden*, he could have said. *You'll never be tethered to a wooden post again. Or forced to defend yourself against a gang of dogs*. But even if he'd said so, she wouldn't have understood him. Somehow, through actions rather than words, he'd have to persuade her to trust him.

Turning the corner they met a plump washerwoman coming towards them, carrying a bundle of laundry in her sturdy arms. "Good evening," she said. "Lovely bear you've got there."

"Thank you," said Pip.

As the washerwoman waddled past, the bear watched her with nervous eyes, mouth open, teeth bared, ready to punish any sudden movement. Luckily, the washerwoman couldn't have moved suddenly even if she'd wanted to, weighed down as she was by a huge armful of shirts and breeches. Calling "God bless" over her shoulder, she was gone.

Pip had passed his first test. He'd saved the life of a washerwoman. He glanced at the bear, wanting to share his sense of satisfaction, but the bear stared determinedly at the ground, refusing to meet his eyes.

Maybe she's shy, he thought. Was that possible? Did bears feel shy? Pip had no idea.

He remembered what his father had said about understanding bears. *Listen to her. Look at her. She'll tell you how she's feeling.*

Pip looked at the bear and listened to her, but couldn't see anything worth noticing. If the bear was trying to communicate her feelings, she had a strange way of doing so. All she did was stare at the ground.

He remembered something else that his father said: *bears are always hungry*. Maybe that was her problem. She was starving. So hungry that her stomach ached. Pip knew that feeling. When you're that hungry, you can't think about anything except eating.

He had an idea. A way to win the bear's trust.

He led her through the streets until they found a festering pile of rubbish clogging a drain, a foul-smelling jumble of mud and manure, pee and poo, twigs and leaves, turnip tops and cabbage skins, chicken bones and sheep's teeth, all the detritus of a hundred families clogged together in one stinking pile, waiting for a heavy rainfall to wash the whole slithery mess down to the river. A battalion of black rats scampered around the sides of the heap and three ravens perched on top like generals in black coats, overseeing the operation.

When the rats and the ravens saw a big bear shambling towards them, they didn't hesitate. They fled. The rats skedaddled across the road and wriggled down the nearest hole. The ravens flew upwards to a safe rooftop and cawed furiously, telling the bear to buzz off, get lost, go home to wherever she belonged.

The bear wasn't interested in the opinions of three scruffy ravens. Not when there was food to be found. Pulling Pip behind her, she stumbled forward, fell face-first in the pile of rubbish, landed with a muddy splat, and starting digging.

Pip had never seen any creature eat with such single-minded dedication. The bear dug until she exposed something edible, popped it in her mouth and then, while chewing and swallowing, dug some more, searching for the next morsel. Soon her fur was covered with mud and long lines of goo dribbled from her muzzle, but she didn't care. She just kept eating with wild enthusiasm as if she'd never known such delicacies. She gobbled turnip chunks and chopped-up carrot and broken celery stalks and soggy lumps of all kinds of other vegetables which had rotted so much that they were no longer identifiable. She chewed on a pig's ear. She chomped fish heads. She licked out eggshells. She ate and ate and ate until she could eat no more. Then she let out an enormous burp, lay down, burped again, yawned, burped a third time and closed her eyes. A moment later, she was snoring.

Pip sat beside the bear, watching the steady rise and fall of her hairy chest as she breathed in and out. He'd have liked to fall asleep himself, but didn't dare. Not in the middle of the street. Someone would pick his pockets or steal his bear.

He wondered where he'd sleep tonight. Not here. Not the Globe either. He didn't have a key, so couldn't get inside when the last actors and stagehands had gone home. Oh, he'd find somewhere. A ditch or an alleyway. Like his first night in London.

He tickled the bear's paws to wake her. She opened an eye, looked at him for a moment, then closed it again and went back to sleep.

Pip stood up and tugged on the rope. This time the bear opened both eyes and stared at him with an angry expression, as if to say: can't you see I'm asleep?

"Sorry," said Pip. "But we have to get going." He tugged the rope again.

The bear just lay there, staring at him, refusing to budge.

Pip tugged the rope again and lifted the whip.

That made her move. Pip could see the fear in her eyes,

the memory of the lashes that the whip had given her. She struggled to her feet and followed him.

When they reached the river, the bear glanced at Pip, as if seeking his permission.

He nodded. "Go on. Get in. If you want to."

She couldn't have understood what he was actually saying, but she must have known what he meant, because she hurried forward, scrambled down the bank and plunged into the water with a big splash.

Pip stumbled after her, pulled by the rope that was still tethered to her collar, and stood ankle-deep in the Thames. He winced. It was cold. Even worse, the sun was just setting, so his boots and breeches wouldn't have a chance to dry out before nightfall.

The bear submerged herself, then lifted her head, opened her mouth and roared.

"GROOOAAAH!"

The noise must have pleased her, because she did it again, even longer and louder.

"GGGRRRRRROOOOOOOOOOOOOOOAAAA AAAAAHHHHHH!"

If you had been there, within earshot, you wouldn't have known if the bear was roaring with fury or pleasure, and you wouldn't have cared. You would just have felt extremely glad that you were sitting in a boat or standing on the other bank, a good long distance away, beyond the reach of her claws and teeth.

Sound travels a long way on water. The bear's voice carried up and down the Thames, all the way north to the houses and piers on the opposite bank, all the way west to Rotherhithe, all the way east to London Bridge. People stared and pointed. Someone waved from a river-taxi. Pip waved back. He felt embarrassed and awkward and oddly proud.

The bear dipped her head and drank for a long time, lapping the river with her long pink tongue, then clambered out of the water and stood beside Pip, sniffing the air. Her nostrils wrinkled. She turned her head slowly from side to side, searching for the source of the smell.

Pip picked up the whip.

The bear cringed backwards, her eyes half closed, and put up her right paw to protect her face.

Pip snapped the whip over his knee and threw the two halves into the river. The current swept them away.

He tied the rope around his wrist, in case the bear was tempted to escape, then lay down on his back and stared at the darkening sky. Soon, he could see the first stars, prickling through the gloom.

44

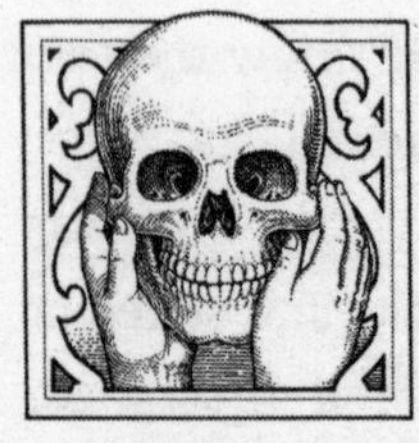

More than anything, Cuthbert Burbage felt disappointed.

The boy was standing in the door to the Globe, looking around the theatre as if he owned the place. He wasn't trying to hide. He didn't even appear to be ashamed.

When Cuthbert first talked to Pip, he thought he'd found a kindred spirit. A boy who, like him, rose early and went to bed early and got the job done. Someone who wanted to work. Someone who knew right from wrong. Someone who shared his own distrust of actors, but could see the financial possibilities of a life in the theatre.

Even as recently as yesterday Cuthbert had nurtured high hopes for that boy, imagining his bright future. Not just a decent job but a steady career path, leading eventually to wealth and responsibility. Perhaps even a partnership in the Globe. Boys who know how to work grow into men who own theatres. And now. . . Now he'd be happy to chase that infuriating child out of the door and never see him again. To Cuthbert's disgust, this boy had turned out to be lazy and unreliable, just like the others. The boy had run away, not even bothering to tell anyone where he was going, leaving his colleagues to clear up his mess. And taking Cuthbert's penny with him.

"Buy a beer for me," Cuthbert had said. "Keep the change."

The boy hadn't just kept the change. He'd kept the whole penny.

Thinking about the boy's behaviour, Cuthbert's disappointment turned to outrage. His trust had been broken. He had been betrayed. The boy had taken his money and probably spent last night getting drunk, chasing girls and placing bets on a dog fights, just like an actor.

Cuthbert stomped across the pit to the doorway, pointed at the boy and said, "You've got some nerve."

"Hello, Mister Burbage," said Pip.

"Don't 'hello' me, young man," said Cuthbert, poking his forefinger into the middle of the boy's chest. "What do you think you're doing here?"

"I've come to make you an offer, sir."

"An offer?"

"Yes. You see, I thought you might be—"

But before Pip could explain what he had been thinking, Cuthbert interrupted him. "Let me tell you, young man, I'm not interested in anything that you could possibly offer me. All I want to know is this: where were you last night?"

"I was. . . I was. . ." stammered Pip. "The thing is, Mister Burbage, I wasn't here."

"I know you weren't. But you should have been."

"Yes, sir. I know, sir."

"We pay you to clean up after the show. You can't just walk out."

"Sorry, sir," said Pip. "It won't happen again."

"You're absolutely right it won't," said Cuthbert. "Because you're fired."

"Fired, sir?"

"That's right," said Cuthbert. "Fired. As of right now. Which means that you have no business being inside this theatre. If I were you I'd get out, before someone throws you out."

"But, sir, you haven't heard what I've got to offer."

"Weren't you listening to me, boy? I don't care about your offers. I just want you to get out of my theatre. And I'll tell you something else. I want that penny back."

"You can have it back," said Pip. He reached into his pocket, found nothing, and remembered what he had done with the penny. "I'm sorry, sir. I've just spent it on some breakfast."

"I'll bet you have," said Cuthbert. "Now get out! Go on – get out!"

At the moment the bear nudged forward, emerging from the doorway, coming to see what was happening.

Cuthbert stared at the bear. "What's this?"

"You don't have to worry, sir," said Pip. "She's with me."

"Don't you know the rule?"

"No, sir. Which rule?"

"The rule which says you can't bring animals into the theatre. Get him out of here." Cuthbert started shooing the bear away. "Go on, get out! Off you go! Out! Out!"

The bear didn't like being shooed. She stood up on her hind legs, waved her front paws, opened her mouth and growled loudly. "GGGGRRRRRRRRHHH."

"Oh," said Cuthbert.

All around the theatre, people turned to see where that extraordinary noise was coming from.

Cuthbert gathered himself. He'd been surprised by the bear, and even a little bit shocked, but he had been surprised and shocked by all kinds of things in life, and none of them had actually killed him. Not yet, anyway. So he took a deep breath and said in an angry tone, "How on earth did this bear get in here? We can't have stray bears wandering round the theatre. Accidents might happen."

"This isn't a stray bear," said Pip, placing his hand on the bear's head and tickling one of her ears. "This is my bear."

"Your bear?"

"Yes, sir."

"You own him?"

"Her," said Pip. "She's a girl."

"Oh." Cuthbert bent down for a moment and peered at the bear's shaggy flanks, then stood up straight again and shrugged his shoulders. "I'd never have known. And she's yours?"

"Yes, sir," said Pip. "She's mine."

Cuthbert was impressed, not just by the bear but by the quiet, calm way that Pip dealt with her. Maybe the boy wasn't so bad after all. He said, "That's a nice-looking bear."

"Thank you, sir. I think so too."

"Does she do tricks?"

"A few, sir. Actually, that's what I wanted to talk to you about."

45

An hour later, the deal was done.

The Burbages drove a hard bargain, but so did Pip. Having worked alongside his stepfather for many years, arguing with farmers and pedlars, he knew how to do business.

The three of them – Cuthbert, Richard and Pip – shook hands to seal the agreement. Both Burbage brothers glanced at the bear, wondering whether they should shake hands with her too, but each of them, without needing to discuss the matter, decided against it.

The bear stared back. Her dark eyes coolly inspected the two men. She looked as if she was taking their measure, deciding whether they could be trusted.

Pip hoped he was doing the right thing. He had rescued the bear from one kind of slavery. Was he now thrusting her straight back into another? After much thought, he had decided that there was nothing wrong with working together with the bear, as long as he made a solemn promise to himself that he would never mistreat her.

In order to keep that promise, he would never – he resolved – ask her to do anything that he would not do himself. They would eat the same food. They would sleep on the same floorboards, covered by the same blanket. They would work the same hours. Whatever she did, he would do too.

Pip agreed with the Burbages that the bear would perform in plays whenever she was needed. She would do a dance or two, but no fighting, and there was never to be any cruelty shown towards her, even in jest. When they weren't performing, Pip and the bear would wander through the streets, putting up posters, or stand outside the Globe, chatting to passers-by, advertising that day's play.

Alongside his duties as the bear's keeper, Pip would be employed as the theatre's smith, mending swords, spears, helmets, clasps, buttons and whatever metalwork was damaged during daily performances.

In return, Pip would be paid fourpence per day for himself and his bear. And, by special permission of the Burbage brothers, they would be given a key to the Globe and permitted to sleep in the theatre until they found a more permanent home.

Cuthbert had initially shown some reluctance about this part of the deal, but Pip had insisted, and Richard had agreed.

"It'll be great publicity," Richard had said. "Other theatres might be guarded by men or dogs. But the Globe will be the only theatre in London – probably the only theatre in the world – to be guarded by its own bear."

46

A crowd of actors and stagehands gathered to look at the bear. People whispered to one another, commenting and making jokes. They knew Pip, of course. And they knew the bearkeeper at the Bear Garden. But they would never have imagined that the two were father and son.

One of the actors was nervous because Pip didn't have a whip. Nor did the bear have a muzzle. At any moment the bear could lunge at someone, knocking off a head or taking a bite from an arm.

The others told him not to be so stupid.

"You don't have to worry about Pip," said Nathan Field. "He's the bearkeeper's son! Bears are in his blood! If he doesn't want a whip, then he doesn't need a whip. He knows exactly what he's doing. Don't you?"

"Yes," said Pip. "I know what I'm doing."

He didn't, of course. But he wasn't going to admit that to anyone. Not when he'd just got a job as a bearkeeper.

The actors pestered Pip with questions. They wanted to know what the bear could do. *Can she fight? Can she dance? What are her best tricks?* Pip couldn't confidently answer any of these questions, so he simply promised that everything would be revealed soon.

William Shakespeare and Robert Armin pushed to the front of the crowd. People stepped aside to let them through.

"Hello, Pip," said Robert.

"Hello, Mister Armin."

"I hear you've found a sweetheart."

"That's right."

"And she wants to be an actor, does she?"

"Yes."

"Well, we'd better give her an audition. That's the rule. You can't join the company until you've had an audition. Has she prepared a speech?"

"No."

"Why not?"

"Because. . . Because she can't speak."

"Well, that's not much good. What are we going to do with an actor who can't speak?"

"I don't know," said Pip. He could feel a hot blush spreading across his cheeks. Anyone else, he was sure, would have replied to Robert's questions with a series of witty remarks, making everyone laugh, but he couldn't think of anything clever to say. He just stood there, embarrassed by all the attention.

He put his hand on the bear's back. Under her thick fur, he could feel her warm skin. She was trembling. Could she be cold? No, she must be scared. She'd probably never seen so many people close up. Pip slowly stroked her fur, tickling her ears and running his fingers down her flanks, trying to calm her down.

Robert Armin took a long look at the bear.

"So, what's her name?"

"I don't know."

"You don't know?"

"I thought bears didn't have names," said Pip.

"No, no, all the best bears have names. Remember Sackerson?"

"No."

"Sackerson was a magnificent bear. I once saw him kill a horse just like that." Robert clicked his fingers. "One punch and the horse was dead. But Sackerson wasn't the only one. Great Ned, Harry Hunks, Henry of Warwick – all the best bears have names." Robert pointed at the bear. "So she must too."

"She doesn't," said Pip.

"I'm sure she does," said Robert. "You just don't know it yet."

"How do I find it?"

"You own her, don't you?"

"I suppose I do."

"Then you should name her."

Pip frowned. He couldn't think of a name for the bear. He thought for a long time, staring at the bear, hoping she would provide him with some inspiration, but his mind was empty. The actors stood patiently, waiting for him to finish thinking. Finally, Pip had an idea. He looked at William Shakespeare. "Will you name her, sir?"

"Me?" William Shakespeare shrugged his shoulders. "Why me?"

"You're good with words, sir."

"That's true. Very well. I shall name her." William Shakespeare cocked his head to one side and stared at the bear. The bear stared back. No one spoke.

William Shakespeare suddenly nodded. "Miranda," he said. "This bear is called Miranda."

Robert said, "Why Miranda?"

"I don't know."

"Oh, come on, William. You can't just say something like that without knowing why."

"Of course I can. And there's no need for you to be so pompous. Miranda is a very good name. Particularly for a bear."

Pip stared at the bear. He tried out the new name in his mouth. "Miranda." He said it a few times, varying his intonation. "Miranda. *Miranda.* Miranda? Miranda!" Then he nodded. Yes, Shakespeare was right. Miranda was a very good name for a bear.

47

William Shakespeare was a pragmatic writer. He didn't mind changing his own work to fit the demands of an audience, the abilities of particular actors, current events, the weather or just about anything else. If the company had been hired to stage a special performance inside some lord's mansion, he'd alter scenes and locations to fit the space. If a new actor was spectacularly tall or unusually ugly, he'd write a part to suit them. If an unseasonal hailstorm had fallen on the city, say, or there had been a particularly ferocious argument between Queen Elizabeth and the King of Spain, he'd add an extra line, just for that day's performance, hoping to get a laugh or make a point. Adding a part for a bear presented no problem. He didn't have time today, he told Pip, but he promised to scrawl a few scenes overnight and deliver them in the morning, giving Miranda lots of time to learn her lines.

At the end of the week, the company would be performing one of Shakespeare's most recent successes, an outrageously funny comedy called *Much Ado About Nothing*. It was the story of a man and a woman, Beatrice and Benedick, who never stop saying how much they hate one another. Of course, Beatrice actually loves Benedick and Benedick actually loves Beatrice, but they just don't know it yet.

Overnight, Shakespeare would take to his desk and rewrite a few of the key scenes, adding a role for a bear. Tomorrow Pip would be relieved of some of his usual duties so he and Miranda could rehearse the part. The following day they would perform on the stage of the Globe in front of three thousand people.

That afternoon Pip and Miranda sat at the back of the theatre, just to the side of the stage. Before the doors opened, letting in the first members of the audience, Pip tied Miranda's rope to a post. She was miserable – the presence of the audience reminded her of the Bear Garden – and Pip felt guilty, but he forced himself to harden his heart. If she was going to be a performer, and he was going to keep his job as a member of the company, Miranda would have to get used to crowds.

As the theatre filled up, Miranda grew even more anxious. She shivered and twitched. Her ears flattened against the side of her head. Her eyes swivelled from side to side, gazing at the mass of people. Whenever anyone came close, she curled her lips, exposing her teeth, and growled. People moved away quickly.

During the performance, as the actors marched across the stage and the audience roared their delight or disapproval, Miranda cringed and whined. Pip sat beside her, stroking her fur, tickling her ears, trying to comfort her, but he didn't have any success.

Once, panicked by a shout on the stage, she swiped at him. Her right paw connected with the side of his head, knocking him backwards.

She hadn't hit hard. If she'd wanted to hurt him, she could have killed him. But she still whacked him hard enough that his head hadn't stopped hurting by the end of the play.

When the audience had gone home Pip swept the stage and cleared up the pit, leaving Miranda tied to one of the timbers. On the middle gallery, under a bench, Pip found a lump of cheese, discarded by whoever had been sitting there. He hadn't eaten since breakfast. Mmmmm, cheese. Just as his mouth opened to take a big bite, he made the mistake of glancing across the theatre. There he saw Miranda, squatting by the side of the stage, looking meek, miserable and very scared.

Pip ran down the stairs, jogged round the pit and stood in front of her, the piece of cheese cradled in his hand.

Miranda lifted her head and, reluctantly, even nervously, took a couple of sniffs. She glanced at Pip. Unlike most of the men that she'd known, he didn't yell, raise his arm or whip her. But she still didn't trust him. Miranda moved closer and closer to the cheese, never taking her eyes from

Pip, prepared to leap backwards if he lifted his hand to hit her.

He stayed very still.

She opened her mouth, lunged, gobbled the cheese from his hands and gulped it down. Then she squatted back on her haunches, cocked her head to one side and looked at him as if she was trying to work out what kind of creature he might be. Pip wiped his hand on his breeches – his fingers were covered with her saliva – and went back to work, clearing rubbish from the galleries.

You can't buy love. Not with cheese, anyway. But you can certainly buy a kind of truce. And that piece of cheese was enough to make peace between Pip and Miranda. They forgave one another.

That evening, when the other actors had gone home, the boy and the bear sat on the stage and ate together, feasting on the discarded scraps that Pip had found earlier. In the darkness, they climbed the stairs to the top gallery. When they reached the place where Pip slept, he tied the free end of Miranda's rope to his ankle, making sure she couldn't sneak off. He knew what happened in the middle of the night. The mice and the rats came out to play, overseen by the owl and the marmalade cat. Miranda might fancy a midnight snack. Tied to Pip's ankle, she couldn't go anywhere. Side by side, they lay down and slept.

48

In the morning, when Cuthbert Burbage arrived at the theatre, he found Pip plumping up the cushions for the expensive seats in the galleries. That was normal. But today, unlike any other day, Cuthbert shouted, "Stop! Stop! Stop that right now!"

Pip looked up, surprised. "Why?"

"Because you're an actor today. And a bearkeeper. Not an odd-job boy. Someone else will do your work for you. Get down from there and come here."

As Pip sprang down from the stage and hurried across the pit, Cuthbert opened the leather purse that was hanging from his belt and removed two coins. He handed the pennies to Pip and invited him to fetch breakfast for both of them.

"There are three of us," said Pip, joggling the pennies in

his palm. "And we'll all be working today."

Cuthbert looked at him for a moment, then glanced at the bear, who was sitting by the side of the stage, picking fleas from her armpit. "Very well," he said. "Get breakfast for all three of us." He reached into his purse and pulled out another penny.

Around midday Shakespeare arrived at the Globe, accompanied by the boy who had been sent to fetch him. He'd overslept, as he usually did, having stayed up all night writing. He was clutching a sheaf of papers.

He glanced round the theatre, saw Pip and sauntered over. "This is for you," he said, not bothering to apologize for his lateness, just handing over the topmost piece of paper.

"Thank you, Mister Shakespeare," said Pip, taking the paper and glancing at the uneven lines of black ink.

Shakespeare must have seen the doubt in Pip's face, because he said, "You can read, can't you?"

"Yes, sir."

"Are you sure?"

"Yes, sir."

"Get one of the lads to help you with your cues. All right?"

"Yes, sir."

"Good luck." Without another word Shakespeare turned his back on Pip and wandered across the theatre to deliver more pages to other actors, extra lines for that afternoon's performance.

Left to himself, Pip hunched over the paper, running his forefinger along the words, mouthing the words to himself as he read what Shakespeare had written.

He'd been worried that Shakespeare would have written some complicated scenes or actions for Miranda to perform on her premiere, but, to his relief, he saw that the playwright had decided to keep things simple. Tomorrow afternoon, during the performance of *Much Ado About Nothing*, she would simply have to:

First, enter from the left, carry a letter to the actor playing Benedick, and exit on the right.

Second, dance a jig alone in the middle of the stage, watched by Beatrice and Hero.

Third, enter from the right, chase Dogberry around the stage, and exit on the left, pursuing him.

Fourth, join the other actors on the stage at the end of the play and dance a jig with them.

Pip lifted his head and looked at Miranda. "This doesn't look *too* difficult," he said. "You'll be able to walk and dance and carry a letter. Won't you?"

Other bears might have been different. Maybe most bears did exactly what they were told, never complaining, never making a fuss. But Miranda was a bear with a mind of her own. She knew what she liked and what she didn't.

She liked eating. She liked sleeping. She liked sitting around doing nothing. She was perfectly content scratching her ears, picking her toes or searching for fleas in her fur. But she really, really didn't like being told what to do.

At first she simply ignored Pip's attempts to rehearse her part in *Much Ado About Nothing*. When he tried to move her from one side of the stage to the other, she watched him with wary eyes, but refused to be moved. Usually she would have followed him when he tugged the rope, but she sensed that today was different. And so today she resolutely refused to budge. When he persisted in his demands, she grew irritable, then angry, growling at him and raising her right paw.

Pip backed away. He didn't want to lose a tooth or get his head broken open.

There was only one thing to be done. He went to see Molly Plunkett, the wardrobe mistress, and asked for half his savings. Molly handed over eight pennies. Leaving Miranda tied to a post, Pip walked to Borough Market and bought six big loaves of bread, a dozen herrings and an earthenware pot filled with honey.

Back at the Globe, the first members of that afternoon's audience were forming a queue, determined to get the best seats in the galleries or the best positions in the pit. Pip ducked past, nodding to the doorkeeper, and went inside to fetch Miranda.

Together, the boy and the bear left the Globe and walked west until they found a quiet spot behind some houses, set back from the riverbank.

Pip had seen farmers training their dogs, repeating the same simple tasks over and over again, rewarding good work with a scrap of food. He'd do the same with Miranda. If she stood when he told her to stand, he would present her with a hunk of bread. If she walked when he asked her to walk, she would get a herring.

That was the plan, anyway.

Pip held a herring in his right hand and the rope in his left. He tugged the rope and said, "Come here!"

Miranda's nostrils twitched, but her body didn't move.

Pip tugged the rope again. "Come on," he said. "Come here!"

Miranda stayed exactly where she was.

"Come on," said Pip. "Look at this lovely fishy! Mmmm, yummy fishy! All you have to do is stand up when I say so and take three paces towards me. Then you can have it." He dangled the herring in the air. "Come on, stand up."

With a sudden movement, too quick for Pip to anticipate, Miranda lunged forward. Her muzzle was wide open. She grabbed the fish from Pip's hand. If he hadn't let go, she'd have eaten his fingers too. Miranda gulped once and the herring vanished down her throat.

Pip told himself that he had to be patient. Learning took time. He picked up another herring and said, "Let's try that once more."

Miranda licked her lips. Then she opened her mouth and chomped the herring right out of Pip's hand.

"No, no," said Pip. "This is supposed to be training, not feeding. You can't just eat the fish; you have to earn it. Let's try again." He picked up a third herring. "Walk towards me. Come on! Walk!"

Miranda looked at him. There was a curious expression in her eyes. Confident. Even mischievous. Back in the bearkeeper's cottage, Miranda had been meek, mild-mannered and mostly terrified, the type of bear that you'd be happy to take home to meet your mother. But now, after a couple of days of freedom, she seemed to be changing. With one swift movement she grabbed the herring from Pip's hand.

"Don't you dare eat it!" shouted Pip.

Miranda swallowed the herring, then pushed Pip aside and reached for the remaining fish. When Pip tried to stop her, she opened her mouth and growled so loudly that Pip almost peed himself with terror.

When Miranda had finished the fish she scooped the honey out of the earthenware pot and made her way through the six loaves. Having looked around to check that there wasn't any more food within reach, she lay down and closed her eyes. A moment later, she was snoring.

Pip sighed. Looking at the scattered crumbs, the crunched fish bones, the broken honeypot and the sleeping bear, he came to the melancholy conclusion that he was going to have to do the one thing that he had hoped he would never, ever have to do.

49

As they walked past the Bear Garden, Miranda seemed to shrink into herself, glancing uneasily at the big wooden doors. She grew more cheerful as soon as she realized that they weren't going inside, but her gloom returned when they headed down the dark alleyway and stopped outside the bearkeeper's cottage. She glanced at Pip with an expression which seemed to say: what are we doing back here?

"Don't worry," said Pip. "We won't stay long."

He knocked twice on the wooden door. He waited a few moments, but there was no answer, so he knocked twice more.

"Yes, yes, I'm coming," shouted a voice on the other side of the door. There was the sound of shuffling footsteps, then George Stone opened the door. "Oh, it's you," he said, peering at Pip through his puffed-up eyes. "If you want to come in, you don't have to knock. You are my son, after all."

George Stone's lips were split and his eyebrows were matted with dried blood. Little half-healed cuts wriggled across his chin and cheeks. One side of his face was covered by a huge purple bruise, stretching from his eye socket to his ear.

Pip was so shocked that he could hardly imagine what to say, but he managed to blurt out the words: "What happened?"

"Nothing," said George.

"That doesn't look like nothing."

George touched his face. "Oh, this? Really, it's nothing at all. I got drunk and fell over. Anyway, what can I do for you?"

"I've come to ask your advice."

"About what?"

"Can I come inside?"

Not bothering to hide his reluctance, George said, "I suppose so." He stepped aside, allowing Pip and Miranda into the cottage.

They were greeted by a scene of total chaos. The house looked as if it had been picked up and shaken. The curtain had been torn down and the chairs broken. Liquid had been splashed over the walls. The bearkeeper's few clothes, plates and other possessions had been smashed to pieces. The bears had gone and their cages had been ripped apart, every wooden bar snapped in half. There was no sign of the dogs.

"This is terrible," said Pip. "What happened?"

"Like I said, I got drunk. When I fell over, I suppose I must have taken a few things with me. To be honest, I can't remember much about it."

"How could you not remember doing all this?"

"I must have been very drunk."

"You must have been," said Pip, staring at the chaos. It reminded him of another chaotic scene that he'd recently witnessed – the interior of his own home after the Weasel and his men had smashed it apart. Then he realized what had really happened here. "The Weasel did this," he said. "Didn't he?"

George tried to deny it, but there wasn't much point. Both of them knew he was lying. Eventually George admitted the truth: the Weasel had been back again, demanding the repayment of his loans. Learning that George hadn't raised a single penny, the Weasel was furious. He and his men tore the house to pieces. They broke whatever could be broken, then confiscated the dogs and the bears, taking them to sell in the market.

"He's given me one more night to find the rest of the money. If I haven't found what I owe by tomorrow morning. . ." George trailed off, not wanting to finish his sentence.

"He'll kill you, won't he?"

"That's what he said."

"Why don't you run? Or hide?"

George shrugged his shoulders. "Where would I go?"

"Anywhere," said Pip. "Leave London. Leave England.

Get on a boat and go to France. Just get out of here!"

"No, no, I'm too old for that kind of thing. I haven't got the energy to start all over again."

"So what will you do?"

"Something will come up. It always does."

"I'll kill him," said Pip.

"Don't be ridiculous."

"Why not? You and me together – we could fight him. I'm a good swordsman. You should see me. I've been practising every day."

"And how many men have you killed?"

Pip didn't answer.

"Exactly," said George. "I don't know how many men the Weasel has killed, but it's certainly more than twenty. Maybe fifty. When a man has killed that often, he begins to forget what killing means. And don't think you'll be protected by your youth. He doesn't care who you are or what you are. I know of one woman whose face was slashed so badly by him, she no longer leaves the house in daylight."

"It's worth trying," said Pip.

"No, it's not," said George. "You told me something when you were last here. You said you'd never be like me. Well, that was a wise idea. Live your own life, Pip. Keep out of my business. And I'll keep out of yours. Will you promise me you'll do that?"

"I promise," said Pip in a small voice.

"Good. Now, what are you doing here?"

Pip explained the purpose of his visit: he wanted his

father's help with the bear. He described what had happened when he returned to the Globe, the deal that he had made with the Burbages and the scenes that Shakespeare had added to *Much Ado About Nothing*. Now he needed to know how he could persuade Miranda to follow her cues, entering and leaving the stage at the correct moments, doing what he ordered, rather than just eating and snoozing as she wished. He explained how he had already tried to train Miranda with bread, honey and herrings, and described his lack of success.

George wanted to laugh, but his bruised jaw and cut lips hurt too much. Instead, he contorted his lips in a strange sort of smile and said, "You can't make friends with a bear, Pip. Not unless you're another bear. And even bears don't have much time for other bears. Angry, bitter creatures, they are. Solitary and foul-tempered. This bear. . ." He pointed at Miranda, who was lying on the floor, her big head resting on her front paws. If she knew she was the focus of their attention, she didn't show any sign of caring. "This bear doesn't want to be your friend. She doesn't even want to be in the same country as you. Given the choice, she'd like to be at home in the woods of the far distant north, roaming free. And whatever you give her – herrings, honey, even a juicy hunk of beef – she's never going to forgive you for being a man. That's why there's only one way to make a bear obey your bidding, and that's the whip. You have to use the whip. A bear born in captivity, here in England, might be different. But a wild bear, a bear who's known the forests, who can still smell the pine needles and feel the wind and taste the snow – you're never going to tame a bear like that. You just have to whip her into shape. Where's the whip that I gave you?"

Pip admitted that he had broken the whip in half and thrown it away.

"I'll give you another," said George.

Pip refused. He had made a vow: he was never going to use a whip on the bear.

"Then the bear will never do what you want," said George.

"Can't I train her like a dog? With snacks. And kindness."

"Kindness?" George smiled and shook his head. "Oh, no, no. If you don't use a whip, you'll never train this bear."

At dusk, Pip left the house. He asked if he could stay the night, but George said no. Pip wondered if this really was the last time that he would ever see his father. Tomorrow morning the Weasel would arrive with his men and kill George Stone. Unless he found a way to raise thirty pounds. And how could he possibly do that?

"Don't worry," said George. "I'll think of something. I've been in worse scrapes than this."

"Really?"

"Oh, yes. Hundreds. I'll see you tomorrow afternoon. I'm not going to miss this show for the world."

"But—"

"But nothing. Just go. See you tomorrow. I'll be in the theatre, I promise."

If his father hadn't sounded so confident, Pip might have protested more, but he allowed himself to be led out of the house and into the street, then pointed in the direction of the Globe. Leading Miranda on her rope, he started walking. At the end of the alleyway he paused and looked back, hoping to catch a final glimpse of his father, but George Stone had already gone back into the house and closed the door.

50

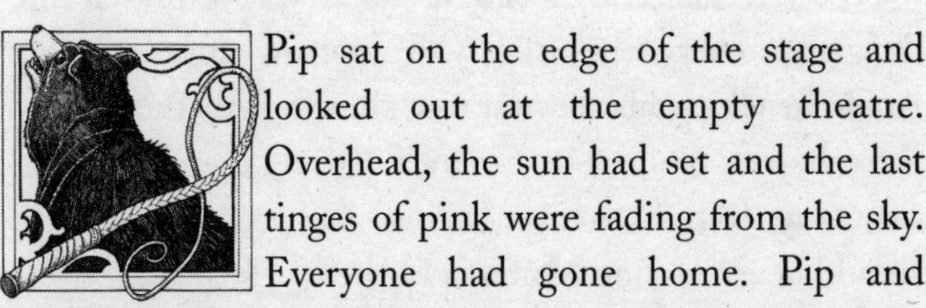

Pip sat on the edge of the stage and looked out at the empty theatre. Overhead, the sun had set and the last tinges of pink were fading from the sky. Everyone had gone home. Pip and Miranda had the whole place to themselves. They could work all night. By the time Cuthbert Burbage arrived in the morning, Miranda's performance would be perfect.

But neither of them felt much like working. In the corner of the pit Miranda was sprawled on a patch of mud, dozing. Pip was sitting on the edge of the stage, swinging his legs in the air and staring into space, trying to reach a decision. He didn't know what to do. He felt as if he were standing at a crossroads, given the choice between two paths, and he had no idea which to take. Should he follow his father's advice and forget the Weasel? Or should he follow his own instincts, which were telling him to jump off the stage right now, hurry to the Weasel's house, draw his knife from its scabbard and take his revenge?

If he was sensible, he'd rehearse with Miranda until the theatre grew dark, then climb the stairs to the top gallery, tie her rope to his ankle, pull the blanket over his body and fall asleep.

And yet, if he'd spent his life being sensible, he'd never have left home in the first place, come to London, met his father or acquired Miranda. If he'd been sensible, he'd still be lying in the storeroom at home, listening to the regular rasp of his stepfather's snores.

And yet, that didn't mean he should throw himself into danger at every opportunity. Tomorrow afternoon Pip would be taking his sternest test, showing whether he had the guts and skill to become a full-time member of the company. Rather than worrying about the Weasel, he should be rehearsing Miranda for her performance.

And yet, he didn't want to stay here, learning the cues for *Much Ado About Nothing* while, less than a mile away, a man was plotting his father's death – a man who Pip had already sworn to kill.

And yet his father was right; fighting the Weasel would be madness. He'd never even killed a man, while the Weasel had murdered maybe fifty.

And yet he trusted his own skill with a knife. He was young and fit, and he knew what he was doing. In a fair fight wouldn't he have a good chance, even against an experienced killer like the Weasel?

And yet he'd made a solemn promise to his father. "Keep out of my business," George had said. "And I'll keep out of yours. Will you promise me you'll do that?"

"I promise," Pip had said.

And yet he remembered how George had treated his mother and him. Marriage was a promise. Not just any old promise. Marriage was a solemn vow made in church before God. George had broken that. So he obviously didn't take promises very seriously.

And yet, and yet, and yet. . . Pip didn't know what to do. As soon as he believed that he'd made a decision, he saw why it was wrong. Thoughts flooded his mind, tugging him in different directions, persuading him of the perfect sense of each possible action, urging him to be brave, to be sensible, to be cunning, to be calm, to be a good boy, to be a good son, to be a man. He glanced at Miranda, but she was no help, just snoozing in a heap, oblivious to his worries. If he was going to make this decision, he'd have to do it himself, without any assistance from anyone.

He stood up. Indecision was driving him crazy. He was being pulled one way, then another. His mind felt as if it were going to break into pieces, torn apart by conflicting thoughts.

He took a few paces backwards and stood in the middle of the stage. If he were an actor, this is where he'd stand when he was talking to the audience. This is where Richard Burbage always stood, for instance, when he was acting Hamlet and discussing his dilemmas with the audience, allowing them a glimpse of his innermost thoughts.

That's it, thought Pip.

Hamlet dithered and dallied, he thought, *just like me, unable to decide what to do, paralysed by all the possibilities. But he finally made up his mind and did the right thing. He drew his sword and took his revenge, driving the blade through his uncle's guts.*

Pip could almost feel the presence of Hamlet here on the stage, standing beside him, whispering what he had learnt. *Do what you think is right. Be brave. Even if it kills you.*

I will, thought Pip. *I'll unsheathe my father's dagger and take revenge on the Weasel for the wrongs that he has done me and my family. Even if it kills me.*

Nothing felt better than making a decision. All the panic, all the thoughts that had been competing for his attention flowed out of his brain and body, leaving him cool and calm and completely confident. He knew what he was doing and why. He knew where he was going. Everything made sense.

He jumped off the stage, ran across the pit to Miranda, picked up her rope and gave it a swift tug. "Come on," he said. "Let's go!"

Miranda lifted her head and looked at him. Go? her expression seemed to be saying. Go? Now? Don't you realize what time it is? But when Pip tugged the rope again, she struggled to her feet without any protest and followed him out of the theatre.

Pip found the house without taking a single wrong

turning. He felt proud of himself. A proper Londoner, finding his own way through the streets of Southwark, even in the middle of the night.

He and Miranda stood in the shelter of the darkest shadows and stared down the cramped street at the Weasel's home. Through the shutters of a first-floor window he could see the flicker of a candle and the movement of shadows cast on to a wall. Someone was still awake.

The moon hadn't yet risen, but it would be full tonight; just what he needed.

The two of them retreated to a dark doorway from where they could just see the half-shuttered window with its flickering shadows. Pip sat cross-legged. Miranda stretched full-length on the ground and fell asleep immediately. Pip didn't even feel dozy. He kept his eyes fixed on the house. He was ready. This was the reason that he'd come to London. This was the test that he'd set himself. Tonight he would finally have the chance to take his revenge.

51

Pip waited until the candle was blown out, then waited another hour or so, allowing the inhabitants enough time to drift into a deep sleep. When he was sure they must be dead to the world, he hauled himself to his feet and shook his arms, trying to get some blood flowing through his veins. His limbs ached, his skin was cold and his belly was empty, but he was too excited to feel any real physical discomfort.

Miranda opened one eye and watched him.

Pip left her there, hoping she wouldn't wander off, and walked down the street. Nothing was moving. In every house, the windows were dark.

Behind him, Miranda hauled herself to her feet. On all fours, she padded down the street in pursuit of Pip. Like any animal who hunts for her own food, she moved without making much noise.

When Pip reached the Weasel's house, he gently pushed the shutters on the ground-floor windows. They didn't budge. He went to the front door and tried the latch. It was locked too.

He took two steps backwards. That was when he noticed Miranda. He whispered, "What are you doing here?"

Miranda didn't reply. She just stared at him. In the darkness, the expression in her eyes was unreadable.

"Just keep quiet," whispered Pip.

I'm being a lot quieter than you, Miranda could have said. But she didn't say anything. She just carried on being quiet.

Pip stood beside her and looked up at the house.

On the first floor he could see open shutters in two different windows. They had probably been left ajar to let some fresh air into a bedroom. One pair of shutters belonged to the window where he'd seen the candle. That room was definitely inhabited. He decided to try the other one. But how was he going to get up there?

He looked at Miranda and whispered, "Will you help?"

Once again she stared back at him without making a sound.

"Come here then," whispered Pip.

Miranda allowed herself to be positioned under the window. But that was her limit. When Pip tried to clamber on to her back she rebelled, pushing him away with her head, opening her jaws, giving him a glimpse of her teeth and making a loud, scary hiss.

"Don't worry," whispered Pip. "I'm not going to hurt you."

Miranda stared at him. In the moonlight her black eyes glistened like wet stones.

"I promise," whispered Pip. "I won't hurt you."

Miranda must have believed him because she didn't protest again. She just stood there, calm and solid and patient, letting Pip place his feet on her shoulders and reach for the first-floor window. At full stretch he managed to get a good grip on the sill. His feet scrabbling on the brickwork, he hauled himself though the window and collapsed face-first into the house.

Pip lay on the floor in a heap, not daring to move, sure someone must have been woken by the thud, but he could only hear one sign of life and that was his own breathing.

He waited for another minute. Now he couldn't hear anything.

When his eyes adjusted to the gloom, he looked around. He was lying on the floor of a tiny storeroom, piled with sacks, crates, boxes, chairs, pots, candlesticks and rolled-up carpets. This must be where the Weasel and his gang kept their loot from all their robberies. Pip considered searching for his stepfather's valuables, then decided not to bother. He was here for something more important than money. He got to his feet and tiptoed out of the storeroom.

A staircase led downstairs. There were two other doorways on the first floor. He went through the nearest door and found himself in a long room. Moonlight seeped through the window's open shutters, casting a pale glow over the embroidered tapestries hanging on the walls and the enormous bed, which held two sleeping bodies. Pip recognized them immediately as the Weasel and his girlfriend.

Pip padded slowly and silently towards the bed, placing his feet gingerly on each floorboard, avoiding the obstacles littered on the floor – a long silk scarf, some discarded clothing, three shoes and a cup of water. He was surprised to notice that he didn't feel particularly scared. When he reached the side of the bed he stood above the two prone bodies, looking down on them.

In sleep, the Weasel's girlfriend looked beautiful, her pale skin dotted with tiny freckles, her long eyelashes splayed around her closed eyelids. Alongside her, the Weasel lay on his back, his eyes closed and his mouth open, his chest rhythmically rising and falling with each slow, steady breath. His white flesh glowed in the moonlight. Naked, his face at rest, his skin scrawled with a few scraps of black curly hair, he looked vulnerable and surprisingly boyish, more like a child than a man.

Stop looking at them, Pip told himself. *I just have to do it. There's no time for thinking. Or worrying. I have to do it now.*

He knew this was his best chance, and perhaps his only chance, of taking revenge. He reached down to his belt, clasped his right hand around his father's knife and drew it from its scabbard.

Do it now, Pip thought to himself, glancing down at the sharp blade gleaming in the moonlight and then looking at the Weasel's white throat.

Do it now, he told himself again.

He knew exactly what he had to do. Many times he had seen pigs being killed. This would be just the same. Although he had never actually killed a pig himself, he knew where to puncture the skin, how hard to thrust and when to jump backwards, avoiding the spray of warm blood that would spurt into the air. It was easy. He just had to rest the blade on the Weasel's exposed throat and push, using all his strength. One swift shove and it would be done.

It would be messy, of course. Just like killing a pig was messy. Blood would jet in every direction, painting the walls scarlet. The Weasel would judder and shriek for a few seconds, his arms flailing, his veins pulsing, the life draining out of him, soaking the mattress, pooling on the floor. When the girl saw the blood she'd probably start screaming too, waking Scar and Tooth and Pigface, but that didn't matter. By then Pip would be halfway down the street.

He was glad he didn't have to kill her too. She had done nothing to him. He was even a bit sorry that she'd wake up beside a dying man, but that was her own fault. She shouldn't have chosen to share a bed with the Weasel.

I'm thinking too much, thought Pip. *Just like Hamlet. Well, I'm not going to make the same mistake as him. The time for thinking has passed. This is my moment to act.*

Step forward, plunge the knife, kill the man. And everything would be better. With one thrust he would free his father and avenge the wrongs that had been done to his family.

Do it, thought Pip, staring at the Weasel's white neck,

the soft skin awaiting his blade. *Do it now.*

Again he tried to urge himself forward, but some force rooted him to the spot, keeping his arm by his side, preventing him from doing what he wanted.

What was wrong with him?

Killing people was easy. He was sure of that. A quick slice with a sharp blade was enough to cut their throats or open their bellies. He'd practised so often against imaginary opponents. A thousand times he'd seen them fall away from his knife and writhe on the grass, coughing out their last breaths. Killing a real person shouldn't be any more difficult.

But something stopped him. The knife stayed in his hand, hanging by his side, the blade pointing at the floor, harmless, useless.

If I can't do a simple thing like this, thought Pip, *I'm nothing better than a coward.*

With sudden, unexpected clarity, he realized the truth. A coward – that's exactly what he was. He couldn't do it. He couldn't kill a man.

As soon as he knew that, there was no reason to stay in the house for another second. He stepped backwards and turned towards the door. If he'd been thinking more clearly, he might have remembered all the objects littered across the floor, but his attention was elsewhere, and so his left boot landed on top of the cup. His ankle twisted. A sharp pain shot through his leg. He managed not to shout out, but he couldn't prevent himself from losing his balance. He stumbled. Flinging his arms out to both sides and wobbling precariously, he just managed to regain his footing, but the cup tipped over, banged against the floor and spilt its contents.

Startled awake by the noise, the Weasel opened his eyes.

Perhaps Pip should have chosen that moment to start running but he simply stood there, terrified, breathless, incapable of thought or movement, hoping against hope that he would not be seen.

From the overturned cup, a small pool of water spread across the wooden floorboards.

The Weasel lay on the bed, staring at the ceiling, not quite awake but not quite asleep either, first closing his eyes, mumbling something incomprehensible, and then opening them again. He turned his head to the right and looked at his girlfriend's profile. He must have liked what he saw, because a sweet smile spread across his lips. Then he turned his head to the left and noticed the shadowy figure of a slim young man, standing upright in the middle of the room and holding a knife in his right hand.

For a moment, nothing happened. No one moved. The smile didn't even fade from the Weasel's lips. The two of them, the man and the boy, stared at one another, both of them too startled to say a word or move a muscle. That moment seemed to last a long, long time, although it can't actually have been more than a second. When it finally came to an end, two things happened in swift succession. The Weasel said, "Who the hell are you?" And Pip ran.

The Weasel roared: "Stop!"

Pip had no intention of stopping. He darted out of the

door and dodged across the landing. A voice pursued him, shouting so loudly that everyone in the neighbouring houses must have been shocked out of their slumbers. "THIEF!!!!"

Pip sprang down the staircase, taking the steps three at a time.

When he'd got about halfway down a figure emerged from one of the rooms on the ground floor. It was Pigface, woken by the roar of his master's voice. Spotting a shape hurtling down the stairs towards him, Pigface turned his head, opened his mouth and said, "Whaaaa. . .?"

Momentum was too fast for either of them. Even if they'd had time to think, they wouldn't have had time to move. Before Pigface could finish his sentence or Pip could alter his course, the boy crashed straight into the fat man's belly.

Blubber cushioned the blow. Pip bounced three steps back up the staircase. The fat man staggered backwards, fell awkwardly, cracked the back of his head against the wall and collapsed on the floor, groaning.

Without hesitating for a second, Pip jumped over the fat man's prone body and grabbed the bolt that was locking the front door. From the room above him he could hear noises. Shouting. Footsteps. Coming closer. He struggled with the bolt. It was stuck. "Come on," he whispered. "Come on!" He pulled harder, but the bolt refused to budge.

52

The Weasel rolled out of bed, completely naked, and sprang towards the open door.

His girlfriend sat up, pulling the blanket around herself, and said, "What's going on?"

The Weasel ignored her. Yelling a stream of threats and curses, he hurled himself down the stairs. When he reached the bottom, he found someone lying in a heap. But not the boy. Even in the darkness the Weasel could see immediately that the enormous body squashed into the hallway couldn't possibly belong to that skinny boy who'd just been in his bedroom. He kicked the fat man, trying to wake him up, and shouted: "Where is he? What have you done with him?"

The fat man just groaned.

"I don't believe it," muttered the Weasel. He grabbed the

bolt that was locking the front door and pulled. As usual, it was stuck. He pulled harder, forcing it with all his strength.

Had the Weasel taken a minute to think things through, he'd have realized that the intruder must still be inside the house. If anyone had gone outside, the bolt would already have been drawn. But he didn't bother thinking. He was too angry. Too upset. And still only half awake. All his available brain power was focused on finding that boy and causing him a lot of pain. He struggled with the bolt, pulling as hard as he could.

Suddenly the bolt slid across. The Weasel swung the front door open and charged into the street.

That was when he saw the bear.

He didn't immediately know that she was a bear. His confused brain just put together what he could actually see – the shaggy fur, the huge paws, the broken teeth – and warned him that there was some kind of monster standing in the street. What was that? A boy in a fur coat? No. An enormous dog? No. Some kind of exotic animal? Maybe. A bear? It looked like a bear. But why would a bear be standing in the street, right outside his house, in the middle of the night?

All these thoughts flashed through the Weasel's mind in the very brief moments before the bear raised herself on to her hind legs, and roared.

"GGRRROOOOAAAHHHH!"

The Weasel shrieked. If he'd been fully awake, armed and clothed, he might have known what to do. But he was confused, defenceless and completely naked. He stumbled backwards, trying to put some distance between himself and the bear . . .

. . . and a lump of timber thudded into his back.

Pip had been standing behind him, holding the timber like a two-handed sword and swinging it with all his strength.

The pain was astonishing. The Weasel cried out and fell to his knees.

Pip dropped the timber, dodged round the Weasel and grabbed Miranda's rope. Together they galloped down the street, him on two legs, her on four, running as fast as they'd ever run in their lives.

The Weasel knelt there, not moving, not even breathing, just watching the boy and the bear sprint away from him. A moment later they had disappeared into the gloom.

53

Spare a little thought, if you can, for Miranda.

As I'm sure you can remember, her life had not been easy. Things had started well, of course, and her first few months on earth had been as good an introduction to living as anyone could ask for, devoted entirely to eating, sleeping and wandering through the forest. Nothing could have been nicer. And then, unexpectedly, horrifically, a gang of brutal hunters had destroyed her happiness. One by one her family was murdered. She had been plucked from the freedom of the far distant north, transported across the waves and locked in prison.

Since then almost every day of her existence had been almost entirely miserable. Her teeth were filed down. Her claws were torn out. She was forced to fight dogs. She rarely smelt fresh air or drank clean water. She spent her days and nights inside a small, dark, damp cage with hardly enough room to lie fully outstretched. Deprived of decent food, her muscles shrank and her bones warped. On an ordinary day in the forest she might have eaten a swarm of moths, some maggots, a rabbit, two fish, six eggs, several pawfuls of honey and a selection of strawberries, raspberries, blueberries, bilberries, cranberries, cloudberries, lingonberries and whortleberries. In London she'd be lucky to get a few rotten vegetables or a ragged old bone, already picked clean of meat and cooked through twice in someone else's soup.

She knew who to blame for what had happened. Men. It was men who had done this to her. Men had slaughtered her mother, her brother and her sister. Men had dragged her out of the forest. Men had forced her to ride across the waves. And even after all they had done to her, men didn't stop mistreating her. One man had clasped a leather collar around her neck and thrust a silver ring through her nose. Another man had confined her inside a small cage with wooden bars, then forced her out of the cage every other day, led her to a large muddy field and made her fight a crowd of furious dogs.

Men had beaten her, tortured her and almost destroyed her. She had grown thin and weak. Her skin itched. Her fur was patchy. Her nostrils bled. Her eyes were sad and damp and downcast. Day by day, month by month, year by year, Miranda had come to accept that life was a misery that just had to be endured.

Now, to her astonishment, things had changed. Another

man had arrived unexpectedly in her life. Although he smelt as bad as the others, and spoke the same incomprehensible lingo of grunts, whistles and coughs, he was smaller and thinner than the rest of them. He seemed gentler too. And he often brought her honey, plums, cherries, cheese and other fine-tasting delicacies.

Food was not the only thing that Pip gave Miranda. There was something else too, something even more important.

He took her away from those ferocious dogs and removed her from the cage which had been her home for two years. He slept alongside her. He shared his own supper with her, halving his bread and herrings. In other words, he treated her more or less in the same way that he treated himself. And so, although she didn't trust him – she couldn't trust any man now and probably never would – she felt a curious kind of gratitude towards him. That was why she had allowed him to clamber on her back when he wanted to get inside the Weasel's house. And that was why she didn't bite his hand off when he tugged her rope, jerking her neck, and forced her to gallop alongside him through the streets of Southwark.

54

It was late at night, and he'd blown out his candle long ago, but George Stone was awake when they arrived.

The house felt different without the dogs and the bears, quieter and lonelier, and he was unable to sleep. The silence wasn't the only thing that kept him awake. He had a lot to think about too. Tonight might be his last night on earth. A few days ago he probably wouldn't have cared much about dying. Then, he hadn't had much to live for. That had all been changed by the arrival of his son.

For the past few years, George Stone had trained himself not to worry about Pip and almost succeeded. Most of the time, he managed to think of himself as being entirely alone in the world. Although he had a few colleagues, acquaintances and drinking companions, he had neither friends nor lovers, and he had never been tempted to marry again. The only living creatures that cared about him were the dogs and the bears, but he had no illusions about the reason that they did. As long as they were given enough food and water, they would hardly have noticed if he lived or died.

He had been lying on the floor, wrapped in an old blanket, burdened by thoughts of loss and failure and death, when he heard a great crash. He sat up. There was another crash, then the sound of voices and footsteps. He barely had time to throw aside the blanket before the first of them, the thin man with a scar spanning the length of his left cheek, burst into the room and said, "Don't you move!"

"I'm not moving," said George, clambering slowly to his feet and letting the blanket drop to the ground.

"I said, don't you move!"

"And I said, I'm not moving."

They stood opposite one another. If George had taken his chance at that moment and grabbed a knife, perhaps he could have fought his way out of trouble, but he was too dazed to lunge quickly, and then the moment was gone. While he stood there, wondering which way to turn, another man came into the room, and then two more, and so he stayed still, knowing he didn't have a chance against so many. Twenty years ago, when he was younger and fitter, he might have been able to fight four men on his own, but not now.

The Weasel was the last man to enter the room, but the first to talk. In a lazy tone, as if he didn't really care about the answer, he asked where he would find George's son.

"My son?" said George, trying to sound surprised. "Which son?"

The Weasel wasn't fooled. "Let's not play games. Earlier this evening your son broke into my house and tried to kill me. Where is he?"

"I don't know what you're talking about. If Pip's in London, he hasn't been to see his father."

"You're lying," said the Weasel. "I know you are."

"I swear to God, I'm telling the truth."

"I swear to the devil, you're lying. I know he's in London because I've seen him. And he had a bear with him. One of your bears, George. Now, let's make things easy for everyone. Where is he?"

"I've already told you," said George. "I haven't seen him for seven years."

In one swift movement the Weasel moved across the room and punched George in the face.

George stumbled backwards, clutching his jaw. "Ow," he said. "I think you've broken my tooth."

"If you don't tell me where your son is, I'll break a lot more than your teeth. Come on, where is he?"

"I've already told you," said George. "I don't know."

"Oh, George," said the Weasel in a soft voice, shaking his head slowly from side to side. "Do you realize how much this is going to hurt?"

"I've got a pretty good idea."

"Would you like to change your mind and tell us where he is?"

"As I keep saying, I don't know where—"

"Last chance," interrupted the Weasel.

"I wish I could," said George. "But I can't."

"I don't want to do this," said the Weasel. "But you're not giving me much choice." He nodded to his men.

They surrounded George Stone and started beating him, thumping him with their fists and boots, showing no mercy. They knocked him to the ground, kicked him and punched him, smothering every part of his body in pain. Just before they drove him into unconsciousness, the Weasel told them to stop. He leant down and put his face close to George's.

"This really is your last chance," whispered the Weasel. "I'm not even asking you to do anything difficult. Just tell me what I want to know. Where's your son?"

George Stone's nose was broken, two of his teeth had come loose and blood was trickling down his face, but he didn't care. Over the years he'd lost a lot of blood and several teeth, and his nose had been broken many times. He hissed, "I don't know."

"Very well," said the Weasel. He drew a knife from his belt and pressed the point into George's body, just about midway down his chest, nudging between two ribs. "Time to choose, George. Life or death."

"Get lost," said George.

The Weasel didn't say a word in response He just smiled and pushed his full weight down on the knife. The blade was so sharp, it cut quickly through George's shirt, dug into his skin and nestled between his ribs. And there, the

Weasel stopped, leaving the knife embedded in George's flesh, not wanting to kill him, just forcing him to endure the most appalling pain.

George's body arched in agony. His teeth clenched. Tears sprung from his eyes. But he didn't make a sound.

The Weasel whispered, "Well, George? Where is he?"

George said nothing.

The Weasel whispered, "Last chance."

And still George stayed quiet.

"I'm sorry," whispered the Weasel. "I don't want to do this." He pushed the blade very slowly into George's body. Before it had gone deeper than an inch George turned his head, unable to look the Weasel in the eye, and whispered, "Yes."

"What did you say?"

"Yes, I admit it. I've seen him."

The Weasel grinned triumphantly. "And you know where he is?"

"No," said George in a small, quiet voice. "I don't know where he is."

"Remember what I said, George. You have to tell the truth."

"It is the truth. He's in London. I've seen him. But I don't know where he is now."

"That isn't good enough, George."

There was a silence which lasted about five seconds, and then George hissed, "He's an actor."

"An actor?"

"Yes."

"Where?"

"I don't know."

"Of course you do. Where does he act? The Swan, the Rose, the Curtain – where?"

"He's an actor," whispered George. "He works in a theatre. Isn't that enough for you?"

"I suppose it is," said the Weasel. In a single sudden movement, he pulled his knife out of George's body, stood up straight and issued a brisk order to his men. "Let's go." He hurried towards the door, not wanting to waste another second.

"Boss?" Scar gestured at George. "What about him?"

"Leave him," said the Weasel. "He's not going anywhere. Come on! Quick!" He hurried out of the door, followed by his men.

When they had gone, George Stone lay on the floor, staring at the ceiling. Every part of his body ached, but the pain wasn't strong enough to bring him the unconsciousness that he craved. He knew what he'd done. Even worse, he knew he had chosen to do it. He had been given the choice between losing his life and betraying his son, and he had chosen betrayal. His own existence was worth nothing, he had known that for years, and yet, like the most disgusting coward, he had turned aside at the sight of death. In a life which had been full of mistakes, this was the worst. He lay there, crippled by self-hatred, hoping to die.

55

The night was quiet. The odd owl hooted, some foxes screeched and there were a few strange rustling sounds in the undergrowth, but Pip didn't hear either of the two sounds that he feared most: footsteps and voices. He hadn't been followed. Not yet anyway.

In the darkness Pip felt safe. No one would find him now. But dawn would be here soon. In daylight he and Miranda would be caught quickly and easily. They had nowhere to hide. Even in London, where the streets were packed with an apparently infinite variety of peculiar people and extraordinary creatures, a boy and a bear would soon be spotted. Someone would send a message to the Weasel. *You know that boy? The one with the bear? I can tell you exactly where he is. . .*

Pip looked at the sky, trying to decide how long he had. At the moment the full moon was shining brightly, glistening on the oily surface of the river, and the edges of the sky were still completely dark. Dawn wouldn't arrive for a few more hours.

How should he spend his last few hours on earth?

Trying to run? Searching for somewhere to hide? Thinking about his sins? Praying for forgiveness? Writing a letter to his mother and his sisters?

He didn't know what to do.

He looked at Miranda, hoping she might be able to make a suggestion, but she was no use at all. She was just lying beside him, her head resting on one of her front paws, staring at the river.

They were sitting beside the bank of the Thames, watching the water flow past. The tide was going out, carrying sticks and leaves and bits of rubbish towards the sea.

Pip had never seen the sea. He wondered if he ever would. Then he told himself to stop thinking like that.

I shouldn't be worrying about death, he thought. *I should be planning how to stay alive. But how do you think about staying alive when you're sure you're going to die?*

Pip looked at Miranda, wondering what she was thinking about and whether she might be able to help him. He'd like to ask her advice. She'd probably been faced with death many times. She must have seen bears die. Dogs too. Probably even people. Every time that she was taken to the Bear Garden and forced to fight, she probably thought she was going to die. So what did she do? Facing the possibility of her own death, what had she thought about?

She turned her head and stared back at him.

For some time, neither the boy nor the bear made a sound. They just peered into one another's eyes as if they were searching for something, although Pip certainly wouldn't have been able to say what he was searching for, and I don't suppose Miranda could have done either.

Pip broke the silence. He whispered, "What are we going to do?"

Of course, he knew she wasn't going to answer him. Bears can't talk. Not even the most intelligent bear in the world can speak a single word of English.

So why did Pip talk to Miranda? Because he had the strange feeling that, even if she couldn't speak to him, she could still understand exactly what he was saying.

"We can't stay here," said Pip. "But I don't know where else to go."

He sighed.

"Wherever we go, the Weasel's going to find us. When he does, he won't hesitate. Not like me. He won't worry about right and wrong. He'll just kill us."

He reached down to his belt and touched his father's knife, remembering the moment when he had stood over the Weasel, poised to kill him. If he'd done it then, he'd be safe now. But he'd also be a murderer. He would be no better than the Weasel.

To stop a murderer, Pip thought, *you have to become a murderer. But I couldn't. So now I'm going to get murdered.*

Miranda stared at Pip. She didn't make a sound. And yet, in a way, she did answer him. She stared at him with an expression of complete calm. Her black eyes showed no sign of panic. Not even nervousness. She seemed to be saying: we'll be fine.

Pip hoped she was right.

Looking into her steady black eyes he began to believe that she was.

"Let's go to the Globe," he said, answering his own question. "If we lock the door, they won't be able to get in. We can sleep till dawn. When Cuthbert arrives, we'll talk to him. We can ask him to help us." With each word that Pip spoke, he felt more confident. "Cuthbert knows a lot of people. He'll find a way for us to get out of London. You know what? He could put us on a boat. We can go to France. No – we can go to Venice. We'll find Inigo Jones. Or we can go to the New World. Wherever we go, we'll keep moving. The Weasel will never find us."

Pip hadn't quite managed to convince himself, but the idea of travelling round the world sounded good. He'd like to see France and Venice and the New World. He felt much better. And then he felt much worse. Staring at the bear, he suddenly realized that he was doing it again. Exactly what he'd done before. He was making her life more difficult and more dangerous.

He whispered: "You don't have to come with me."

She was still staring at him, calmly and blankly, giving nothing away. He reached out his right hand and touched her warm flank with the tips of his fingers.

"I'm sorry," he whispered. "I should have left you where you were. Locked up in the cage. At least you'd still be safe."

Pip paused, as if he was waiting for Miranda to respond, and then he whispered: "Come with me if you want. Or don't. You can choose."

This time he really hoped that she might make some kind of signal. Raise her paw. Shake her head. Even sneeze. But she didn't do anything.

Pip stood up.

Miranda stared at him.

Her eyes looked different now. There was an expression in them that Pip couldn't understand.

He could have hugged her, tickled her ears or stroked her fur. He could have told her that she was his best friend. Or he could have picked up the rope that was tied to her collar and tugged it, forcing her to follow him. But he didn't do any of those things. Instead he just said, "Bye." Then he turned his back on her and walked away.

He was desperate to look over his shoulder and see what she was doing, but he made himself stare straight ahead.

It was Miranda's decision. He wanted the choice to be hers and hers alone. So he kept walking, never looking back.

Miranda raised herself on to her hind legs and stood upright. Turning her head from side to side she peered through the gloom, letting her eyes wander over the river, the trees, the houses and Pip.

Lifting her head, closing her eyes and wrinkling her

nostrils, she took several deep breaths, drawing the city's air through her nose and deep into her lungs. Each breath provided her with a vast amount of information about her environment, telling her all about the people, the animals, the food and the vegetation that surrounded her.

A bear's nostrils are astonishingly sensitive. If the wind is blowing in the right direction a bear can smell food from several miles away. She can tell what it is. She'll know if it's alive or dead, good to eat or horribly rotten. She can even follow the scent back to its source, finding exactly where its coming from, tracking it for miles through the countryside.

Right now Miranda was almost overwhelmed by the amazing variety of scents that assaulted her nostrils from every direction. She could smell cows and sheep, trout and lamb, sparrows and parrots, pears and plums, mushrooms and marrows, honey and pepper, saffron and cinnamon, all the smells of a city that held not just thousands of houses but hundreds of ships which had sailed here from all around the globe.

Sniffing the air, she peered at the nearby houses and trees, trying to decide which way to go and what to do.

A new world was opening to her. A world that had been hidden for the past two years. During that time, while she languished behind the bars of her cage, her world had shrunk. Now it felt big again. For the first time since she wandered through the forest as a cub, she was smelling freedom. And not just smelling it. Hearing it, seeing it and tasting it too.

She could have done anything. She could have plunged into the river for a midnight swim. She could have gone down to the docks and tried to board a boat. She could have sauntered round the houses, broken down a door or searched in the rubbish heaps, and scavenged some of that delicious-smelling food. Or she could have curled in a heap under a tree and had a nice quiet snooze till dawn.

Instead she dropped down on to all fours and set off at a quick trot, the rope trailing along the grass behind her.

When she reached Pip, he glanced at her for a moment and allowed himself a small smile. Then he concentrated all his attention on the shadows ahead, searching for any sign of his enemies.

56

That night The White Swan was packed. Whenever the door opened, people turned to see who had arrived. But when a thin man in smart clothes came through the door, no one waved, shouted or called for a beer to be poured for their friend. Instead, several actors went pale and several more turned their faces to the wall, trying to hide.

They all knew the Weasel. Not just because he was a notorious thief and bully. No, many of them had a much more intimate knowledge of his business: they had borrowed money from him. Which was why none of them wanted to be seen by him.

When the Weasel opened his mouth and shouted a name across the pub, all of them breathed a sigh of relief and turned back to their conversations. All except one.

"Eccles!" shouted the Weasel. "Eccles!"

When William Eccles heard his name being shouted across The White Swan, he stood absolutely still for a second, rigid with panic. Then he thrust his beer into a friend's hand and rushed towards the back door, pushing people aside and ducking under outstretched arms.

If he could just get to the door, thought William Eccles, he would be safe. The Weasel would catch him eventually, he knew that. He couldn't keep running for ever. But he just didn't want it to happen today.

He reached the back door. Glancing over his shoulder, he saw the Weasel several feet away, trapped between two fat drinkers. He'd done it! He'd escaped! He would live to fight another day! He opened the door and sprinted into the cold air of the street . . .

. . . straight into the waiting arms of Scar and Tooth.

"Oh, look," said Scar. "It's our friend Eccles."

"What a nice coincidence," said Tooth. "You're just the man we're looking for."

"I-I-I have to go," stammered William Eccles.

"Don't worry," said Scar. "It won't take long."

"We'll be quick," said Tooth.

And they were right; it didn't take long. A moment later the Weasel emerged from the pub and strolled down the street to his men, who had thrown William Eccles against the wall. They held him there. When he saw the Weasel coming towards him William Eccles started speaking very quickly. "I promise, I'll get your money. I promise. You have to believe me, I'm telling the truth.

Please, don't hit me."

"I'm not going to hit you," said the Weasel.

"You're not?"

"No."

"Oh." William Eccles smiled. Then he suddenly looked suspicious. "Why not?"

"I want some information. If you tell me what I want to know, I'll forget what you owe me."

"Forget it? Completely?"

"I'll wipe the slate clean."

William Eccles grinned. "What do you want to know?"

"I'm looking for someone. I think he might be an actor. I want you to tell me who he is and where he is."

"If he's an actor, I'll know him. What's his name?"

The Weasel started to describe what he knew about Pip.

William Eccles interrupted him. "You mean the bearkeeper's son?"

"That's exactly who I mean," said the Weasel.

"Sure, I know him. His name's Pip. He'll be in the Globe."

"Now? At this time of night?"

"That's where he sleeps." William Eccles described precisely where Pip made his bed, explaining that the Burbage brothers had given Pip a key and allowed him to sleep in the theatre.

"Thank you," said the Weasel. He nodded to his men. "Come on." They hurried down the alleyway in the direction of the Globe.

William Eccles stood there for a second, watching them go. A big grin slowly spread across his face. He couldn't believe what had just happened. His debts were gone! He was free! He went back into The White Swan, summoned the landlord and ordered a round of drinks for everyone.

57

Pip couldn't breathe.

He was being suffocated. Someone was trying to kill him.

He opened his eyes but he couldn't see a thing. They'd covered his face with a blanket.

He was just about to start struggling with all his strength, fighting for his life, when he realized that the blanket was the bear's fur. In the night they must have rolled together and hugged, huddling side by side for warmth.

He sat up.

Beside him, Miranda was standing on all fours, her head raised, her ears perked up, her mouth open. She hadn't been hugging him. She had been pushing his face with one of her front paws. Maybe she wanted to play.

Pip whispered, "What's going on?"

The bear glanced at him, then looked away and growled.

"GRRRRRR."

Pip could hear another sound too. Footsteps on the stairs. He slowly raised his head above the balcony and looked down at the theatre. The moonlight was still strong enough to cast clear shadows. From here he could see the stage, the pit, the other galleries and the staircases which connected them. On the opposite side of the Globe, four men were nearing the top of the stairs.

The front gate hadn't presented them with any problems. Scar had been picking locks like that since he was nine years old. Now they were hurrying to the uppermost gallery, following the instructions that they'd been given by William Eccles.

They were being very careful to make as little noise as possible. If Pip had been alone he'd never have heard them. He would have carried on sleeping until they climbed all the way to the top gallery and caught him without a struggle. He owed his life to Miranda.

Of course, that might not mean much. He probably wasn't going to be alive much longer.

He looked up and down the gallery, trying to think of a plan.

A boy against four grown men.

What did he have to help him? A knife, a blanket and a small brown bear. He wondered whether Miranda would be much help. Probably not. The blanket should offer a little protection. But the knife – his father's knife – yes, that short, sharp knife might just save his life.

He wrapped the blanket tightly around his left forearm, making a very basic shield, then drew his knife and watched the four men emerging from the staircase.

One of them spotted him and alerted the others. They conferred briefly, then came towards him. In the moonlight Pip could clearly distinguish their familiar silhouettes: Scar's skinny frame; Pigface's bulk; Tooth's muscular shoulders; and, hurrying ahead of the others, the unmistakable profile of the Weasel.

58

The Weasel was the first to see the bear. He had been trotting along the gallery, a smile on his lips and a sword in his hand, ready for action, when he realized that the boy wasn't alone.

At that moment the bear raised herself on to her hind legs, lifted her front paws into the air, opened her mouth and roared.

"GROOOOOOOOOOAAAAAAAAAH!"

The sound echoed around the Globe. Under the stage, mice froze. On the roof, the owl took flight. In the middle of the pit, the marmalade cat hissed. On the top gallery, the four men stood still, staring at the boy and the bear.

Scar was the first to speak. He said, "I don't like the look of that."

"Me neither," said Tooth. "Nasty vicious creatures, bears."

"Shut up, both of you," said the Weasel. "It's only a cub. Nothing to be frightened of."

As far as Scar and Tooth were concerned, a bear, even a small bear, was definitely something to be frightened of, but neither of them wanted to admit that, so they kept quiet, waiting to see what the Weasel would do next.

The bear must have sensed their fear, because she took a step forward, shook her head violently from side to side, then roared again. "GROOOOOOOOOAAAAA AAAH!"

Scar and Tooth glanced at their boss and, hoping he wouldn't notice, took a step back. Pigface sheltered behind them.

Seeing what they'd done, the Weasel smiled. He might have been shocked by the bear when he was naked and defenceless, but he felt much stronger now, dressed in his best leather breeches and armed with a long sharp sword. He wasn't scared of anything or anyone. Especially not a small brown bear. He'd been to the Bear Garden a hundred times and seen how the bearkeeper dealt with them. Swinging his sword back and forth through the air, he advanced down the gallery, shouting as he went. "Yah! Yah! Yaaaaaaaaahhh!"

Miranda took a step backwards, then another. She knew how much a sword could hurt. When the metal was swinging so close that it almost touched her, she dropped on to all fours, turned round, dodged past Pip and ran down to the end of the gallery. There she crouched on the ground, her back against the wall, watching the men with wary eyes.

Now Pip was on his own. Although Miranda had deserted him, he wasn't cross with her, nor even surprised by her behaviour. Why should she risk her her life to save his? The Weasel meant nothing to her; he hadn't robbed *her* family or threatened to kill *her* father. This battle was Pip's, not Miranda's, and he should fight it alone.

Here they came, the Weasel first, the others just behind. Walking in unison, their swords raised, the four of them marched down the gallery.

As the four swishing blades came closer, Pip did what he could to protect himself, dodging from side to side and blocking blows with the knife or the blanket, but neither offered much protection. The small knife was knocked sideways by any half-decent swipe. The blanket was quickly slashed to pieces; it slithered from his forearm and fell to the ground. A blade sliced his arm. Another chopped his shoulder. Pip started to panic. Against four swords he didn't stand a chance. If he stood here, trying to fight, he would be cut to pieces. But what else could he do? Where could he go? There was only one possible direction. He leapt sideways. Four swords skewered the spot where he had just been standing.

Pip landed on the balcony with both feet. Momentum sent his body forward, threatening to hurl him over the edge and into the void. He flung his arms out to either side and just managed to keep his balance. When he was standing steadily he turned round to face his enemies . . .

. . . and saw all four of them charging towards him. The

Weasel came first and fastest, his sword already swinging through the air.

Pip realized immediately that his situation was even worse than before. He was balancing on a narrow balcony, forty or fifty feet above the ground. If he fell backwards he'd break his neck. If he leapt forward he'd plunge on to the swords of his attackers. If he stayed here he'd be cut in half. In other words it was time to say his prayers. But he didn't have a chance to say anything before a length of cold steel swept through the air, heading for his knees.

Pip jumped as high as he could, drawing up his legs, letting the sword travel under his feet, then landed back on the balcony.

"Very good," said the Weasel with a smile. He looked as if he was enjoying himself. "But not quite good enough." He raised his sword again and this time thrust directly forward, pointing at Pip's heart.

Pip sprang to the left. The blade cut a long gash in his shirt, but missed his skin.

Gripping the sword with both hands the Weasel drew the blade back, then swung it again.

This time Pip didn't have enough time to be clever or enough space to be athletic. There was only one thing to do. Only one way to go. He hurled himself off the balcony and plummeted towards the ground.

The Weasel yelled furiously at Scar and Tooth. "Get him! Get him!" They sped round the gallery, heading for the staircase. As Pigface waddled after them, the Weasel stopped him. "You stay here. Guard that bear."

"Why me?" said Pigface. "Why can't I—"

"Just do it!"

"Fine," said Pigface.

The Weasel looked over the balcony. Down in the pit, the boy was sprawled in the mud. He didn't seem to be moving. Not even breathing. Maybe he'd been knocked out by the fall. *With any luck*, thought the Weasel, *he's dead already*. Only one way to find out. Sprinting after his men, he ran round the gallery and down the stairs.

59

George Stone was lying on the floor. Something was licking his face. Something warm. Something wet. Something with terrible breath.

He opened his eyes.

A dog was licking his face.

"Hello, Snapper," whispered George.

The spaniel wagged her tail.

Using the wall as a support, George slowly hauled himself into an upright position. He looked around the room, staring at the appalling mess, then touched his face, feeling for broken bones. When he'd spoken to the dog his jaw had hurt. Come to think of it, just about everything hurt.

He couldn't understand what was going on. Not only did everything hurt, but his home seemed to have been torn apart by a tempest. The table and the two stools had been smashed to pieces. The walls and the floor were splashed with blood. Whose blood? His?

He turned to Snapper and said, "What happened?"

The spaniel didn't reply. She just stared at him with wide eyes, then darted forward and licked his hand.

Looking at her, George suddenly remembered what had happened yesterday. More than that: he guessed what Snapper was doing here. The Weasel had taken the bears and the dogs to the market. The bears would have sold immediately, and he'd have found buyers for the sleek hounds and the sturdy mastiffs without too much trouble, but Snapper would have been trickier to shift. The only people who bought spaniels were rich ladies who wanted a cute little doggie to hug on their laps, but no lady would look twice at Snapper. Not with her torn ears, her battle-scarred muzzle and her scrappy coat, pockmarked with half-healed scabs and misshapen patches of missing fur. Unable to sell her, the Weasel must have turned her loose.

"Good dog," whispered George, tickling Snapper's ears. She might not be the most beautiful spaniel in the world, but she was certainly intelligent. All alone, she'd managed to negotiate the streets of London and find her own way back home. "You're a very clever dog, aren't you?"

Snapper's tail wagged furiously.

With each second that George was conscious, more memories came flooding back. He remembered the Weasel coming here again with his men. The questions. The beating. The pain. The knife sliding between his ribs.

His own absolute refusal to say a word. And then, just as he was beginning to feel proud of himself for staying silent and keeping a secret, he remembered that he hadn't.

Pip was in danger.

George tried to lift himself up but his feet wouldn't take his weight and he fell immediately, crumpling on to the floor.

Snapper jumped backwards and stood in the middle of the room, staring at her master.

George tried again. He grabbed the wall, using it for support, and hauled himself to his feet. The effort exhausted him. He'd lost a lot of blood. He waited there for a moment, cursing and catching his breath. When he'd gathered his strength he pushed himself forward once more. Pausing only to grab a knife and tuck it into his belt, he hobbled towards the door. Snapper followed at his heels. Together, the man and the dog stumbled down the street and headed for the Globe.

60

Falling was like being free.

Without a thought in his head Pip whistled through the air, his arms and legs outstretched, and everything felt good.

The only problem was landing. He would have been happy to carry on falling for ever, but the ground soon reared up and met him. The breath was knocked from his body. He lay there stunned, unable to move, wondering whether he might be dead.

No, he was definitely alive. If he'd been dead, all the different parts of his body wouldn't be hurting so much. Nor would he have been able to hear the shouts and footsteps of the men who were coming to kill him.

Time to go. *Quick*, he told himself. *Quick, quick. Move, move. Or I really will be dead.* He rolled over and forced himself to his feet. His legs moaned in protest. Tomorrow his skin would be covered with bruises. If he was still here tomorrow.

Here they came. The three killers. Pip hobbled in the opposite direction. Gaining speed with every step, he darted across the pit and hauled himself on to the stage. The men were just behind him. He could hear their footsteps, their curses, their breathing.

In the centre of the stage Pip turned to face his opponents. He could have kept running, but he wouldn't have got far. He didn't intend to die with a sword in his back. No, he wanted to die like a soldier. Like a man. Staring into his killer's eyes.

The three men clambered on to the stage and surrounded Pip.

Pip turned on the spot, glancing at each of them in turn, wondering who would come for him first.

Three against one. Three swords against one dagger. Three men against one boy.

He didn't have a chance. In a minute or two he would be dead. He felt scared, although he wasn't sure which actually scared him most: fighting, dying or suffering all the different pains which would surely be inflicted on him in the next few moments. Probably the pain. He didn't mind fighting. Dying shouldn't hurt. And it would be interesting to see where he ended up, heaven or hell, after he died. But pain. . . He was definitely frightened by the thought of enduring yet more pain.

What do you do when you know that you're about to die? How do you spend your last few seconds on earth?

Some people weep. Others beg for mercy. If you're worried about the reception that you're going to get from God, you say a prayer, confessing your sins and asking for forgiveness. Or you just close your eyes, breathe deeply and wait to see what will happen next.

Pip didn't do any of these things. There was a small chance – a very, very small chance – that he might be able to survive, if he was brave and fought well and, most importantly, got lucky. He watched the three men, remembering what he knew. The more you have learnt about your opponent, the better you can fight him. You must watch him constantly. Study him. Search for his weaknesses. He stared at Scar, Tooth and the Weasel, wondering if there was any way that he could fight all three of them at once and win.

He didn't have to wait long to find out. After a few seconds of inaction the Weasel nodded to Tooth, then to Scar. Together, all three men raised their swords and advanced.

The Weasel lunged first.

Pip ducked, avoiding the blow.

As he raised himself from the ground, Scar's sword flew through the air and sliced a long gash along his chest.

Yelling in agony, Pip stumbled. It was lucky that he did. If he had been standing upright Tooth's sword would have run straight between his shoulder blades. Instead, it nicked his forearm. Pip yelled again, this time with fury rather than pain, and rammed his body backwards.

"Owf!" The breath was knocked out of Tooth's lungs.

Pip flung his right arm behind him and stabbed with his dagger, hoping to connect with some part of Tooth's body.

"Aiieee!" The blade sliced the length of Tooth's forehead, opening a long wound. Blinded by the curtain of blood running down his face, Tooth didn't have a chance to see the foot which slammed between his legs.

"Uuuhh!" Gasping in agony, Tooth fell to the ground.

George Stone could see four men fighting on the stage.

Three men, actually, and a boy.

George lurched through the pit, ignoring the agony shrieking from every nerve in his body, and headed for the stage. The spaniel ran alongside him, yapping.

Pip whirled on the spot, checking the other two men.

They were standing still, considering their tactics.

The odds had hardly improved. A boy against two men doesn't have much more chance than a boy against three men.

He had nowhere to run. He raised his dagger and looked at each of the two men in turn, trying to decide who to attack first.

Before he could reach a decision he received some unexpected assistance. A shape flashed across the stage and attached itself to the Weasel's ankle.

The Weasel sprang into the air, shaking his foot and howling in agony. The spaniel might have been a small dog with shaggy fur and droopy ears, but she had a full set of sharp teeth.

This was better. One against one. Pip charged at Scar.

Scar watched him coming.

A kid with a knife. Against a man with a sword.

No contest.

Scar grinned, lifted his sword and stepped forward for the kill.

Tooth rolled across the stage, roaring with fury. The pain was appalling. But the humiliation was even worse. He wasn't going to be defeated by a boy. Not him. No chance. He rolled over once more and put his hands flat on the stage. He was just about to push himself upright when George Stone fell on top of him.

Tooth was pinned to the stage, unable to move. He yelled, "Gerroff! Or I'll rip your—"

But we'll never know what he was going to rip, because that was the last word he ever spoke. He groaned quietly, then slumped on to the stage, a knife wedged in his heart.

Shaking his leg backwards and forward, the Weasel dislodged the spaniel. As she whirled round, her mouth open, coming back for a second attempt, he delivered a vicious kick to her middle.

With a shocked yelp the spaniel flew through the air, bounced twice on the wooden boards, rolled over and came to rest at the edge of the stage.

The Weasel lifted his sword and turned round. The smile had faded from his face. This wasn't fun any more. Now he just wanted to kill the boy as quickly as possible.

Scar knew exactly what he was doing. An experienced fighter like himself would never be outwitted by a kid. He stood his ground as Pip ran towards him. At the last possible moment, just before Pip reached him, he lunged with his sword.

Pip chose exactly the same moment to shimmer sideways, dodging past the blade.

Scar slashed the air again and Pip dodged the other way.

Holding his sword with both hands, Scar chopped the air like an axeman swiping at a big old tree.

This tree moved. Pip dropped to the floor. The sword whistled over his head. Pip jumped forward and, thrusting with all his strength, buried his father's dagger in the middle of Scar's belly.

"Oh," said Scar. He blinked and dropped his sword.

Pip pulled the dagger out of Scar's stomach and turned round. He didn't see Scar sinking to the ground, both hands clasped around his middle, trying to dam the stream of blood. He hardly even heard the low, desperate moan that seeped from Scar's mouth. He had forgotten Scar already. All his attention was focused on the only man still standing.

They stared at one another.

Pip had just killed a man, but he didn't think about that. Later, if he was still alive, he could worry about being a murderer and what that meant to him. For now, he only had enough space in his mind for one idea. How to fight the Weasel.

A boy against a man. A knife against a sword. The odds certainly weren't even. But one against one is always better than one against three. Pip felt more confident. Maybe he'd survive. He raised himself to his full height and stepped forward.

He had practised for this moment over and over again, standing in the heart of the woods, conjuring up opponents, watching them emerge from the trees, walk into the clearing and take up their position opposite him. Just as he had always imagined, he was armed with his father's knife. He advanced, waving his dagger through the air, ready to put his training to good use.

Pip and the Weasel exchanged a few blows, the knife clashing against the sword, nothing serious, just enough to try one another out, and then, without any warning, the Weasel darted forward and lunged at full length. His sword dug into Pip's thigh.

Pip screamed and staggered backwards. He couldn't believe how much his leg hurt. But he didn't have time to think about that. Already, the Weasel was attacking again, this time hacking rather than lunging, digging his sword into Pip's shoulder.

Pip screamed again, louder, then looked down at his body. Blood was leaking on to the stage. He lifted his head and saw the Weasel advancing on him. What could he do? How could he save himself? He raised his right hand, hoping his knife might offer some protection, but it didn't.

The Weasel's sword flashed through the air, left and right and left again, each blow clashing against Pip's dagger, and then thrice more, left and right and left again. The last blow sent a jarring pain along the entire length of Pip's arm, reverberating from his wrist to his elbow, and he dropped his knife. The blade clattered on the floorboards. Before Pip had a chance to pick it up again the Weasel was advancing on him, chopping and cutting, covering Pip's arms and legs with nicks and bruises, forcing Pip backwards, further and further away from his knife.

None of Pip's rehearsals had prepared him for this. He didn't know what to do. Without a weapon, he could only try to avoid being stabbed. Darting to one side, then the other, he retreated with every step, leaving a trail of scarlet spots on the wooden boards, until he tripped over his own feet, fell over and sprawled helplessly on the stage.

The Weasel allowed himself a quick smile. With two swift paces he was standing above Pip.

There was no hurry. No need to take any chances. Steadying himself for one final attack the Weasel gripped the sword with both hands, then swung.

His blade whistled through the air.

This is the end, thought Pip. *This is what it means to die.*

At that moment a figure leapt across the stage and flung himself in front of the Weasel's sword.

61

Pip rolled aside, surprised to find himself alive, but not waiting to find out how or why. He scrambled across the stage, grabbed his knife and turned round to see who had saved him. He'd thought it must have been Miranda, but the inert shape curled at the Weasel's feet was definitely a man, not a bear. George Stone had taken the full force of the blow. For the second time in his life, Pip owed his existence to his father.

The Weasel stepped over the body and strode forward.

Pip stood very still. Holding his knife with a firm grip, he waited for his enemy. Now he was no longer nervous. He felt completely calm. He knew what his father had done: sacrificed his life to save his son's. Now Pip was ready to repay the debt.

Until this moment, Pip had merely been struggling to

save his own life. He hadn't wanted to murder anyone. If he'd been given the opportunity to run away with Miranda rather than fight, he would have taken it immediately.

Things were different now. He wasn't fighting for himself and he no longer cared whether he lived or died. That made him very dangerous.

A strange kind of confidence filled him, unlike anything that he had ever felt before, pushing aside pain, fear or any other emotion which might have caused him to hesitate. He knew exactly what he wanted to do and he was determined to do it. Nothing was going to stop him.

The Weasel wasn't conscious that anything was different. He was simply impatient for the fight to be over. He'd had enough. Striding across the stage, he thrust his sword through the air and lunged at full length.

Pip jumped to the right, avoiding the blade.

The Weasel lunged again and Pip jumped to the left.

The Weasel lunged once more, but Pip was too quick for him, dodging backwards. For the third time, the sword missed him.

It shouldn't have happened like this. A grown man versus a skinny boy, an experienced killer versus a child, a sword versus a knife – no one would put money on that.

But this particular boy refused to be beaten. He dodged and ducked, jumped and ran, avoiding every swing of the sword, keeping himself just beyond the blade's reach.

And now the boy darted forward, his arm outstretched, and drove his dagger into the Weasel's left arm.

"Ow!" cried the Weasel. He whirled round, his sword raised, and stabbed at the place where the boy had just been standing.

Somehow the boy was already six paces away, waiting and watching, his dagger clutched in his fist. A few drops of blood dribbled from the blade's tip.

The Weasel swung his sword.

Pip ducked and leapt to the side.

The Weasel swung again. This time the sword clipped Pip's shoulder, knocking him off balance.

The blow hurt, but Pip didn't notice it. Pain seemed to have lost its ability to affect him. He felt calm and oddly relaxed, as if he were sitting in the audience, observing his own predicament, rather than standing on the stage, experiencing it. He straightened up again and faced his enemy.

The Weasel was already stepping forward, gripping his sword with both hands, preparing to deliver the final blow. In one swift, sudden movement he twirled his sword through the air and brought the blade crashing down on the top of Pip's head, right between his eyes, slicing his skull in half.

Or rather, he brought his sword down on the place where Pip's head had just been. By the time the sword got there, Pip had already swerved aside, letting the blade plunge past him and thump down on to the wooden stage. The force of the impact threw the Weasel off balance, which allowed Pip to dart forward and drive his knife across the Weasel's fist.

"Agghh!" cried the Weasel. The blade ripped his knuckles, carving through the skin of all four fingers. He couldn't keep hold of his sword. It fell from his hand and clanged on the stage.

Pip was the first to react. He sprang forward, transferring his dagger from his right hand to his left, and grabbed the sword.

Now their positions were reversed. Pip held a sword and a dagger. The Weasel had nothing. No, not nothing. Like all the best warriors, he kept one weapon in reserve. He reached into his belt and pulled out a long, slim knife with a serrated blade.

They wove around the stage, watching one another.

The Weasel knew he had to make a choice: fight or flee. He chose to fight. Grasping the knife in his right hand he ran forward, screaming at the top of his voice.

The Weasel was a big man. He had mad eyes. Confronted by him, most people would have turned and run.

Not Pip.

He stepped to one side, avoiding the knife, then drove his sword into the middle of the Weasel's chest. The blade shuddered for a moment, meeting resistance, then plunged through layers of cloth and flesh, sliding between a pair of ribs and puncturing a lung.

The Weasel stumbled to a standstill. He blinked and looked down at his shirt with an expression of astonishment. Where had that sword come from? Why was it sticking out of his middle? Gripping the blade with both hands he tugged, but the sword didn't budge. Blood frothed through his fingers. The Weasel dropped to his knees, swaying gently from side to side, then toppled backwards and lay on the stage, staring at the sky.

When people died in plays they usually spoke a few final words, asking forgiveness for their bad deeds or begging to be remembered kindly by those who survived them. The Weasel didn't do any of that. He just shuddered, gurgled and gasped for breath. A pool of blood spread across the stage, soaking into the wooden planks.

Pip stood very still, his hands by his sides.

He knew he should feel guilty. He should go and help the Weasel. Even if the dying man was beyond help, he should offer him some comfort in his last moments on earth.

Love thy enemies. That was what Jesus said. And Jesus was right about most things.

But I don't love my enemy, thought Pip. *I hate him.*

And then Pip remembered his father.

62

Mice and rats emerged from the shadows. An owl swooped through the gloom. A marmalade cat padded along a balcony. A fat man walked slowly down the stairs from the top gallery to the pit.

Just as the Weasel had ordered, Pigface had stayed at the far end of the top gallery, guarding the bear. Well, that's not quite true. In actual fact, he had stood about fifteen feet away from the bear, hoping she wouldn't come any closer. Every now and then the fat man and the bear each gave the other a nervous glance.

Neither of them wanted any trouble.

At first Pigface had enjoyed watching the fight, but the smile had slowly faded from his face. As each of his friends was killed, his unease turned to fear.

When the fighting finished, Pigface came down from

the gallery and walked across the pit. He knew exactly what he ought to do now. Stride across the stage and finish off the boy, making sure he was dead. That would serve as some small measure of revenge for the deaths of his friends.

Instead he headed out of the theatre and went home. As another fat man once said, the better part of valour is discretion. In other words: why die if you don't have to? In the house, he grabbed as much money as he could carry, then left London.

Some time later, the bear came down from the gallery.

Around the theatre, other creatures gazed at her. All of them – the mice, the rats, the owl, the marmalade cat and the spaniel – were wary of the bear, knowing their lives could be ended with one swipe of her paws.

They needn't have worried. Miranda was a peace-loving bear and she had no intention of killing anyone. She lay down on the stage, not far from Pip, placed one paw on top of the other and rested her head on both of them. A moment later she was asleep.

Pip didn't even notice her. Nor did he see the spaniel, who came and curled up on his other side. As the moon sank, and the sky turned from black to blue, Pip remained entirely oblivious to his surroundings, sitting cross-legged on the stage, cradling his father's limp head on his lap, all his attention focused on his father's face.

63

As the first rays of sunlight were creeping into the sky, Cuthbert Burbage left his lodgings and hurried through the streets of London, heading for the Globe. Today he was planning get to work even earlier than usual, because today was a very important day. For the first time in its history, the company would be performing a play which featured not just actors, dancers, singers and musicians but a real live bear. Cuthbert was determined that this afternoon's show should be a success.

Outside the theatre he stopped, confused. Although he was unusually early, someone else had arrived before him. The gate was open. Suddenly nervous, wondering if the theatre had been robbed or vandalized, Cuthbert hurried into the Globe. Once inside he was greeted by a horrible sight.

Within these walls Cuthbert had watched hundreds of tragedies. He'd witnessed hangings, poisonings, garrottings, disembowellings, amputations and just about every other imaginable variety of violence, but he'd never seen anything like this. The theatre was splashed and smeared with half-dried blood. A contorted body was spreadeagled across the pit, leaking guts and goo. Another corpse dangled over the edge of the stage. A third lay flat on the wooden boards, a sword sticking upright in the middle of his belly. Nearby, two more bodies, a man and a boy, were huddled in a heap, as if they'd wanted to face death together, taking some kind of comfort from one another's presence.

Cuthbert walked slowly round the theatre, trying to reconstruct what must have happened. He peered at the corpses. One of them he definitely recognized. Another looked vaguely familiar. As for the boy. . .

"Oh, my God," whispered Cuthbert.

The boy was alive! His clothes were drenched in blood. His arms and face too. He didn't have the strength to lift his head. But Pip was definitely still breathing.

Cuthbert locked the main gate, preventing any passers-by from wandering into the Globe, then hurried through the streets to his brother's house and roused him. Together they summoned more help and returned to the theatre.

While the bodies were carted away and the stage was washed clean, Pip was taken to Robert Armin's house and put to bed.

There was no need to hold an inquest into the death of the

Weasel. When he was alive no one would have dared say a word against him, but that changed as soon as he was dead. People talked freely, informing the authorities all about his illegal activities. When the Weasel's house was searched, piles of stolen property were discovered alongside evidence linking the gang to seventeen unsolved murders. By killing the Weasel, the authorities decided, Pip had done a public service.

A few days later, reports arrived in London that a gang had been robbing travellers on the Great North Road. All the victims agreed on one fact: they had never seen a man as fat as the gang's leader.

The trail of robberies headed north and stopped somewhere near Newcastle. There, who knows what happened. Pigface might have picked a fight with the wrong Geordie and died in a pub brawl. Or perhaps he settled down and become an honest man. Whatever he did, and however he lived or died, he was never seen again within the walls of London.

For the first day or two Pip didn't know where he was. He wondered if he might be dead. Was this heaven? Or hell? He'd never imagined either of them would look like this: a small room, a window, strange people standing at the end of his bed. He had the feeling that he recognized some of their faces and voices, but he wasn't sure where he knew them from. He tried to ask them, but his voice didn't seem to work, and all the different pains in all the different parts of his body soon overwhelmed him, dragging him back into a feverish darkness, full of weird hallucinations.

Sleep cured him. That and the delicious chicken soup cooked by Robert Armin's housekeeper. By the third day he was able to sit up and talk coherently to his visitors. Cuthbert Burbage visited two or three times a day. Richard Burbage, William Shakespeare, Nathan Field and Molly Plunkett came when they could. Best of all, every morning and evening, Robert Armin spent hours sitting beside his bed, keeping Pip entertained by reciting speeches from all the plays that he'd acted in.

Outside Pip's bedroom, the bear and the spaniel were tied to posts on opposite sides of the yard. They hurled themselves across the yard at one another, trying to fight, or perhaps just play, but their ropes were so short that they couldn't reach. Robert wanted to put them somewhere else, but Pip begged him to leave them. "They're not disturbing me," he said. So Robert left them there, right below Pip's window, close enough that he could shout to them from his bed. "Hello, Miranda," he called out. "Good morning, Snapper." They answered him with a chorus of yaps and growls.

Later Pip discovered that he'd stayed in bed for eight days. At the time it felt like much less time and much more: less because he had so little understanding of when one day ended and the next began, more because he did very little but lie under the blanket and think, and his thoughts seemed endless.

He went over and over the events of the past few weeks, remembering everything that had happened. More than anything, he thought about all the mistakes that he'd made. There were so many of them. So many things that he could have done differently. He could hardly believe that he had been so stupid and so reckless. If only he'd been more sensible, he kept telling himself, his father would still be alive.

64

Robert Armin and the Burbage brothers had a whip-round and raised enough money to pay for George Stone's funeral.

He was buried in the graveyard of St Mary Overy. More than a hundred actors came to the ceremony, showing their support for a fellow performer. Outside the church they queued up to shake hands with Pip. Afterwards they trooped to The White Swan and spent what remained of the money that they had donated.

Late that night Robert Armin turned to Richard Burbage and said, "Where's Pip?"

Richard Burbage peered drunkenly round The White Swan and said, "Under a table, I'd guess. Or being sick somewhere. Lad like that probably can't hold his drink."

"Have you seen him since the funeral?"

"Not sure I have."

"We should find him," said Robert Armin. "He shouldn't be alone, not tonight."

Robert Armin went one way, Richard Burbage went the other, and they searched the pub. Gradually more and more actors joined the hunt, until it became a kind of game. Everyone was poking behind benches, looking into barrels, peering out of the windows and stumbling through the nearby streets.

Wherever they went, they called out Pip's name, but there was no sign of him. Eventually they decided that he must have gone to bed. They returned to The White Swan and ordered another round of drinks for everyone.

The next morning they still couldn't find him. Nor that evening. Nor the day after. Without telling anyone where he was going, Pip had gone.

65

They walked for three days.

Walking would have given Pip time to think, but he didn't want to think. He'd done enough thinking. Too much, actually. He just wanted to walk fast with an empty mind, taking deep breaths of the clean air, sluicing London from his lungs.

He had a pair of good companions. Silent, too. Neither of them said a single word for the entire journey.

The bear plodded slowly alongside Pip on all fours, keeping a steady pace, while the spaniel darted ahead and behind, sniffing whatever seemed interesting.

In his right hand Pip held two ropes, one attached to each animal's collar. Although he trusted them both, he didn't want to take any unnecessary risks. If they dashed into the woods, chasing a scent, he'd have to spend hours finding them again.

Over his shoulder Pip was carrying a lumpy brown sack filled with apples, cheese, walnuts and loaves of fresh bread, enough to feed himself for a week or the bear for a day. He had a few pennies in his pocket, the dregs of his savings, and he bought a few more provisions whenever they walked through a village, keeping his sack full.

On the afternoon of the third day they reached Mildmay.

Children came running from the fields, shrieking with glee at the sight of the bear, and then stopped, amazed, when they saw who was leading her. They all knew Pip. They knew him as several things – the blacksmith's apprentice, a loner, a fighter, a fatherless child – but they'd never imagined that he could be a bearkeeper.

One of them shouted out, "Make him dance!"

Pip shook his head.

"Go on, Pip, make him dance! I'll give you a farthing if you do!"

"She doesn't dance," said Pip.

Emboldened, the other children came closer and pestered Pip with questions. By the time he reached the other side of Mildmay he'd gathered an entourage of forty people, almost half the population of the entire village. They followed him all the way home. As they walked through the forest he was so busy answering their questions, explaining where he had been, what he'd seen and how he'd acquired not just one animal but two, he didn't have time to worry what he'd say to his family.

As they came close to the cottage there was the sound

of furious barking. Pepper had heard the conversation and laughter before anyone else. He bolted out of the workshop and came charging down the lane. In the time Pip had been away, the puppy had doubled in size.

Seeing Pip, Pepper darted forward, his tail wagging like mad. Then he saw Miranda. He stood there for a moment, hardly able to believe his eyes, before his tail dropped between his legs and he scampered back to the cottage, barking even louder.

The others came to see what all the noise was about. Samuel emerged from the workshop, wiping his sooty hands on his apron. Isobel hurried out of the vegetable garden. Bridget and Susannah scrambled after her.

Samuel and Isobel weren't used to visitors, not in such numbers. They stood together and stared at the villagers, the spaniel, the bear and, standing at the head of the crowd, a small boy with skinny limbs, messy hair and a huge smile on his face.

With a cry of joy, Isobel ran down the lane and wrapped her arms around her son.

tectum
orchestra
proscænium
planities siue arena

The Swan Theatre

No one knows exactly what the Globe looked like. No pictures of its interior have survived the past four hundred years. But we do have a drawing of another theatre on the south bank of Thames. It was called the Swan.

In 1596, a Dutchman named Johannes de Witt visited London. He went to see a play at the Swan. Writing home to a friend, he drew a sketch of the theatre. His friend made a copy of the sketch, then lost the original letter.

In his drawing, you can see the stage, the pit, the galleries and the flag flying on the roof. Johannes de Witt didn't bother drawing the audience, but he did place three actors on the stage: a woman sitting on a bench, a man standing behind her and someone who looks like a clown. Perhaps he is just about to sing a song or tell a joke.

The Names of the Principall Actors in all these Playes.

William Shakespeare.
Richard Burbadge.
John Hemmings.
Augustine Phillips.
William Kempt.
Thomas Poope.
George Bryan.
Henry Condell.
William Slye.
Richard Cowly.
John Lowine.
Samuell Crosse.
Alexander Cooke.

Samuel Gilburne.
Robert Armin.
William Ostler.
Nathan Field.
John Underwood.
Nicholas Tooley.
William Ecclestone.
Joseph Taylor.
Robert Benfield.
Robert Goughe.
Richard Robinson.
Iohn Shancke.
Iohn Rice.

These are the names of the principal actors who performed in Shakespeare's theatrical company, as published in the first collected edition of his plays.